# THE CULMINATION
## a new beginning

# THE CULMINATION

## a new beginning

Gwen M. Plano

Fresh Ink Group
Guntersville

**The Culmination:**
**a new beginning**

Fresh Ink Group
An Imprint of:
The Fresh Ink Group, LLC
1021 Blount Avenue, #931
Guntersville, AL 35976
Email: info@FreshInkGroup.com
FreshInkGroup.com

Edition 1.0     2020

Book design by Amit Dey / FIG
Cover design by Roseanna White Designs
Associate publisher Lauren A. Smith / FIG
"This Is My Song" by permission of Lorenz Publishing Company

Keywords: Action and Adventure, Suspense, Military, World War, International Politics, Terrorism, Mystery, Nuclear Weapons, Denuclearization, Assassination

Cataloging-in-Publication Recommendations:
FIC002000 FICTION / Action & Adventure
FIC032000 FICTION / War & Military
FIC031090 FICTION / Thrillers / Terrorism

Library of Congress Control Number: 2020920027

ISBN-13: 978-1-947893-89-4 Papercover
ISBN-13: 978-1-947893-91-7 Hardcover
ISBN-13: 978-1-947893-92-4 Ebooks

# Dedication

With gratitude

To retired Lieutenant Colonel John V. Smith,
And to all those who have worn or wear the uniform.
Because of your service, we live.

And

To Rebecca Mantey
Of the International Refugee Committee.
You open our hearts to the suffering masses.

# Table of Contents

# Author's Note

*The Culmination* is a military thriller that travels across several continents and into the competing interests of Heads of State. Though real countries and cities are mentioned, they're situated within a fictional story with fictional characters and fictional events. The military ships, aircraft, and armaments exist, but their locations at sea, on the ground, or in the air reside within the author's imagination.

The writing of this book required extensive research into the ongoing tensions within the Middle East, the mounting unrest in the South China Sea, the worldwide threat of nuclear arsenals, and much more. I've tried to represent these findings faithfully within the context of the overall story; however, my suppositions are mine alone and may bear little resemblance to reality.

Most characters within *The Culmination* are military or veterans. For consistency purposes, I've marked time with 24-hour increments, written as 16:00 rather than 1600 or 4:00 PM. I've also followed the U.S. Department of Defense's guidelines regarding capitalization of active duty military. At the book's end, I've included a brief glossary that may assist readers unfamiliar with unique military terms.

The creation of this book has provided an unexpected and unforgettable journey. I glimpsed the weightiness of decisions made behind closed doors, the terror of innocents caught in battle, and the manifest bravery of men and women who fight to save us all. I'm grateful to editor Harmony Kent, who accompanied me on this journey. Her brilliance, wisdom, and grace offered an invaluable roadmap.

*The Culmination* begins at the conclusion of *The Choice*, with two gunshot victims from the Begert Air Force Base arriving at a hospital. The victims, an Admiral and a journalist, were apparently shot because they exposed media as controlled by outside entities. And so, the story begins.

# Chapter 1

*A*n ominous alarm wails in the Trauma Center of the University Medical Center, signaling an incoming critical situation needing immediate attention. *Gunshot wounds, two victims, gunshot wounds, two victims* an announcement declares. At this Level I trauma center, response teams rush to the helipad on the 13th floor and watch as a U.S. Air Force helicopter lands.

"Tell me what happened," a doctor says to the medics accompanying the victims.

"Sir, the woman was addressing a crowd of reporters at the base. The Admiral spotted the sniper and jumped in front of her just as the rifle discharged. The bullet hit one of his service medals, passed through him, and hit her. Neither is conscious. The medal is embedded. We were afraid to remove it because we feared he might bleed to death."

The doctor darts forward as two gurneys are pushed to the aircraft and the motionless victims put onto the mats. "Get them to the Trauma Center now! Call for the cardiac team."

Nurses scramble to help the victims. A medic applies pressure to the officer's chest but is unable to stop the bleeding. As they move toward the elevator, the surgeon speaks to the medic, "Thank you, Airman, we'll take it now."

"You may have a crowd here soon, sir."

"Why's that?"

"Respects is all, sir. Respects."

"From the looks of things, respect won't be enough. If they hope to see these two healthy again, tell them to get on their knees." The surgeon turns quickly and moves with the bodies.

The medic stands at attention and watches as they disappear behind the closing elevator doors.

Admiral Joseph Parker gets taken to a locked-down surgical unit. He has suffered massive blood loss. When the bullet penetrated his chest, it hit a service medal and pressed the decoration next to the left ventricle of the heart. The projectile then exited his body and hit the second victim. There remain no signs of life, no gasping respiration, and no palpable pulses.

The cardiac surgical team works at speed. One doctor intubates the Admiral and hooks up the ventilator. Others set up a central line and an arterial line. In a matter of minutes, the surgeons are ready to crack open the rib cage. They nod to one another and begin.

\*     \*     \*

In an adjoining operating room, a second team works on the female victim, Julie Underwood. She is also unresponsive. Though she stood behind the Admiral, when the bullet exited him, it struck her shoulder and lodged next to the subclavian artery. She, too, has lost much blood. Suspected head injuries complicate her gunshot trauma. When the Admiral took the hit, he fell backward onto her. She hit the platform hard and got knocked unconscious.

The team moves swiftly to intubate her as she is not breathing. They insert a central line and an arterial line and then focus on the removal of the bullet. After they have recovered it, they close the wound. The lead doctor orders a CT scan of her head and spine to evaluate injuries to the vertebral column. Because she continues in a vegetative state, he suspects that the fall might have fractured her skull.

This locked-down unit treats patients at risk for retaliation. The surgical teams are accustomed to managing the worst of life, but this is the first time they have dealt with an attempted assassination at the Air Force base. They race against time, as the patients are not responding.

Finally, Julie takes a breath.

"We have a response!" a nurse shouts.

"Great job, team," the surgeon responds. "Let's get that CT scan."

*　　*　　*

Down the hall in the other operating room, the Admiral's heart begins to beat.

"Oh, my God, he's alive. Let's do this now." The two cardiac surgeons work in concert with one another, cutting through the Admiral's breastbone to open his chest. Once they have him hooked up to the heart bypass machine, they focus on the medal lodged near his heart.

An intern speaks over the intercom in the first operating room, "Doctor Aguirre, the President wants a status report on the Admiral."

"Can't you see we're busy, intern?"

"Yes, doctor, but the President is insistent."

"Who the hell does he think he is? The president of what?"

"The United States, doctor."

Everyone looks at the intern through the barrier glass with disbelief. "Tell him we're doing our best. The Admiral remains unconscious, but he has a heartbeat. We have no further updates."

"Thank you, doctor."

Dr. Aguirre notices the reaction of his team and responds, "Focus, team." Everyone's attention returns to the Admiral. They locate the medal and dislodge it.

Another interruption comes when the intern uses the intercom again. "Doctor, General Taylor, the Commander of Begert Air Force Base, wants an update on both of the patients."

"This is not a zoo, intern! Tell him the Admiral is alive. I'm not sure about the female. She's in the next operating room." The intern starts to leave the observation area, and the doctor calls out.

"Intern …"

"Yes, doctor?"

"No more disruptions. I don't care what the person's title might be."

"Yes, doctor. Understood. One more thing, the General said these two are lovers."

"Lovers? Could be helpful information." The doctor turns to his resident. "Try to get an update on the female."

Within minutes, the resident returns and reports that she's stable but still unconscious. "They've successfully removed the bullet, but the CT scan revealed a simple linear fracture of the skull, no compression or distortion of the bones. However, the scan of her spine uncovered a rapid cerebrospinal fluid leak along the thoracic vertebrae. The team is consulting with a neurosurgeon at Cedars-Sinai, who specializes in CSF leaks."

Dr. Aguirre nods his approval and continues to focus on the Admiral. "Ahh, I've got it." Proudly, he holds up the mangled medal for the team. "No damage to his heart. The rhythm is regular. Let's close him up. Tonight, we all have much to celebrate. Great job, everyone."

As the nurses prepare the Admiral for the Recovery Room, Dr. Aguirre goes to the other operating room.

"Is she going to be medevacked?"

"We can't risk it. Our team is ready to proceed."

"Can I observe?"

"Of course."

The neuro team works efficiently. One surgeon makes an incision along the Thoracic 4, 5, and 6 vertebrae, while another spreads the wound to expose the bleed. They shave the spine to allow for the insertion of titanium clips to stop the spinal fluid leak. Once they've stitched her up, the lead surgeon acknowledges a job well-done and directs that she get taken to the Recovery Room, and if possible, to a bay next to the Admiral.

# Chapter 2

*A*t Dr. Aguirre's insistence, the Admiral and Julie get taken to a multiple-bed Intensive Care Unit in a locked-down area of the hospital. Gunshot victims get brought here for safety purposes because of the possibility of reprisal. More than a few eyebrows raise over the protocol breach, but the doctor remains firm and explains that they're life partners and dependent upon one another.

✳    ✳    ✳

General Taylor sits in a waiting room, tapping his fingers on the armrest. He goes to the nurses' station, again, and demands to see the patients.

"Sir, we're doing everything we can."

"Your *everything* is not good enough. What room are they in?"

An aide responds, "Sir, I'll take you." He leads the way.

At the door, Taylor stops abruptly. Multiple monitors with unfamiliar beeps, as well as IV lines of medications, are attached to the motionless bodies of the Admiral and Julie. They now breathe on their own, but neither one is conscious.

A shrill alarm sends nursing staff running into the room. The nurses check the Admiral's heart monitor and buzz for the surgeon. His blood pressure has fallen precipitously, and the heart arrhythmias appear dangerously exaggerated. Aguirre rushes into the room, sees the complication, and shouts. "Move their beds next to each other."

"Let me help," Taylor says and then pushes one of the beds.

"Good to see you, sir." Aguirre places Julie's hand into the Admiral's. As soon as they touch, the Admiral's blood pressure returns to normal, and the arrhythmias regulate.

The nurse interrupts, "Doctor, I need to show you something." She presses a pointed instrument into the Admiral's extended hand. "I think he might have nerve damage. I don't think he can feel anything in his left arm."

"You may be right, but fortunately for him, love isn't limited by physicality. Please, make sure these two stay together."

"I will, doctor. This is a first for me."

"For me as well," Taylor says. "I've visited many bedsides over the years, but I've never seen anything like this before."

"Sir, I take it you're family to these two?"

"Yes, doctor. The Admiral is my best friend, and Julie is my sister-in-law."

"Well, they both remain in critical condition, but it appears they've decided to live. I suspect whatever lies ahead, they've agreed to face it together. Are you the one who let us know they're lovers?"

"Yes."

"Your comment prompted us to push their beds together so that their hands could touch. They're alive because of that action."

"I don't know what to say. I don't even know why I said it."

"Thank goodness you did. It's not unusual for surgeons to experience miracles. Most of us are quite aware of our limitations, and we have a healthy respect for the divine. Love keeps us humble, that's for sure."

"Doctor, do you know when they might wake up?"

"The Admiral shows signs of awareness, so I expect him to awaken first. Try talking with him. Tell him about recent events, anything that might interest him. You just may bring him to life."

"I'll do that. Thank you, doctor."

"I'll be back to check on them in an hour. If you need me, I'm just down the hall."

Taylor scans the room for a chair and moves one to the Admiral's bedside. Just as he sits down, his phone rings. It shows a FaceTime call from his wife, Becka. He lowers his voice, "Hi, dear, I'm in the room with them now. Let me show you." He walks over to Julie and then to Parker. "I know it looks bad, but they're doing well. I'll be home soon with a full report." He says goodbye and moves closer to the Admiral.

"Hey, Parker. You've slept long enough. I've got a few things to tell you. I bet you don't know that Becka stayed here through the surgery. She didn't want to go home until Julie showed signs of improvement."

The Admiral moves his foot, which encourages Taylor to continue, "Ahh, you're listening to me. Well, your son should arrive within the hour, so you need to snap to. You don't want Johnny to see you just lying here, do you?"

The Admiral stirs, and Taylor says, "Let me tell you what's going on. You remember the journalism students you invited to the base? Well, a group of them have been at the hospital since you arrived. They've set up their cameras and are reporting news on independent stations right from the grounds. Also, remember the confidential materials Julie and the team sent to the journalism departments? Well, that information is getting shared broadly, and every time one of the networks tries to manipulate the information, there's a huge outcry. It's like the sixties all over again with young people demanding change. But the cry is different. Instead of Peace and Love, it's Truth. Things have shifted, Parker."

The Admiral moves more and then moans.

"Parker, you've been shot. Do you remember that? You'll have to take it easy. How about opening your eyes? By the way, do you know who's next to you? Julie. She's right next to you."

The Admiral struggles to open his eyelids.

"You want to see Julie, don't you? Well, she's sleeping, but she looks stronger by the minute. The surgeons repaired her injuries, so there's no cause for worry. When all this is over, I bet she writes a best-seller about this adventure."

The Admiral's eyes open. He tries to smile and whispers, "Thank you, Taylor."

"Hey, buddy, I'm glad to see you awake. Can I get you anything?"

"Julie?"

"She's next to you. Can you feel her hand in yours?"

"I don't feel anything. Maybe it's the meds."

"Probably. I'm going to step out for a minute to let the nurse know you're conscious. You okay with that? I'll be right back."

"Okay."

Taylor steps into the hallway and flags down a nurse. He explains that the Admiral is now talking but doesn't feel anything.

"I'm not surprised," she responds. "I'll let the doctor know that he's alert now."

When Taylor returns to the room, the Admiral is trying to remove the covers.

"What's going on, Parker? Is there something I can do?"

"I want to see Julie."

"That's not going to happen for a while. You're not strong enough to get out of bed. Let me show you something." Taylor walks to the left side of the mattress. "Parker, I'm holding your arm. Now, watch. You see this hand. Do you know whose it is?"

"Julie's?"

"Yes. Now, I'm putting her palm in yours and laying your hands on the bed. You may not feel it, but you can see it. She's with you and will be okay."

"Why can't I feel her hand?"

"Your doctor is on the way, so ask him."

The door opens, and the surgeon walks in. "Hey, Admiral, it's good to see you awake. How're you feeling?"

"Good, I think. But I can't feel much."

"So, let's figure that out. I'll touch different parts of your body, and you tell me what you feel." The doctor pokes the Admiral's toes and moves up the body. Parker responds to each prod. But when the doctor pokes his left arm, Parker doesn't respond. The doctor moves down the arm to the fingertips. The patient feels nothing. The doctor goes to the right arm, and Parker reacts immediately.

"We've got a challenge, Parker, and together we'll figure it out. You don't have sensation in your left arm. This could be a matter of compression neuropathy because of the fall, but it could also mean nerve damage from the gunshot wound. Either way, we'll fix it."

"I appreciate your confidence, doctor. I need both arms."

"No worries. We'll take good care of you. I'll come back in another hour."

As the doctor leaves the room, the Admiral smiles and calls out, "Johnny!" His son, Lieutenant John Parker, an MP with the Army's military intelligence, has just arrived.

"Hey, Dad."

"I didn't want you to see me like this, son, but I sure am glad you're here. I must be in trouble, given you're wearing your dress uniform."

"Come on, Dad. Do you think I wouldn't have come? I'd have gotten here earlier, but I had to get clearance to carry my weapon. By the way, last I knew, you were on some island enjoying yourself. I had to get the details from NPR. That's not right, Dad."

"NPR?"

"You don't even know what's going on, do you? You're a household name now."

Taylor says, "I told him a little bit, Johnny, but maybe you can fill him in. Now that you're here, I'll return to the base." He gives Parker a pat on the shoulder. "I'll see you in the morning. Ask Johnny to call me if there's anything you need. Anything."

Parker nods. "Thank you. I appreciate it."

As the General leaves the room, Johnny moves closer and tells his dad about the upheaval. "YouTube has footage of the shooting at the base. It also has interviews with the students who saw the whole thing. Social media has gone crazy with conspiratorial theories."

"What do you think, Johnny?"

"I'm not sure, but it seems plausible that there's an unknown group calling the shots. What's important, though, is that you've broken through."

"What do you mean?"

"You sent the documents implicating key international elites in a scheme to kill the President. Remember? The materials also included evidence of a plan to create a single world government with themselves at the helm. Pretty heavy stuff. The whole world knows that mainstream media is controlled."

"That wasn't me. Julie, Taylor's sister-in-law, did that."

"Your girlfriend?"

"Well, yes."

"No need to feel shy about that, Dad. Knowing you have a girlfriend makes me feel better than thinking you're alone."

"I didn't expect to love again after your mom died, but then I met Julie. It was easy to talk with her because she's a widow, too. I didn't have to explain myself—she just understood."

"Dad, you have my blessing. Mom would be glad to know you're happy."

"Thank you. I believe she'd like Julie."

"So, Julie came up with the idea of distributing the documents?"

"Yes. We scanned the papers, sent several journalism departments the files via the cloud, others we sent by USB flash drives, and still more by hardcopy. We blanketed the U.S. but also hit international sites. We got responses almost immediately. It was brilliant, but it had consequences, as you can see."

"Dad, I want to show you something." Johnny picks up the television remote and turns the TV on to PBS. A young man talks about the need for honesty. He points to the documents as evidence that a few self-centered billionaires have held the world in their grips for a long time. He claims that these few created divisions to control the masses. "When the population at large turns against one another, this secretive group has won. So, ask yourself:

when the activists get involved, who pays for their transportation and housing, their effigies, and posters? Who, ultimately, gains?"

"Well, I'll be. Who is this man?"

"He's one of many spokespersons for the student journalists. I'm not
sure of his name, but I *am* sure that you, Julie, and your team have awakened the country. Just as the Sixties prompted monumental social and
political change, your actions have sparked a different kind of revolution."

"What are you saying? Are people marching? Are they getting hurt?"

"No. Fifty years ago, people marched. Now, people use social media. If
the internet is taken down, or if their message isn't heard, we'll see people
in the streets, but it won't be a love-in. People want the unadulterated truth,
and they're insistent. Powerful stuff, Dad, and you and Julie lie at the heart
of it."

# Chapter 3

When the General arrives at his office, he finds a lineup of folks waiting to see him. Upon noticing Staff Sergeant Gruner, he calls him in.

"What do you have for me, Gruner?"

"The assassin wasn't Air Force. Somehow, he secured a uniform, had the layout of the base, and knew our precautions. He disguised himself as Special Forces and blended in. No one noticed. We're going over every tape now to find out who this guy was and see if he had an accomplice. One thing for certain, this was a professional hit, and we should've caught it."

"Copy that, Sergeant. Keep me posted."

The General walks Gruner to the door and motions for his assistant. "What's most pressing?"

"Sir, POTUS wants an update. Here's the number he said to phone."

The General grimaces and makes the call.

"General Taylor?"

"Yes, sir."

"Give it to me straight."

"Sir, Admiral Parker and Julie Underwood steadily improve. The assassin wasn't Air Force. We don't have much information yet. I still have the base on lockdown because we have too many variables."

"I'm relieved to hear about Parker and Underwood. As for the investigation, spare no expense. This could have international consequences, and we need to get to the bottom of it. Keep the base locked down. Frankly, it's hard to know who you can trust."

"Yes, sir."

"And, Taylor, report in every day. You have my number, so call if you gain information or need my help. Got it?"

"Yes, sir."

"All right. Later, then …"

"Goodbye, sir." The General takes a deep breath and mutters, "We need to get to the bottom of this."

His assistant stands in the doorway. "Sir, you had a call from the hospital. Julie has regained consciousness."

"Thank you."

Taylor makes a call to Becka, who tells him, "I'll return to the hospital."

"Give me an hour, and I'll join you. I don't want you to travel by yourself. There's too much going on."

The General disconnects and calls in his assistant. "I'm heading out in an hour. Please reschedule my appointments and tell my driver we're going to Sacramento."

"Yes, sir." The assistant salutes and leaves the room.

The General calls Gruner and explains that he'll be leaving soon. "I want updates at any time of the day."

Gruner says, "We've tracked the assassin. He first appeared by the Exchange loading dock, out of uniform. We have footage of him talking with the delivery drivers. We're questioning them now. The assassin then moves into the Exchange and re-emerges in uniform. We're checking the inside cameras as well. I suspect that he obtained a uniform at the base cleaners, and if he did, this was a carefully organized attack."

"Do you see a weapon on the man?"

"None that we've seen so far."

"Well, keep digging. POTUS wants me to give him regular updates, so check in with any findings."

"Will do, sir."

The assistant knocks at his door, and then Becka enters, carrying a flower arrangement and a tote bag. Taylor walks over and gives her a kiss.

"The flowers are beautiful. What's in the bag?"

"Just a few things. Julie's robe, a change of clothes, and a hairbrush."

"Excellent. I'm certain she'll appreciate that. Okay, give me five minutes, and we'll get on our way."

The General makes one last call, then turns to his wife and nods. "Let's get on the road."

# Chapter 4

At 30 Rockefeller Plaza in New York City, a UPS delivery man places three boxes on the floor beside the receptionist's desk for NBC's *The Nightly News*. A tour guide and twenty-six visitors exit an elevator and walk toward the studio. The delivery man pushes them aside in his hurry to take the elevator to the ground floor.

Emma Delaney, the tour guide, apologizes for the rude behavior and walks over to the receptionist. Emma provides the names of her guests, shows her identification, and then turns to her group to explain what they will soon see. Mid-sentence, one of the boxes behind her explodes and unleashes a fiery hell. Shrapnel and flames engulf the room.

Thrown all the way to the far wall, where she lands with an agonizing impact, Emma yells, "Help!" Her legs have become bloody masses. She cannot move. She cannot see. She cannot hear. The smoke and debris have taken the light. Only silence roars in her ears. Emma struggles to breathe and, finally, gives in to deadly unconsciousness.

Emma drifts in and out of awareness. She is vaguely aware when the police and first responders arrive and set about identifying those most in need of help. Emma is one of the severely injured. A medic puts tourniquets on her legs. After a few minutes, she rouses more, gasps for air, and sees through the clouds of dust to those helping her.

"A man with boxes," she whispers. A police officer bends over her to listen.

"UPS," she mutters and, again, loses consciousness.

The team moves at speed, putting the injured on stretchers and taking them to the many waiting ambulances. A few in the tour group manage to stagger to their feet and, though unstable, they evacuate with the assistance of police.

"Did you notice anything unusual?" an officer asks Emma once she rouses again.

She shakes her head and winces in pain. A woman off to the side whimpers, and through her tears, says, "A UPS delivery man brought in boxes. He must've been in a hurry because he pushed past us."

A nearby teen says, "He was an ass; he shoved us. He wasn't an American."

Another officer asks, "Why do you think he wasn't an American?"

The teenager appears confused and just stares. The officer repeats the question, and then the young man says, "He couldn't answer the secretary's question."

"What did she want to know, son?"

"Where his clearance papers were. That's all she said."

"Can you describe him?"

"Middle Eastern, mustache, 5'11", about 190 lbs."

"Would you be willing to come to the station to help identify this guy?"

The teenager glances at a man leaning against the elevator wall. "Dad?"

His father stares at the floor without speaking. His face is pale and speckled with tiny cuts and debris.

"Dad? Can we go to the station?"

The police officer says, "I think your father has gone into shock. We'll have an officer accompany you to the hospital and will talk later."

The teenager acknowledges the policeman, and then shuffles off with Emma on a stretcher and into a free elevator. From the stretcher,

Emma looks at the faces of the other ash covered victims with her. *They look like zombies*, she thinks. *No one's talking. Maybe they can't. Maybe they're all in shock.* Then she notices blood pooling on the floor and reaches for the medic by her side. She points to the gory mess.

"Step back out of the way, people," the medic says, but no one moves. He pushes his way over to a woman crouched in the corner and calls to her. When she doesn't respond, he shakes her. Blood drips from her torso. The medic radios for another emergency crew to meet them at the elevator doors. Within minutes, the car arrives on the ground floor, and two more medics whisk the woman away.

The police officer turns to the teenager. "Stay with your dad, and we'll meet with you at the hospital."

As the crew lifts Emma into an ambulance, she stares around at the crowds of spectators, the reporters demanding information, and the helicopter flying low above, and decides, *This is what war is like.*

# Chapter 5

---

The General's car nears the hospital entrance, but the driver spots the swarms of reporters and camera crews and turns down a side street. He heads for the loading dock at the rear of the complex. "Much better here, sir."

"Thank you. We'll visit for an hour and be back down. See you then."

Taylor and his wife disappear into the service elevator and head to the eleventh floor. Becka takes a deep breath before stepping out. The General leads the way.

"Look who's here," Johnny calls out.

"Hey, team. Becka and I decided a visit was imperative, especially since Julie is doing so well."

Becka rushes to Julie's side and puts the flowers on the bedside stand.

Taylor turns to the Admiral. "You're looking good, my friend. You've got color in your face. How are you feelin'?"

"Well, I can't complain. For an old guy who got shot in the chest, I'm doing super. It turns out that the Medal of Honor saved me."

"You're kidding, right?"

"No, I'm dead serious. The bullet hit the medal, pressed it against my heart, but caused no damage there, and then exited. It's a good thing you instructed us to wear our dress uniforms, or I wouldn't be talking with you now."

"Sometimes you wonder, don't you? What about your left arm? Has feeling returned?"

"A little. Johnny massaged it earlier, and since then, I've felt a tingling in my fingers."

"That sounds hopeful. At least you have sensation."

Johnny interrupts to ask if anyone would like a cup of coffee. "I'm headed down to the cafeteria and can bring back a cup of brew if you like."

Taylor speaks up, "You know, some coffee would be great. Black."

Parker says, "Wish I could join you, son, but the doc has me on a pretty limited diet."

Johnny nods. "Okay, one coffee it is. I'll be back in a few."

Taylor watches him leave and comments, "You've plenty to be proud of, Parker."

"I know, he's an impressive young man. What's happening at the base?"

"We're still locked down. Actually, all bases are on high alert. POTUS is deeply involved and expects regular reports. He knows that security is compromised and even feels cautious toward some of his staff."

"What have we come to?"

A message to General Taylor beeps on his phone and interrupts their conversation. He reads the text and says, "Well, this isn't good."

"What's wrong?"

"There's been an explosion at NBC. Thus far, they have three wounded and might have more. Reporters suggest this is the result of those critical of network news."

Parker's jaw drops. "Unbelievable. So, they're attributing this terrorist act to student journalists? I doubt any of the students would go near NBC, and they certainly wouldn't be allowed in."

"Didn't you say that Johnny knows officers in the NYPD? Military buddies, who joined after their tour was up?"

"That's what he told me. And, as far as I know, they respect him."

"When he gets back, let's ask him if he has any connections that might shed light on this craziness. Who knows, there could be a link."

A couple of minutes later, Johnny hurries back into the room and gives Taylor his cup of coffee. "Black, just like you wanted. Did you hear?"

"About NBC?"

"Not just NBC, Dad. A few minutes ago, CNN in Atlanta got hit. One fatality for certain, many more injured."

Taylor shakes his head and frowns. "By chance, do you know anyone with the NYPD?"

"You think they might have inside information, and maybe surveillance footage?"

"You read my mind."

"Well, I have a few contacts. I can't be sure of what they know or not, but they'll give it to me straight." Johnny walks to the far corner of the room and soon enters into an animated conversation. When he returns to the bedside, he looks troubled.

"They know it's not the students. They obtained footage of a person leaving a package by the receptionist's desk. They have the person's identity but won't say who. They're working with the Atlanta PD. All they'd tell me is that the terrorists aren't American. Homeland is handling both cases."

The General's eyebrows raise. "Do they believe this was a random act of terror or part of a larger plot?"

"Part of a larger plot. It involves another country, apparently."

Taylor grimaces and shakes his head. "I need to get back to the base." He looks over at Becka and motions that it's time to leave.

Julie rouses and squeezes Becka's hand. "Don't worry about me, sis. I'm doing great, and look at all this company. We'll see each other tomorrow."

Taylor calls his driver to explain that he'll be down shortly and to pick him up at the loading dock.

"Yes, sir. There's quite a gathering at the front of the hospital. Reporters are clamoring about a conspiracy to block their coverage of the news."

"We'll avoid them. See you in five."

All eyes settle on General Taylor. "We've got a mess. I'll see you guys in the morning. Take care, Parker. No tricks tonight."

"Hey, drive safely. This thing is exploding."

The Admiral laughs and says, "Ha. Pardon the pun."

The others join him in the laughter, but the shared mirth has a tense edge to it.

Then Parker tells Johnny, "I need to get some sleep. Leave with General Taylor to avoid the media frenzy."

"Are you sure, Dad? I can spend the night. The easy chair in the corner looks pretty inviting."

"There's nothing you can do here, and I'm certain your Commanding Officer needs you to report in. Stop by in the morning."

"Well, I'll decide one way or the other when I see you tomorrow, Dad."

"Okay, I'm feeling the love."

Johnny gives his dad a pat on the shoulder and leaves the room with the General and his wife.

✳    ✳    ✳

The Admiral looks over at Julie. "This has escalated in a way we didn't expect. We're dealing with entities that want to destroy, and we don't even know who they are."

"Joe, my dear, when you put it that way, it sounds like Armageddon."

"But, don't you feel it?"

"Yeah, and I suspect we're in this hospital because we came too close to exposing the predators. It tells me that we're in danger now."

"They have more to worry about than us. Too many people have the files—thanks to you. But we've rattled someone's cage, and they don't like it."

"And you don't believe we're in danger?"

"I see your point. At least this part of the hospital is a locked-down unit. Nobody can get up here without clearance."

Julie reaches for him. "I'd sure like to hold your hand right now."

"I'll call the nurse. We should be able to manage that." He punches the call button, and a nurse comes in a few minutes later.

"Could you help us? We'd like to move our beds closer so that we can hold hands."

The nurse smiles. "What a sweet request. Give me a second, and I'll have you two next to each other."

Once they lie close enough together, Parker takes Julie's hand. "The world could end, but I'll leave this life happily if I'm holding your hand."

Julie chuckles. "You're quite the romantic, Joe."

"That may be, but I mean it. With your hand in mine, I feel at peace."

"Let's pray for a long life. I need more time with you, my dear man."

"A long life it is."

# Chapter 6

*E*arly the next morning, Lieutenant John Parker pushes through the mob of reporters outside the hospital. Once inside, two student journalists approach and ask to speak with him privately.

"Sir, we've received a call from an associate in Berlin. We think it's important."

"All right, let's hear it."

"Two photographers on assignment in a remote area of the Lofoten Islands sent these photos to a reporter in Berlin. Perplexed, the reporter sent the pictures to us." The student hands over his phone. "Take a look, sir."

Johnny pages through the images.

The reporter says, "The photographers traveled to Norway to shoot the Aurora Borealis. Their cameras focused on the horizon when the sky lit up with aircraft. One-by-one, the planes flew into the Harstad/Narvik Airport, Evenes. This struck them as odd, so they switched to their telephoto lenses and shot what they saw. Not that we know much about this type of thing, but it appears to be an international gathering of the elite."

Johnny studies the pictures, which show two Bombardiers BD-700, two Gulfstreams, and a Falcon 7x.

"Can you forward the images to me?" The student nods and sends them. "Thank you. I've got them now. I'll check it out and get back in touch soon."

While Johnny rises with the elevator, he considers how he'll track down the owners of the private jets. He sends a quick text to his intelligence team.

Dr. Aguirre leaves room 1130, as Johnny arrives to see his dad. "How's he doing, doctor?"

"Remarkably well. If you can, try to get him to take a few small steps. Just a few. It will help his circulation."

Johnny walks into the room, and it surprises him to see his dad sitting up and eating breakfast.

"Wow, you must have had a good night's sleep."

"Couldn't have been better. I feel like a new person today. Doc said he might let me go home within the week."

"That's great news. Where's home? Not Annapolis, I assume?"

"I need to stay local until I'm strong enough to fly. I have a nice setup at the base, and the General has assigned an Airman to help me. What more could I ask for?"

"Sounds good, but I want you to know that I'm prepared to stay as long as you need me."

"I appreciate that, I truly do, but I'm certain the Army needs you more than I do. Too much is going on right now."

"I'm not making any plans yet. Let's see how the day goes."

"Do you have any updates about the attacks?"

"Only what I've mentioned already. It's troubling. The police believe the students are being scapegoated."

"They use that language?"

"Oh, yeah. The authorities believe it's a setup and that someone will get hurt if it isn't stopped. Speaking of setup, look at these photos. What do you see?"

Parker takes Johnny's cell and pages through the images. "I see a lot of money."

"Exactly. The jets landed in Norway last night. And, …" Johnny's cell phone beeps to indicate the arrival of a text, which reads: *International. One has ties to the Federal Reserve.* Johnny looks at his dad, who studies him intently and says, "We may have stumbled upon the cabal. I've got to tell the students to be extra careful."

"Go ahead and go. I'm fine."

Down in the waiting room, Johnny meets with the student journalists. He explains, "The police departments are assisting Homeland Security and the FBI. They're aware that it isn't the students' fault, but they're not free to release information yet. The assumptions voiced by the networks, intentional or otherwise, are wrong and dangerous."

One of the group says, "We need to notify our team leader, sir. May we have permission to do so?"

"Anything I've mentioned, you're free to use. However, you cannot divulge my name."

"We understand that, sir. We'll be careful."

"I wish I had more information for you, but I believe there will soon be a formal press release. I'll give my liaison your contact information so that you get the notification simultaneously with the networks. Then we'll all know what's going on."

Johnny glances at the group. "I need to get back to my father, but there's something else. The photos from your contact in Norway remain a mystery. Until we find out more, please don't share them. I'll get in touch soon. Take care."

He walks to the elevator and presses the button for the eleventh floor. As he exits, he gets a call from his contact in the NYPD and walks into his dad's room as he listens. "Homeland Security has apprehended two Iraqi nationals, who set the explosives in the news stations. They were paid in new bills to plant the explosive. No tracking evidence. And their instructions came from untraceable iMessages. The terrorists never met their benefactor, nor did they know his name."

"Thanks, Frank. Is this information I can share?"

"Homeland has authorized a news release, which we're preparing and will have available within the hour. So, I need you to hold for now."

"Can you send the report to non-network reporters as well?"

"Yeah. Anyone in particular?"

"How about I give you a list?"

"Get it to me within the hour, and I'll make sure your folks receive a notification at the same time."

"I owe you one, Frank."

"A beer at O'Toole's?"

"For sure."

Parker listens with care to the one-sided conversation, and when his son ends the call, he speaks up, "What's happening?"

Johnny repeats the information for his dad's benefit.

"I don't know what I'd do without you, son. Thank you."

"Hey, I'm near useless here, so if I can do anything like this, then I don't feel so worthless."

"I know what you mean. I feel as if our way of life is at risk, and here I lay, unable to do anything."

"Stop that. You're a hero, and you've got the wounds to prove it. There is something you can help me with, though."

"What's that? Anything I can do, I will."

"The contact information for the alternative news reporters. Do you have that?"

"Check the drawer on the side table. The list should be there."

"I've got it. I'll go through the list and . . ." Johnny freezes. "Did you hear that?"

Shouts and screams come from the hallway. Two gunshots echo down the corridor. Johnny darts to the door. Armed men approach.

Johnny pulls out his gun and ammunition and turns to his dad and Julie. "I've got to get you out of harm's way. We've got trouble. You guys ruffled the feathers of some nasty people."

His father demands, "What's going on?"

"I don't know, but we've got company, and it's not friendly."

Johnny gets a text from Taylor. *The hospital's locked down. I can't get up to the floor. What's happening?*

Johnny writes back. *Shots down the hall. I'm ready.*

Taylor sends an immediate response. *I'll try to get up to you.*

Johnny pushes his dad's bed next to Julie's. Then he shoves the cabinets against the door and wedges the stops in place. Next, he moves the end table into a position that offers him some protection and sets his aim at the exit.

"What's happening, Joe?" Julie cries out, fear audible in her voice.

Parker whispers, "We must stay calm and silent. Hospital security will get here momentarily, but 'till then, we're on our own. Johnny has his weapon, so we're protected."

The door pushes open, and the barrel of an automatic weapon pokes into the gap and protrudes into the room.

"Push it open, Tom," one of the gunmen calls out.

"I'm trying. It's stuck. Get over here and help me."

Focused, Johnny crouches into firing position with his gun pointed at the opening in the doorway.

Parker motions for Julie not to speak or move.

The attackers force the door open. One of the gunmen raises his gun to shoot, but Johnny fires first. He makes a direct hit. The intruder falls, and his automatic lands next to him.

Johnny grabs the weapon lying to the side of the assassin and returns to his original position.

Another gunman calls out to his sidekick, "Tom's been hit. We've got someone in there."

"Get the bastard!"

More shots sound from down the hall.

Security has arrived.

"What the fuck? I thought we had a clear path," an intruder yells.

"We have to get out of here."

"It's locked down, you fool."

"Get behind the desk over here."

More gunfire rumbles. "Davis, I'm hit. Shit, it wasn't supposed to end this way."

Parker motions to Julie again, not to make a sound, not to move.

Johnny stands ready.

Multiple shots blast down the hallway, and then silence falls.

Johnny eases to the door just as a security officer arrives. "We'll have this cleaned up in five," he calls on his radio and then turns to Johnny. "Did you check the body?"

"Haven't touched it," Johnny says. "I'd sure like to know who the bastard is."

"Let's take a look."

The security officer rolls the body over and looks up at Johnny. "Clean shot."

Johnny acknowledges his recognition with a nod.

The officer then checks the guy's pass lanyard. "Robert Sayer." He checks the pockets and finds a wallet. "Interesting. His driver's license says Thomas Brown. With the right uniform, it seems like you can breach security without a problem."

"What about the others?"

"We'll know soon. You had help."

"Who?"

Taylor walks into the room, and the security officer salutes. "Couldn't have done it without you, General."

Taylor salutes back. "These are my people. I'd do anything for them."

Johnny salutes, "And I for you, sir."

Parker breaks the seriousness by saying, "Hey, you two, let's clean up my room."

They all laugh and push the furniture back into its usual place. Hospital staff arrive with a gurney. They pick up the body and lift it onto the stretcher. The security officer speaks to them privately.

Once the staff has left with the gurney, the security officer says, "There'll be a full investigation. But, given who we're dealing with, I doubt we'll make much headway."

Johnny asks, "What do you mean?"

"They had approvals from the White House. That trumps our security. Two are dead, and the third won't be talking for a while. I doubt he'll leave here alive."

Johnny says, "Is he critical?"

"The thug who ordered this hit won't want him to speak. I've seen this scenario before. It's just a matter of time."

"Whoever is behind this will send in an assassin to finish him?"

"Yes."

Parker looks at Taylor. "The sooner we get out of this place, the better."

"Let's make it happen."

Taylor turns to the security officer. "Will you keep me updated? I'll try and get these two released for their own well-being. But I'd like you to keep me in the loop in terms of discovery."

"Normally, that wouldn't be possible. But you've proven yourself, sir." He hands Taylor his business card. "Call me directly, and I'll share what I know. This stays between you and me. I served two terms in the Army. I know a good man when I meet him."

Taylor nods. "Thank you, I appreciate the confidence."

# Chapter 7

Johnny and Taylor grab chairs next to Parker, who relaxes in a wheelchair. The three sit deep in thought about the attempted assassination. Their questions have no answers, and yet they review the incident over and over again. Nothing adds up.

In the opposite corner, Becka helps Margaret transfer into a wheelchair and pushes her over to the windows, out of the way of the cleaning staff busy sterilizing the room. She sits next to her sister in the only available chair. Together, they stare out over the rooftops of the hospital complex.

The late afternoon sun pours through the windows, and Becka reaches for Julie's hand. "It feels good, doesn't it?"

"Like old times, sis. I can't thank you enough for being here with me."

"There's no place else that I'd rather be. It's strange, isn't it? A week ago, who could have imagined what we're going through? On the bright side, we can look outside together and pretend to breathe fresh air." They stare, saying little. The rhythmic chuff-chuff sound of helicopter blades catches their attention. Three helicopters approach. They glance at each other.

Becka says, "Guys … did you expect the President?"

Parker speaks up, "No. Why?"

"Three choppers just flew past the window, and one has landed. I reckon it might be a Marine One transport."

Johnny darts over to the window. "Tell me what you saw." He bends to try and get a better look at the landing pad but can only see propellers.

Becka says, "Not much, really. The helicopters appear military, and they have an American flag painted on the side with *United States of America.* Makes you wonder."

"Hmm." Parker looks over at Taylor. "Could, easily, be Marine One. But it doesn't make sense. Why would the President or any of his staff come here?"

Taylor purses his lips. "If it's the President, he must be in the area for some other purpose and then decided to pay you a visit."

Parker nods. "I guess that's possible."

A ruckus comes from out in the hallway. Johnny goes to the door and opens it slightly. In disbelief, he stares at the approaching entourage. Then he turns around and says, "The President is here."

"You talkin' about me, son?" President Williams asks as he walks into the room, escorted by several Secret Service agents. Parker sits up straighter in his wheelchair while Taylor and Johnny offer a formal salute.

"Hey, Parker, by the look on your face, you didn't expect me." The President's belly shakes when he laughs.

"No, sir, I did not. What brings you here?"

"You, of course. I'm told you suffered another assassination attempt this morning. My team didn't even want to stop. What the heck is going on, Parker?"

"Sir, I've tried to understand it myself, but I'm not sure I do."

"We'll have to get into that, but first things first. Who're the beautiful ladies by the window?"

"General Taylor's wife, Becka, and his sister-in-law, Julie Underwood, sir."

The President glances over to Taylor and reaches for a handshake.

The Admiral says, "This young man is my son, Lieutenant John Parker. He's an MP with the Army military intelligence."

"Glad to meet you, Lieutenant. You remind me of your father when he was your age."

Williams moves closer to Parker. "So, have you told your family how we became friends?"

The Admiral bites his lower lip and says, "No, sir. That's a story best told by you."

"All right, then. I suspect each of you've heard aspects of the story I mean to share. But today, you'll hear why Parker has so many medals on his uniform, and you'll understand why I came here."

The President nods to Johnny. "During Vietnam, your dad served on a submarine off the Mekong Delta. Some of our troops got cornered near the opening of the Delta. They needed help badly, but no one was available. When the pleas came over the radio, your dad offered to go in. Against the better judgment of his Commander, Parker swam to shore and tried to help the men. He arrived too late. Most had been slaughtered, and others were left for dead.

"While he walked through the rubble, he stumbled on a mound and heard a moan. Unknowingly, he'd stepped onto my arm and broke it. I was barely conscious and had made my peace. I assumed I would meet the Lord that day. But my anguish got your dad's attention. He turned around, searched through the debris, and found me buried in mud. My being dark-skinned and all, I was well concealed. Your dad pulled me out of that grave and said, 'Soldier, you need a shower. Let's see if I can find you one.'" The President chuckles.

"Then he called in for a Patrol Boat Riverine and carried me onboard at great risk to himself. When he laid me on the deck, he asked for my name. 'Samuel Williams,' I told him. Then he said, 'Samuel Williams, I expect to see you in a clean uniform when we meet next. Take care of yourself.' The small boat charged down the delta and got me to a make-shift hospital. They fixed my arm as best they could but mostly focused on the gunshot wound to the chest. It if weren't for your dad, I'd be dead. It gave me great honor to be present when your father was awarded the Medal of Honor for his valor in combat."

Johnny shakes his head. "I'll be ... I'm familiar with this story, sir, but Dad never mentioned who he rescued and, certainly, didn't tell me what he'd said."

"Yep, that's your dad, never wanting the spotlight." Williams turns to the Admiral and says, "Is it true? Was it the Medal of Honor that saved you?"

Johnny answers instead, "It was, sir." He opens up his rucksack and pulls out the badly damaged decoration.

A big grin stretches across the President's face. "Life brings us together again, Parker."

"What do you mean, sir?"

"Just like you visited me while I recovered from my injuries, I'm visiting you now. A lot of years have passed, haven't they? And we've kept in touch through the highs and lows of those decades. But now, I can't help but smile because, in a roundabout way, my actions saved you. Think of it, if you hadn't been in dress attire when the sniper took his aim, we wouldn't be having this same conversation. But you were, and the assassin hit the only medal associated with me."

The Admiral's eyes water. "You're right about that, sir. Amazing but true."

"Well, for the skinny 19-year-old who got pulled out of the mud in 1972, carried through hellfire, and put into a Pibber, that's an event I'll never forget. But it took a sniper to make sure we *all* remember what occurred that day." He looks over at Johnny. "Your dad risked his life for a stranger, a black one at that, who lay covered in mud." He chuckles and shakes his head. "Yep, life is full of surprises, isn't it?"

Johnny grins. "That it is, sir."

The President addresses Parker, "So, tell me, why are you a target?"

"I assume the attempt on base happened because I challenged the reliability of the media. But, now, I think there must be another reason."

The President's gaze becomes more focused. "Anything specific?"

"Sir, I don't have any answers. I've even reviewed conversations I've had that might be construed as problematic."

"To whom? What outside entities would care about what you think? Unless you're discussing classified information, which I doubt, I believe you need to focus on your work with the Navy. You designed ships. What is it about those ships that could prompt an enemy to perceive you as a risk?"

"I have no idea. And besides, why now?"

"Uh-huh, now you're on the right track. Why now? Why have you, all of a sudden, become a target? What do you know that we all need to be aware of? Some unidentified entity wants you gone for a reason."

"I hadn't thought of it in that way, sir."

"Well, I need you to think like that now. You must know the attacks aren't over. You're still here. The bounty will get offered to someone else, and then yet another until the job gets done." The President looks at Parker with determination. "We need to figure out which country wants you dead because—somehow—they believe you have the ability to foil a larger attack they plan to make."

"Mr. President, it's hard for me to believe there's anything I know that's consequential in the ways you're suggesting."

The President chuckles, which breaks the tension. "I know you well enough that I suspect you'll now obsess about this non-stop. You'll find the answer, and when you do, give me a call."

Julie has remained silent throughout the exchange, but now she says, "Sir, do you have a recommendation for us? Is there something we can do?"

"Ms. Underwood, your only job right now is to stay alive, and given the circumstances, that may prove a challenge. You've endured a sniper's bullet, as well as a failed attempt in this hospital. Do you imagine yourself safe now?"

"Sir, if I can help, then I want to do my part."

"I admire your patriotism, but your task is to stay alive." He turns to Parker and Taylor. "You two need to make this your principal focus.

Tensions are mounting with Saigon, and that's a force to reckon with. I believe these attacks are related, somehow."

Taylor receives a message from Gruner. He grimaces and holds up his hand. "I just got an important text from my assistant. We should watch the news."

The conversation stops, and Taylor turns on the television. Together, they watch as the Secretary of Homeland Security explains, "The terrorist attacks on the network buildings in New York and Atlanta were conducted by non-national mercenaries. The investigation remains ongoing, but we feel confident that only two people were responsible, and we have them in custody."

After glancing over at Taylor and Parker, the President says, "Gentlemen, I need to go. This will escalate, and folks will demand that I step in." He smiles and adds, "Folks always want me to solve their problems. But, in this case, I wouldn't be surprised if you solve it for me."

Parker says, "Sir, I'm honored you came to see me. Thank you very much."

"This was as much for me as it was for you. When I had the opportunity to visit Vandenberg to discuss space launch activities, I took it with the knowledge that I could visit you. Get well. Our country needs both of us."

"Yes, sir, I intend to do just that."

"It's been a pleasure. Stay the course. Ms. Julie, Ms. Becka, I'm honored to have met you. Sorry to leave abruptly, but I'm due at Vandenberg to watch the launch of our newest unarmed intercontinental ballistic missile. It's not just North Korea who plays with fire. Besides—" He grins. "—traveling south offers a fantastic view of Yosemite National Park."

The two officers stand at attention and salute. Parker salutes from his bed. The President offers the gesture in return and says, "At times like this, I feel proud to be an American. Not a day passes that I don't think of that muddy riverbank in Vietnam and the man who pulled me to safety. Thank you again, Parker. You gave me a second life—one I've tried to be worthy of." With those words, he turns and leaves with his Secret Service.

Johnny goes to the door and watches the President stride down the hallway. "Oh, my God, Dad, that was amazing."

"Certainly unexpected. If I weren't in the hospital, I'd say our President's visit calls for a drink."

Taylor says, "We need to get you back on base. I'm ready for that drink!"

# Chapter 8

The national news interrupts its account of the captured terrorists with Breaking News. Taylor shushes his companions. Everyone in the room watches intently while the news anchor says, "Yosemite National Park Rangers report that Marine One—while flying in thick fog—has crashed into a canyon wall in the park. A full investigation is underway. We have no word about who was in the chopper—or if it carried the President of the United States. We've been told that the other two helicopters are safe and headed to Vandenberg Air Force Base."

Becka gasps. "This is surreal. How could this happen? They were just here."

Julie sobs and grabs Becka's hand. Together they watch the horror as it unfolds on television.

At the commotion, a nurse comes to the door.

"Did you see it? Did you see it?" Julie cries. "The President might be dead. A Marine One plane has crashed." The nurse gasps and stares at the television then rushes out the door.

Taylor glances at Parker and catches his attention. This was more than fog. Taylor signals that the room might be bugged, and Parker grimaces in agreement. Johnny nods and follows their lead.

Taylor pulls a pad of notepaper from the bed cabinet, walks over to Julie and Becka, and writes, *The room is bugged. Say nothing of our plans. Keep your conversation focused on the news. I'll get you and Parker out of here and back to the safety of the base.*

Julie looks into his eyes and nods her understanding. Then she stares blankly into the distance.

Becka takes the pad. *Should I pack up her things?* Taylor motions for her to do so. Then he scribbles a note to Parker and Johnny. *I'll set up a diversion.*

Once they acknowledge his note, he says, "With all that's going on, I need to get back to the base. I'll call for a chopper. It's the fastest way for me to return. Several times, Gruner has asked if he can pay his respects. This seems the perfect time, as he could ride in the helicopter. Are you good with that?"

Parker says, "Of course. I hope he's not worried. I'm doing well."

"I've told him so, but he still wants to visit." Taylor texts Gruner. *Need Parker's room checked. Come ASAP. If anything found, state "just as you said, sir." Nothing more. Understood?*

*I'll be ready in minutes,* Gruner texts in reply.

Taylor doesn't want to text that he plans to airlift Julie and Parker out of the hospital. Instead, he lets him know, *I'm mobilizing the Search-and-Rescue team. You can ride in the bird with them.*

*Roger that, sir.*

Taylor then sends a text to the Search-and-Rescue team leader, directing that the S-92 SAR be deployed to the University Medical Center. *Mobilize. ASAP. Gruner will ride with you to the site. You'll pick up two on stretchers and two others. Bring armed Airmen, prepared for engagement. Await my direction. The bird is a target, guard at all times.*

*We'll be ready, sir.*

Taylor turns to Parker, "I expect that Gruner will visit within the hour."

Becka looks at Julie and says, "Dear, let's take a break from all of this and sight-see. I can push the wheelchair down the hall, and if no one is in the family room, we can go inside. It's on the corner and has wrap-around windows. We'll be able to see the whole area. Doesn't that sound like fun? Would you like to get dressed first? I brought clean clothes for both you and Joe."

"Thank you for doing that, sis. I'd love to get out of this hospital gown, and I'd so like to escape the room for a bit."

Becka draws the curtain between the beds and helps Julie dress. She puts Julie's other items into a bag, which she'll carry back to the base for her.

Johnny follows their lead and helps Parker get changed. They don't say anything but acknowledge the steps they're taking with raised eyebrows.

Taylor's phone beeps a message from Gruner. *In flight.*

Taylor follows with a text to his driver. *Head back to the base now. I'll return via chopper.*

Johnny looks over at his dad. "I need to check in with my Commander. I'll be right back." He walks out into the hallway to speak with his superior. When he returns, he explains, "The Commander approved four more days of leave and also said there's no update on the President."

Taylor asks, "Where do you spend your nights?"

"Just across the street, at the Marriott. My rental car is there as well."

"Good to know you're close by." Taylor writes a text to Johnny. *Meet us at the base. I'll notify the guards at the entrance that you're coming. A bird will arrive shortly to pick us up.*

Johnny acknowledges and looks at his dad. "I'm going to take a walk while you've got company. I need some fresh air, and I'll check in with the students while I'm downstairs. They're probably in as much distress as we are."

Parker nods. "Of course, take all the time you need. I'm doing great."

✳    ✳    ✳

Johnny offers a playful salute and heads to the ground floor. As he exits, three students come to his side.

"Sir, we work on our website and need to talk with you. Something has come up. Something serious."

"I'm here, so let's talk now."

"Is there a space where we can talk privately?"

"I don't know. Is it *that* urgent?"

"More than we can tell you here."

Johnny walks over to the front desk and asks, "Do you have a private space where we can chat about a sensitive matter?"

The receptionist points to a vacant consulting room. Johnny motions to the students to follow him.

✳    ✳    ✳

On the eleventh floor, Taylor makes final preparations for the evacuation. He talks with Parker about everyday matters while he gathers Parker's belongings and puts them in a rucksack. Then he presses the help button. When an attendant arrives, Taylor explains, "My wife and I will give these folks a tour around the floor. Can you remove the monitors just for a short while?"

The attendant checks the charts. "That should be fine. Both are doing well, all things considered. I'll disconnect the machines. When you return and settle back down, just hit the buzzer, and I'll come back."

Taylor nods. "Okay." Beeps sound from his cell and indicate a text. *On the ground.*

Taylor acknowledges, *Take the elevator to the 11th floor. Wait for me.* Then he swings around to Julie and Parker, "So, who wants the first ride?"

"I do, I do," Julie says.

"You finished your housekeeping, Becka? Let's walk together."

"Yes, I'm all set."

"All right, see you in a bit, Parker."

Taylor sends another text. *Meet me by the 11th-floor elevator.*

An MP replies, *Yes, sir.*

Taylor pushes Julie down the hall and heads to the elevator where the soldier waits. When they near the doors, four armed Airmen, a nurse, and Gruner step into the corridor. Taylor directs the nurse to take Julie to the helicopter. Becka follows. The MP uses his key to access the roof helipad.

Taylor directs two Airmen to stand at the elevator exit, and then he tells the other two Airmen to accompany him back to Parker's room. Within minutes of reaching the medical bay, Gruner finds mics. "Just as you said, sir." The MP's eyes widen when he sees what Gruner has found.

Taylor acknowledges and motions for the Airmen to move quickly. They gather the last of the belongings and walk toward the exit.

Just then, Johnny rushes in. "General, I've been with the student journalists downstairs. They showed me video footage that I believe you need to see. It was posted on the student website a few minutes ago but hasn't been made public. It would be wise for Gruner to look at this as well."

Gruner joins the General, and they look at the footage saved on Johnny's cell phone. Horror spreads across their faces while they watch. The footage captures Marine One traveling near the mountains. One of the helicopters turns perpendicular to the other two and gets struck by a projectile. It explodes on impact. No one speaks about what they have just seen.

"Do you know who took this footage?" the General asks.

"The students have no idea. They showed me how personal photos and videos are submitted. And they also explained that all submissions must receive approval before they get published on the site. According to them, the contributors identify themselves, but this person didn't."

Taylor asks Gruner, "Does it look real to you?"

"Very."

The General motions for silence. "Interesting." He glances at Johnny. "Forward it to me, and I'll review it carefully. Thank you."

Then he turns to Parker. "Well, it's time to get this show on the road. Are you ready for a tour, buddy?"

"I'm eager to travel outside this room, that's for sure, even if only for a few minutes."

Taylor pushes Parker into the corridor, and the entourage follows.

As they approach the elevator, a nurse calls out, "Where are you going, sir? Do you need help?"

"No, we're giving my friend a tour of the building. All's well. Thanks."

The nurse appears baffled but turns away. The team enters the elevator, and the MP uses his key to allow access to the roof. They travel upward in silence. Julie and Becka watch their approach from the chopper. Airmen lift Parker and lay him on a gurney, which they load onto the helicopter. The Airmen hop on after Gruner and the General get settled inside.

The SAR climbs out of sight.

*     *     *

Johnny takes the elevator down to the first floor. When he exits, the three young journalists walk over to meet with him.

"Let me ask if we can use the consulting room again." He walks to the receptionist, speaks, and then waves for the students to join him. The group takes seats, and Johnny closes the door so that they can talk freely.

"I want to thank you again for showing me the video clip and not posting it publicly. You have respected the pilots, their families, and the President by doing so. When this video gets aired, it will be through officials in Washington, D.C.

"I want you to imagine the courage of the two pilots. When they volunteered for this assignment, they knew the risk. They knowingly committed to protecting the President at the cost of their lives. How extraordinary. These heroes would have had a moment's notice of an incoming rocket-propelled grenade. Had they hesitated, the outcome would have been very different. Instead, they moved into formation and paid the ultimate price. They gave their lives so that the President might live.

"You have honored their valor by giving this footage to me to pass it on. Your thoughtfulness and selflessness move me. The General asked me to tell you that he'll get in touch real soon."

The assembled students exchange glances and smiles. A few blush.

Johnny waits until they focus on him again. "It's important that you remain silent on this matter. The video shows the attempted murder of the President of the United States and the death of two pilots. Extremely dangerous information. The story the networks have carried is quite different from what we have with this footage. They attributed the crash to fog. Someone told them to say this. Whoever this someone is, they won't want anyone to come up with an alternate story, and especially not one of murder. With D.C. leaking the information, which they will do soon, the burden leaves your shoulders."

One of the young women says, "Thank you, sir. We've removed it from our website completely. Only you, and those you choose to give it to, have the information now. This has been a first for us, and we've learned immensely. Thank you for everything you've done for us. We're honored to have met you."

They stand and say their goodbyes. When Johnny walks out of the hospital, he discovers a mob of reporters. He shrugs, shakes his head, and quickens his pace. At the hotel, he pays the bill and asks for directions to Route 5 North. Once he reaches his car, he takes a deep breath—glad to be on his way.

# Chapter 9

*A*t the Trauma Center, an alarm blares. Throughout the locked-down floor, police move from room-to-room. The medical team searches for Julie and Parker. They check their files and discover that the backup person is General Taylor. Dr. Aguirre telephones him.

"Sir, Julie Underwood and Admiral Parker have gone missing. Are you aware of this?"

"I am, doctor. My men and I removed them. They are now en route to the base hospital."

"But . . . we didn't release either patient. They weren't ready for transport. You could endanger their lives."

"Doctor, you had them in a bugged room. A medical bay in which the President of the United States spoke of classified matters. He left here and, mysteriously, a Marine One helicopter flew into a mountainside. I can't help but think that his final words to us put him at risk because of the mics in that room.

"I had to get Admiral Parker and Ms. Underwood out of your hospital as soon as possible. Because we all might face the same fate as the President, I couldn't let anyone know what we planned."

"There were mics?"

"Go look for yourself. At the head of the bed, under the table, behind the bedside stand. We stopped looking after finding three. I'm sure you could find more. We didn't remove any of them, so you'll discover them easily."

"I don't know what to say. I have no idea how bugs could've got there. This is a tight hospital. It has to be."

"Well, that's for you to figure out, doctor. On my end, I will do every-thing possible to make sure Admiral Parker and Ms. Underwood heal safely. We need them. These next months will be rugged."

"I'll release their medical records to you today."

"Perhaps you'd like to visit them? If so, let me know ahead of time, and I'll clear the way. Thank you for your medical expertise. Your extraordinary efforts got them through this ordeal." The General says goodbye and ends the call. He feels impatient because he needs to make two crucial calls.

His first contact is to his Special Tactics Officer. "Thank you for your assistance. The recovery went smoothly, and we'll need an ambulance at the airfield to transport the patients to the base hospital. Please, put them in the President's Suite. It has more space, and those two want to stay together."

"Consider it done, sir."

He then rings the Secretary of Defense. His call gets put through immediately.

"Taylor, this is a surprise. How can I help you?"

"Sir, we received footage of an RPG hitting Marine One. Should we share the video?"

"Because it will get judged as a cover-up if we don't, and it gets out through other means?"

"Our thoughts, sir."

"All right. Please, send me the footage. I'll have it checked out."

"Thank you, sir. Should this go out anonymously, or from your office?"

"Good question. My office should take the lead."

"I'll send the footage now, sir."

"Thank you, Taylor. I'll have my team handle this. You'll hear from us soon."

A few minutes later, the helicopter makes its descent. As promised, an ambulance waits on the runway. Carefully, the Airmen lift the stretcher holding the Admiral and move him to the transport. Once they have him situated, they do the same with Julie's stretcher. After both are in place, Taylor steps forward. "My wife and I will visit in another hour or so."

Parker says, "Thanks for everything. Don't worry about us. We're in good hands."

A TH-73 Marine helicopter sits on the other side of the runway. "Airman, who brought in that chopper?"

"I don't know, sir, but they came to see you. They arrived just a couple of minutes ago."

"The pilot?"

"Inside, talking with the crew. Do you want me to get him?"

"Marine?"

"Yes."

"All right. I know what this is about. Thank you."

Taylor signals for his driver. "Take me to my office first, and then drive Becka home."

When they reach the front of his office, Becka says, "FBI, maybe?"

"My thoughts exactly. I'll call you after my meeting."

When Taylor goes inside, his assistant appears concerned. Behind the assistant, two men donned in dark suits wait for him.

"Am I to assume you two wish to see me?"

"You've assumed correctly. We're with the Federal Bureau of Investigation and have a few questions for you."

"Might this have to do with the assassination attempt on the President?"

"It does."

"In that case, I'd like to invite Staff Sergeant Gruner to join us. I think you'll find his insights enlightening. Shall I?"

"Certainly."

Taylor sends a text to Gruner. *Come to my office ASAP. FBI is here and has questions.* "He'll be here momentarily. Let's go into my office, gentlemen, and get comfortable."

Taylor directs them to his conference table. "I'm not surprised by your visit, but I didn't expect to hear from you this soon. Please, have a seat."

As they get comfortable, Gruner walks in.

"Ah, perfect timing, Gruner. I was just getting ready to ask these agents how they got here so soon after I called the Secretary of Defense. Gentlemen?"

The taller of the two agents responds first, "General, the FBI's been tracking the journalism students since the attempted murder of Admiral Parker. My buddy and I were at the Marine One crash site when the conversation between their group and Lieutenant J Parker was relayed. Once we knew you had the footage of the RPG, we decided it was time for a visit."

Taylor smiles. "There's not much that stays private, is there?"

"Not much."

"Well, Gruner is working on the case and is one of our best OPS specialists." Taylor turns to Gruner and motions for him to take over.

"I've only just begun to examine the footage, but some things we know for certain. I'll bring the clip up on the monitor so that we can all see it." Once the footage displays, he continues speaking.

"Given the trajectory and the impact, Marine One got hit by a rocket-propelled grenade. The footage doesn't show the origin of the launch, so we can't identify the assassin. We have aerial footage of the 2019 white Ford F-150 long-bed truck involved in the attempt, but the plates aren't visible. I checked, and unfortunately, about a million F-150s sold last year, and about a third of those were white. The likelihood of us finding this vehicle is slim.

"When the President visited Admiral Parker, he mentioned specifically that he looked forward to seeing Yosemite from the air. After the attack, we searched the hospital room for mics and found three. There might be more. Whoever masterminded this attack knew the President's intended flight plan. He directed the assassin to position himself along that path."

Gruner studies the two agents. "Would you like to hear my personal opinion?"

The elder of the two nods. "Certainly."

"Let me show you something first." Gruner opens his laptop, positions it in front of the agents and Taylor, and brings up a video game. "Take a look." Gruner plays the video, and the four men watch as a character shoots down a military helicopter with an RPG that he carries in the back of his truck.

"Familiar?"

The younger agent murmurs, "I'm speechless."

"Just so you know, millions play this simulated war game. The attack on Marine One was, likely, a contract killing. But I suspect this assassin has trouble distinguishing a simulated war game from the real thing. Entertainment and reality might be one and the same for him."

"Do you think he operated alone?"

"Yeah, I do, but I have no evidence one way or the other. My gut says he's a loner—one of those types with a garage full of every toy you can imagine. When this offer came up, my guess is that he felt thrilled that someone recognized his skills, and he got to use one of his toys. Perfect world."

"So, the attempted assassination wasn't personal?"

"I don't believe so. This guy's whole world is impersonal."

"That's frightening to think about," Taylor says.

"Agreed. I doubt he'll live much longer."

"What makes you say that?" The younger agent asks.

Gruner and the older agent exchange world-weary glances. Gruner says, "Whoever contracted the killer to fire that rocket will want him gone. Because he's an unknown, that shouldn't prove difficult. I suspect that he will get silenced soon, and we'll never know about it. The guy's a nobody—someone who spends his life in a synthetic world."

The younger agent shakes his head. "It gives me the chills to think about it in that light."

"Yeah, well, there's more, and it's even more concerning. I looked into who produces the game." He gives the General a look. "It's created and produced in China. They could, easily, track players, nab this one, and set up the attack. All remotely and anonymously."

# Chapter 10

*A*t Vandenberg Air Force Base, crowds have formed at the gate. Security Forces stand guard and do not permit entry. Reporters shout that they want to interview the President, but their demands fall on deaf ears.

Marine One circles the base and approaches the helipad from the west, flying over the ocean. The President stares out of his window at the growing mass of people crowded at the base's perimeter. He glances over at his Secret Service team, and they shake their heads, *no*, anticipating his request to speak to the crowd. As he exits the chopper, he hears the shouting and mutters, "unbelievable."

The Commander welcomes the President with a formal salute and then explains, "We'll go to my office where it's quiet."

The driver takes them past the chaotic gathering and to the front door of the Commander's office complex.

"I must apologize for this disruption, Commander. The reporters can be relentless. They want more information, and if my Secret Service team would allow me, I'd address them, because then they'd go away."

"How about an alternative? You could address the crowd through our audio system. Your message will carry throughout the base, and those at the gate will hear it too. It may not satisfy the most disruptive visitors, but your words might calm the majority, who want to hear that you're okay."

President Williams considers the offer and then decides to utilize the audio system. The Commander leads him to the OPS center—the location from which messages, typically, get sent. The Commander ushers him into a private room equipped with a microphone. The President sits at the desk, positions the mic, and prepares to speak. When the President's voice issues from the speakers, the crowd quiets and listens intently.

"Ladies and gentlemen. Today is a day of mourning. Two of our finest pilots lost their lives in protecting mine. I order that all flags get flown at half-staff for a full week, out of respect for these brave Marines. They embodied the best of our military and are heroes. Their names are Major Sarah Jameson (married with one child), and First Lieutenant Simon Vesey (married with no children). Our hearts go out to their loved ones.

"This is an emotional day for all of us, but especially for me. Two Marines just sacrificed their lives to save mine. To say that I'm overwhelmed is an understatement. Every morning, I offer thanksgiving for one more day, knowing full well that it might be my last. The presidency is the most targeted position in our country. Death threats are common, and attempts are just about as frequent. Because of the Secret Service and our military, I am alive.

"Daily, I commit to doing what I can to foster life, to make this a better world. Do you? I am serious. Do you? Circumstance has taught me that we are one family. It's irrelevant whether we're Republican or Democrat, Christian or Muslim, or Black or White. We are family, and as family, we need to help one another. In two days, I leave for Iceland, where I will meet with the nuclear powers. We will focus on denuclearization. On making our world a safer place. Each of us has a role to play.

"These two Marines died trying to help our world become a safer place. They acted without hesitation, without a thought to their own safety. I consider them part of my family, and today, I mourn. Please, allow me the emotional space I need to process my sorrow. I will have much more to say once I return to the White House, but now is not the time. One of my sisters and one of my brothers just died because of me." His voice drops and he adds, "Thank you."

The President turns away from the mic and faces the Commander. With a slight shake of the head and tightened lips, he communicates his grief. He looks across the room. All the Airmen and officers stand at attention. He acknowledges with a salute and then accompanies the Commander back to his office.

"Mr. President, the rocket launch happens in 45 minutes. We understand if you need to return to Washington before it's sent forth."

"Thank you, Commander. I had looked forward to the launch, but now I'm faced with identifying an assassin, or assassins, and more importantly, trying to offer comfort to the families of those brave Marines. Please prepare Air Force One for immediate departure."

"I assumed you would decide as such and requested Air Force One prepared and ready whenever you are, sir."

"Let's make this happen, Commander."

The Commander picks up his phone and tells his subordinates that it is a go. Air Force One will leave within minutes.

"Thank you for everything, Commander. You run a tight ship, and I'm most impressed."

"Thank you, Mr. President. I'll take you to the plane now."

# Chapter 11

In his hospital suite, Parker sits by the wall of windows. Since the second attempt on his life, he's found himself unable to sleep. Parker keeps hearing gunshots and has flashes of scenes from his service in Vietnam.

Drowsy, his head grows heavy and falls to his chest. His mind takes him back to Vietnam. Grisly scenes flash before him of mangled bodies, thundering missile explosions, and shrill screams. He shudders and recoils. Then he startles when someone touches his shoulder. When he opens his eyes, he finds the base chaplain stands next to him.

"Hello, Admiral. I'm told you might appreciate a friend to talk to. I'd like to be that friend if it's okay with you."

Parker shrugs his acceptance. "I suspect you're here because I'm remembering things. I, ah … I don't know what's wrong with me. I keep having flashes of Vietnam. It's like I'm reliving it, but why? Why now?"

"My understanding is that the sniper's bullet came within a hair of your heart. One centimeter more, and we wouldn't be talking right now."

"That's true, but still …"

"And, it was the Medal of Honor that protected you."

"Yes …"

"Awarded because of your extraordinary valor in Vietnam, right?"

"Correct."

"Maybe it's time to remember your experience there and make your peace."

"Some things are best to forget, chaplain."

"And yet, you've discovered that you haven't forgotten. The experience lives and haunts you with its devastation."

"I don't understand it. After all these years, it feels like it happened yesterday. I keep seeing the same scenes over and over."

"Tell me about what you see."

Parker looks away, his eyes welling, and his jaw tightening. "Marines got trapped at the Delta. They needed help, badly. The sub Commander asked for volunteers to go ashore, and I offered. The sub got as close to land as possible, and I swam to shore and found mayhem. I could barely see through the smoke. The thumping sound of the Hueys mixed with desperate cries for help. It was a scene from hell. Bodies strewn everywhere. Torsos without arms. Without legs. Arms and legs without bodies. Hell."

Parker stops and wipes his eyes. "I arrived too late. Yet I searched for any injured. There were none. It was a graveyard. I decided to go back to the sub, and when I drew close to the shoreline, I heard a moan. It turns out that I'd stepped on a Marine's arm and broken it. The Marine lay buried in the mud but was alive. That man was Samuel Williams."

"As in *President* Samuel Williams?"

"Yes. I called in for a patrol boat and got Williams into the craft. Though I did what I could, I was too late, except for Williams." Parker slumps, and his head falls.

The chaplain breaks the silence with a question, "Do you pray, Parker?"

"Yeah."

"Do you mind telling me *how* you pray?"

"I say the Lord's Prayer, and usually, I hold my mom's beads." He raises his hand and shows the chaplain an old wooden rosary.

"Do you bring that prayer into your memories?"

"Not really. The past is past. Until recently, I thought I'd moved on."

"Time isn't linear. We can be a young child one moment, and an old man the next. The past is as real as the present through our memories."

"I see your point. So, what do you suggest?"

"Well, if we understand prayer as our conversation with God, then we talk with God about what we experience."

"About memories? About something that occurred fifty years ago?"

"Yes, those memories live in you. The horror, the fears, become part of who you are now."

Parker runs his hand through his hair, "I don't know what I think about this conversation. It sounds weird ..."

"Parker, I'm being straight with you. You remember the battlefield because the memory got triggered, and you're ready to remember. Now is the time to invite God into your recollections."

"I don't know how to do that."

"I shall accompany you. Prayer isn't complex but simply speaking with God. All I ask is that you make it real. God isn't just a figment of my imagination or yours. God is our creator, *Our Father.*"

"I'm not sure I understand where this is going, but I'm on-board if it will help."

"Okay, then, let's focus on the second and third sentence of the Lord's Prayer. *Thy Kingdom come. Thy will be done, on Earth as it is in Heaven.* What do these words mean to you?"

"Well, we're asking for God's Heavenly Kingdom to manifest here on Earth."

"Good. Remember that when emotion overwhelms you and nothing seems right. Say *this prayer* and make the words real."

"Chaplain, I'm not sure I can. I was 23-years-old when I got deployed to Vietnam. I'd never seen such horror, not before or since. I stumbled over bodies. So how do I bring the Lord's Prayer there? I just don't get it."

"Okay. Describe the scene as graphically as possible."

"I don't know that I can."

"You can. As graphically as possible . . . I'll go with you."

"When I got on shore—" Parker pauses. "—when I got to shore, I didn't know which way to turn. Bodies lay everywhere. I walked and searched for survivors but didn't find any … except, later, I discovered the President." Parker clutches the rosary, and the veins on his fist distend. His breathing becomes rapid and shallow. "Young Marines, 18 or 19-years-old were spread across the muddy banks. I tried to check each body. I did what I could . . . I did what I could. As instructed, I gathered dog tags."

The chaplain lowers his voice, "Stay with the scene, Parker. You're safe. We'll pray now. *Our Father who art in Heaven. Hallowed be thy name. Thy Kingdom come. Thy will be done on Earth, as it is in Heaven.* Loving Father, bring your perfect, healing peace to this moment, to this scene. May your *Kingdom come.*"

After a few minutes, Parker's breathing quiets.

"What's in your mind now, Parker?"

"They're not alone. The Marines aren't alone. They have many others with them."

"Can you tell me who's there?"

"I'm not sure, but they're loving. Family, maybe, or friends. The spirits seem to have come to help the Marines with their transition. Maybe they're angels?"

Parker smiles. "Oh, they're saluting me and saying thank you. But I didn't do anything. They say I was with them, and that's why they feel grateful. And they seem happy."

Tears roll down Parker's cheeks. His breathing has slowed.

The chaplain leans forward. "What do you see now?"

"They're leaving. The Marines are going with their friends and platoon. Their bodies still lie on the ground, but the dead aren't with their bodies."

"Ahh, the Father's Kingdom has come."

Parker opens his eyes and turns to the chaplain. "I don't know what to say, except thank you."

"You were ready, Parker, to see what most do not see—the life that awaits us."

# Chapter 12

Seated alone by the windows, Parker glances up when Becka walks in and hugs him. A woman he doesn't know stands to the side.

Becka says, "Hey, how're you doing?"

"Every day's a little better. Thank you."

Julie rouses from her nap.

Becka smiles. "I've got a surprise for both of you."

Parker says, "I'm all ears."

"I've arranged for this lady to wash and trim yours and Julie's hair. She even offered me a discount when I mentioned you were an Admiral. Seems she likes officers, particularly. Isn't that right, Mei?"

"It gives me a way to show my respect."

Parker says, "Thank you, Mei. To let Julie wake up properly, I'll go first."

Mei pushes Parker's wheelchair into the bathroom—an ample space made to accommodate multiple people and a wheelchair. She closes the door, an alarming action that prompts Parker to text Gruner. He doesn't like this woman. He doesn't trust her. But now chills run down his spine. *Come NOW!* he writes.

"I can take that for you," she says, her hand outstretched.

"That's okay. By regulation, I must keep it on my person."

"Hmm, interesting. Have you been here long, Admiral?"

"Not that long. I came for a visit, which ended up more prolonged than I'd expected."

Mei picks up her scissors and runs her fingers down its blades. "So, Admiral, you must have served on many ships."

Parker stumbles for words, "Y-yes, several. Recently, however, my work has been limited to an office." He hopes Gruner arrives soon.

"The USS Gerald R. Ford is an impressive ship. Are you familiar with it?"

Heavy pounding rattles the bathroom door. Mei had jammed the exterior lock before closing the door, thus making it impossible for anyone to enter. Parker reaches to release the lock, but she stops him. "Your days of being in charge are over, Admiral. You follow my directives now."

More pounding shakes the door. "Can I help you?" Mei calls out.

"We need the Admiral. He must come with us."

"He's not going anywhere, sir. He's busy right now." She pronounces each word in a slow and surly fashion.

A click sounds when the lock disengages. Security Forces rush into the room. The beautician stands behind the Admiral and holds the scissors at the tight skin over his jugular.

"Don't come any closer. Put your weapons on the floor. Do it!"

Gruner turns to the two security officers. "She's in charge now."

"Correct. I'm in charge. Put your weapons on the floor."

The Airmen, in different positions in the bathroom, reach to put their handguns on the tiles.

Gruner asks, "Why are you doing this, Miss? You must know this threat won't end well for you. What did the Admiral do to you?"

"He's part of the establishment. That's enough."

"I don't understand what you mean."

"Oh, I think you do, but I don't have time for this conversation. The future is no longer yours. It's best you realize that."

The Admiral looks down and pleads, "My rosary. I dropped my rosary. It was my mother's. Please, let me pick it up."

Mei moves the scissors. "Make it quick."

The Admiral bends to pick up the rosary and falls onto the floor. In that split second, the Airmen pick up their weapons and open fire. The hits prove fatal. One bullet to the head, another round to the chest. The Admiral picks up the rosary and whispers, "Thank you, Mom."

Taylor runs into the room. Becka lays on the bed with her body positioned to protect Julie.

"Are you two okay?"

"We're fine, but what about Parker? We heard two gunshots."

"He's okay. I believe our Security Forces shot the assailant twice. I'll get back to you in a minute." He rushes into the bathroom area and sees that Parker has a surface wound on his neck, but otherwise, looks fine.

"Gruner, fill me in."

Gruner says, "Sir, I believe there's an active Chinese cell in the area. When Mei said, '… the future is no longer yours. It's best you realize that.' it gave me the chills. I have the feeling that she expects China will take over America. I know that sounds far-fetched, but something big is afoot, and I wouldn't be surprised if this group is one of many. Also, I suspect they may lie behind the assassination attempts. They're angry, impatient, and want revenge."

"Let's talk more in a minute."

Taylor turns to the Security Forces, "Clear the area and leave no stone unturned. We need to check that woman's cell phone and the contents of her purse. Find out how she got clearance to come onto the base and how my wife met her and arranged for this encounter. This is of the highest urgency. We may have stumbled upon the cell that tried to assassinate the President. Report all findings to Gruner." He nods to Gruner and says, "Meet with me as soon as you find out anything."

Once more, Taylor addresses his Airmen, "Are we clear?"

They respond in unison, "HOOAH!"

Parker sees his reflection in the mirror—his face appears chalky, and his hands tremble. Taylor rests a hand on his shoulder. "Let's get you out of here." He pushes Parker through the gathering to his bed. Then he calls the nurse, who takes one look at Parker and puts a cuff on his arm to check his blood pressure. As suspected, it reads as dangerously high.

"Admiral, we've got to bring down your blood pressure. I'm going to put in a saline line with a little labetalol. You may feel sleepy, but it will help. I also want you to try a simple deep breathing exercise. I'll get you the directions."

Julie says, "We'll do it together."

*     *     *

Taylor goes back to his team and checks on developments.

"We're taking the cell phone, sir. It appears that the woman made several calls to Beijing. We also need her purse. The bag contains some questionable items that we need to test. Finally, and this will dumbfound you, the Airmen at the gate told us that she presented them with a pass signed by you."

"Good grief. Do what you need to do, Airmen, and get to the bottom of this. Consider it your highest priority. When I call the President, I want to impress him with our thoroughness and conclusions. As I said, leave no stone uncovered."

"We still need to speak with Mrs. Taylor, sir."

"I'll have her come to you. Just a moment." Taylor returns to the main room and asks Becka to come with him. He explains the need for questioning and promises to stand beside her.

First Lieutenant Kate Smith says, "Hello, Mrs. Taylor. We have a couple of questions regarding Mei Huang. Could you tell us how you met her?"

"I saw a card posted at the Exchange. I have it here." She pulls the slip of card out of her purse and hands it to Smith. "As you can see, it offers discounts to military personnel and their spouses. I called, made the appointment, and met her for the first time just this morning."

"Do you remember anything she might have asked you?"

"When we were setting up the appointment, she asked how long I'd been here and wanted to know my husband's rank. She seemed particularly interested in Admiral Parker and even asked me if he'd served on the USS Gerald R. Ford."

Smith nodded and made notes. "What did you tell her?"

"That he'd served on several ships and that the USS Gerald R. Ford was his last deployment. Because it seemed odd that a beautician would have an interest in military ships, I asked her if her father was in the service. She said he was and that he had a book about ships and would point to ones with the names of states, like the USS Nevada, California, Oklahoma, West Virginia, and Arizona."

The Airmen look at each other and over at the General.

"What's wrong?" Becka asks.

"Mrs. Taylor, those ships sank during the December 7th, 1941 attack on Pearl Harbor."

Becka's face pales, and she reaches for her husband's hand.

Smith says, "Because you inquired about her interest, we have a chance of solving this crime. That was excellent thinking on your part. Please, let us know if you remember anything else. Here's our contact number." She hands the card to Becka and turns to leave with her team.

"I should have known," Becka says to Taylor.

"You were talking with her about haircuts. Given the context, few people would have realized what she was saying."

Becka appears visibly distraught. She looks down at the floor and shakes her head. "I should have known."

"Come on. Let's get you home. I think Parker and Julie need some quiet time."

# Chapter 13

--------·--------

*A*cross the Atlantic, in an unidentified area of Reykjavik, Iceland, President Williams meets with the leaders of the eight most powerful nuclear nations—Russia, China, the United Kingdom, India, Pakistan, France, Israel, and North Korea. They've drafted a treaty to ban nuclear weapons, but notable disagreement delays progress. These countries didn't support the *2017 Treaty on the Prohibition of Nuclear Weapons*. That lack of support is evident in this meeting. Russia claims that, with their new weapons, they're invincible to the U.S. missile defense systems. China asserts the same. North Korea won't consider any settlement. The tensions grow palpable, and the lack of trust evident.

Williams asks each participant to identify what would make it possible for them to sign a binding treaty. The leaders articulate that disarmament will need to be staged carefully to facilitate an incremental reduction in each country's arsenal and that such a reduction would need objective verification.

North Korea is the most antagonistic. It wants equal holdings in each country and proposes the first step should be an assessment of each country's depository and then the elimination of nuclear warheads in excess of the country with the least holdings. Russia challenges this proposal and suggests the reduction be proportionate to the size of the respective country. China counters and proposes that population be the determining factor. Williams intervenes and reminds the leaders that current stockpiles could kill every living thing on the planet many times over.

He asks, "What would we achieve by exerting such devastation? What would we prove? If we're all dead, who is victorious? We need to move this discussion to steps we're willing to take to preserve life. I'm ready to commit to incremental disarmament, but I need partners in this effort."

China says, "I can commit—with certain requirements in place."

"Such as?"

"Verified reductions in other countries."

"I agree absolutely. Others?" Williams looks around the room.

Russia says, "I could agree if reductions are verified. We need to specify clearly what forms of verification we would use."

The United Kingdom offers its support, as does France, India, and Israel. Pakistan finally concedes. But North Korea's leader sits cross-armed and grim-faced. Williams looks at the Supreme Leader and says, "You've stayed silent. Could you tell us your position?"

"I want equal holdings in each country."

Williams's eyes narrow. "Are you willing to accept incremental reductions?"

"If the goal is equal holdings, then I support it."

"You have the smallest population and the smallest area of our nine countries. You expect the largest countries to reduce their holdings to match yours?"

"Or, provide me with the warheads. That is correct."

Outraged commotion disrupts the meeting. Williams says, "As you can hear, your suggestion is not supported. We need to find an alternative that we can all endorse. Let's consider options over lunch and reconvene at 14:00."

Williams scans the room and locks his gaze on the Russian President, who sits talking vigorously with China's President. The North Korean leader sits alone, smug, and seemingly amused by developments. Williams grows more concerned. They must reach an agreement, but he doesn't know how that can happen.

The restaurant maître d invites everyone to relocate to the dining room. With the seating prearranged, Williams finds himself assigned to sit between the North Korean Supreme Leader and the United Kingdom's Prime Minister. Lost in his thoughts, he jumps a little when the waiter asks him if he'd like to order a drink.

"Thank you, I'll have a Brennivin. I love the flavor of caraway."

"Excellent choice, sir."

He turns to his Korean comrade. "Have you thought more about disarmament?"

"Why should I? I don't accept your proposal."

"I suggest that you look at alternatives to make the current proposal more attractive to you and your people."

"Like what?" he says, and his voice comes out at a near snarl.

"Perhaps an expanded trade agreement?"

"You want to barter?"

"If that will help us move forward on behalf of our people, then yes."

The Supreme Leader purses his lips and squints his eyes. "I need the trade embargos lifted."

"And, if we provide that, will you cooperate with the disarmament effort under discussion?"

"Perhaps."

"I cannot move forward with a *perhaps*. Tell me what steps you will take toward disarmament."

The Supreme Leader's tone changes, and he slams his fist on the table. "I don't need to tell you anything. You provide me with a proposal."

Williams excuses himself and walks over to the window. He doesn't like this man, but he must find a way to secure an agreement on disarmament. Sharp pain buckles his stance, but he manages to correct. His kidney disease has flared. Because of the disarmament meetings, he delayed his regular dialysis. A glance back shows the Supreme Leader talking with one of his team. The leader then gets up and walks over to speak with China's President. Williams sighs and stares out through the window. The meeting chair calls time. The President turns and looks over at his seating place. Someone has moved his drink. He studies the room. All the servers appear busy. Only his Korean colleague and his assistant went near the glass. A chill runs through him. Williams suspects that someone has tampered with his drink and motions to his Secret Service detail.

"Did you notice anyone touch my glass?"

"Sir, the Korean Supreme Leader's assistant moved it while the two of them talked. You suspect foul play?"

"Perhaps. Take care of things."

# Chapter 14

As planned, Williams reconvenes the leaders at 14:00. "Your Excellencies, we have cause for great celebration. The United States has offered to end its trade embargos with North Korea. With this move, North Korea has accepted progressive nuclear disarmament. Madam Prime Minister and gentlemen, our nine countries have reached an agreement." The gathering erupts into loud applause.

"Over the next couple of days, we shall work through the details of how to implement the treaty, but today, we celebrate. The clerks have prepared a binding covenant for our signatures. In front of you is a pen. Join me in signing this historic agreement."

The leaders push back their chairs and dart glances about the room as they step forward. Unlike the *2017 Treaty*, this one is endorsed by the nine most powerful nuclear nations on the earth. Photographers stand to the side, waiting to capture the historic moment. Within minutes of their camera flashes, photos of the nine leaders circulate in most newspapers, and footage of the nine signing the agreement airs on most television news stations.

After the last signature, the Russian President calls out, "Let's toast!" A waiter brings out a tray with flutes of champagne. Each leader takes a glass, raises it high, and repeats after the Russian President, "To a new beginning."

The leaders return to their seats, where the conversation continues with more drinks poured, and appetizers served. The North Korean leader turns to President Williams. "You and I have had our differences, but we're working together now to solve the armament problem. Let's toast one another."

Williams darts a look at his Secret Service detail. At their nods, he understands that his concerns have been addressed. The President picks up his glass, raises it, and then takes a swallow. He wonders what might have happened if he hadn't noticed the displaced glass. Sharp pain again riddles his mid torso and prompts a gasp. He decides he must call Margaret Adler, the Vice President. He excuses himself and slips into one of the meeting rooms.

"Margaret, this is sudden, but I need your help. Please mobilize Air Force Two and fly to Reykjavik as soon as possible. It's a six-hour flight, so you can sleep on the way. I wouldn't ask, except I'm struggling with a physical problem."

"I'll get on the plane momentarily, sir."

Williams returns to the conference room and addresses the group, "Colleagues, this is the proudest day of my presidency. We've looked upon one another as adversaries and not allies, as competitors and not friends. Today, we declare that we are interconnected. Whatever our differences, we have chosen to work through those differences for the survival of humankind. Thank you for joining me in this effort. Our children now have reason to hope."

President Williams lifts his drink again, "To each of you and to our joint efforts to rebuild our world. Cheers!" After setting down his flute, he adds, "In front of you is a packet of information that includes lists of questions and concerns that have been raised and possible solutions for each. Please, review this carefully and let's reconvene at 19:00 to discuss. Dinner will be served at 17:00. Until then, thank you."

Williams returns to his room and collapses on his bed. *Just a few more hours, just a few more hours. When Margaret arrives, I can leave.* He calls his assistant and asks him to prepare the team and Air Force One for departure at 22:00 tonight. Then he considers what he will say to his colleagues.

He writes a few thoughts on a notepad and drifts into sleep. A knock on the door prompts him to sit up.

"Yes?"

"Sir, the group awaits you before beginning dinner."

"Please tell them I'm on my way."

Williams takes a deep breath, and with measured movements, he stands. He reaches for his notes and walks to the dining room. With a fist raised high, he greets everyone with, "We did it! Let's enjoy our meal together."

Before sitting down, he goes from one leader to the next and shakes their hands or pats them on the back and thanks them for their efforts in moving the negotiations forward. When he reaches his seat, he notices that the North Korean Supreme Leader is missing. He turns to the U.K. Prime Minister and asks about him.

"We were told that he felt unwell and ordered a special meal to be delivered to his room."

Williams nods. "Thank you, ma'am. I hope he feels better soon, because he has more questions than anyone, and we plan to address every concern at our meeting."

"If he can't make it, perhaps his assistant could?"

"That's an option, but I doubt it's one he'll support. You know how he is. After dinner, I'll try to visit with him and see how he wants to proceed."

As they near the end of the meal, Williams catches Smirnov's attention, and the two walk over to the windows.

"I'm having some medical issues," Williams confides, "and I need to return to D.C. this evening. I've asked my Vice President to step in. Ms. Adler will arrive in a few hours. I wanted you to know that I trust her implicitly, and you'll see why. Margaret's as straight as they come. You don't need to pull punches around her. She can handle most anything."

"Will you be okay?"

"Yeah, it's my fault. I delayed my dialysis, and I'm paying the price."

"Well, your health is more important than anything else. I'll miss you tomorrow, but I trust your assessment of the Vice President." Smirnov smiles mischievously and adds, "I'll let you know what I think after this is over."

Taylor chuckles. "I look forward to that call."

Later, when the meeting convenes, it is without the Korean leader. The President explains to the group that he attempted to speak with him, but to no avail. He suggests that they begin discussions about the concerns. Then, in the morning, the group will address each issue and come to an agreement. He expresses hope that the Korean leader will be well enough to attend at that time. Everyone agrees to the compromise, and they proceed.

After an hour, Williams calls for a break. "Colleagues, I have an important announcement. Tonight, I must return to the United States for medical treatment. The problem is long-standing but has worsened and needs attention. My Vice President, Margaret Adler, will arrive shortly, and tomorrow with your approval will act in my stead. You will find her an excellent leader, trustworthy, and clear-thinking. Her decisions are my decisions.

"It has been a pleasure working with each of you. Together, we've created a future for our families and our countries. We've achieved what few would have imagined as possible. How extraordinary. Madam Prime Minister and distinguished gentlemen, we are adjourned. Have a good evening."

\*   \*   \*

Vice President Adler and her team arrive on schedule and head to the hotel. As she walks past a limousine parked in front of the hotel conference site, she hears a familiar voice.

"Margaret, thank you for coming on a moment's notice. Please, join me for a few minutes." She steps inside the limo, and the President updates her about the deliberations, the remaining challenges, and the schedule for the next day.

"Sir, are you okay?"

"Yes and no. I'm dealing with a blood disorder that requires dialysis. I had hoped I could get through the deliberations without needing treatment, but unfortunately, I was wrong. I must return to D.C."

"Mr. President, you can trust me to do the best that I can."

"Yes, of course. You'll find a packet of information in your hotel room, along with my personal notes. We've reached an important juncture, but I feel confident you can manage it well. When I concluded our last session, I informed the leaders that you would act in my stead and that I needed to return to the United States for medical treatment. They expect you."

"I appreciate your confidence, sir. Hopefully, I can live up to your expectations. Safe travels."

# Chapter 15

At the hotel, the North Korean leader lies down. He complains of nausea. "I blame this illness on the Hakarl. I didn't enjoy that fermented shark dish they served us." He orders his staff to bring him rice and porridge. "It might help my upset stomach." The leader also tells his aide to bring him some antacid.

The tablets seem to help a little, but not enough. The leader yells at his staff. He's impatient and wants relief. They give him more antacid, but the improvement seems minor. As he lies on the bed, he sweats profusely. Annoyed and suffering, he orders, "Open the windows and turn on the fan." Eventually, he falls into a restless sleep. When he awakens, he stumbles to the restroom and collapses.

Concerned, his staff go in search of him. They find him unresponsive on the bathroom floor.

The leader's companions call the front desk and request immediate assistance. The hotel staff calls the police and asks for an ambulance.

The police arrive first and determine that the North Korean leader has died. They examine the situation and decide that the Supreme Leader lost his balance, fell, and hit his head on the floor. "It appears that he cracked his head when he hit the hard tiles. That is the reason his blood has pooled on the floor."

When the medical team arrives, the police inform them of their findings. The paramedics proceed to check the body and point out the blood seeping from his mouth. They set the time of death as 22:00.

\*    \*    \*

No sooner has Margaret walked into her room than the phone rings. "Ma'am, this is the front desk. We were told to contact you if an urgent need arose. Could you come downstairs for a few minutes? A serious situation has developed."

"Certainly. I'll be right there." Margaret grabs her purse, not knowing what to expect, and heads to the reception area. When she walks into the foyer, hospital personnel carry Korea's Supreme Leader on a stretcher to a waiting ambulance. She looks for someone she might know but sees no such person.

"Madam Vice President?"

"Yes. Can I help you?" She turns to see a member of the North Korean delegation approaching her.

"Our Supreme Leader has died. It appears he fell and suffered severe head injuries. We will have no representation during the last phase of these negotiations. Still, our leader signed the agreement, and we will abide by the group's decisions."

"I'm deeply sorry for your loss, and I'm grateful for your consideration in wanting to speak with me tonight. Please, express my heartfelt condolences to his family and to your people."

"I will do so. Now, I must go." He bows and proceeds to the exit.

Margaret walks to the curb with him and offers a deep bow to the Korean assemblage. Once their vehicles disappear into the night, she returns to her room and, immediately, calls the President. His Chief of Staff answers and informs her that President Williams is currently receiving medical attention and is unavailable. Margaret offers an overview of the Korean leader's demise and tells the CoS that her staff is preparing a detailed report, which she'll forward shortly. Then she asks, "When you can, please inform the President that the conference is proceeding as planned, and I have matters in hand." After she hangs up, she crosses to the desk in the corner of her room and begins reading the documents President Williams left for her.

❋    ❋    ❋

The following morning, Margaret gathers the papers and her notes and goes to the conference room. She walks around the gathering, greeting participants and introducing herself to those she doesn't know. Then she walks to the podium. Margaret pushes her hair behind her ears, shuffles the papers in front of her, and looks intently into the assembly.

"It's a pleasure to join you, Madam Prime Minister and distinguished gentlemen. President Williams asked me to facilitate the remaining meetings, as he had to return to D.C. for urgent matters requiring his immediate attention. I know most of you, but allow me to introduce myself once again. I am Vice President Margaret Adler. I have served in this position for six years, and prior to this, I was part of the legal counsel team for the defense department. I look forward to working with you to craft the details of this treaty, but before I proceed as President Williams asked, I have two questions for you. Firstly, do I have your support in facilitating the discussion? And, secondly, do you have any questions of me?"

The group quiets and looks, nervously, to other members of the assembly. No one voices any questions.

Margaret clears her throat. "Thank you for your endorsement. I will do all that I can to help us reach our stated goals. However, before beginning, I suspect you've noticed that North Korea's Supreme Leader is not with us today. Last night, he had a fall and, tragically, passed away. His attendants accompanied him back to his grieving people. Before they left, the Vice Chairman of the Workers Party stated that his country will support our collective decisions. Let us begin our deliberations with a moment of silence."

After a few minutes, Margaret says, "President Williams suggested that we pair up according to the size of our country's stockpile of nuclear warheads. Should we agree to his suggestion, the matchings would go as follows: the United States and Russia, China and France, the United Kingdom and Pakistan, and lastly, India and Israel.

"It's inevitable that we might get paired with a country that thinks quite differently than we may. Our task is to find common ground. Already, you've taken the hardest step—in that you have authored a binding nuclear disarmament treaty, which stipulates progressive actions toward our goal. This next step focuses on implementation and how we will disarm. Any questions?"

"What if we can't reach an agreement?" The Chinese leader, President Zhang, says with defiance.

Without flinching, Adler responds, "I know you will reach an agreement because you've promised to do so. You are wise leaders. You love your countries, your people. You know better than anyone the consequences of nuclear war. How can you not reach a resolution?"

Adler pauses and looks around the room. "Colleagues, we don't need to like each other; we don't need to trust each other. We do need to believe in the value of life and make decisions accordingly. Yesterday, you watched the simulation, *Plan A,* developed by researchers at Princeton's Program on Science and Global Security. We're not far from a worldwide conflict. As you learned, within three hours of deployment of the first nuclear weapon, about 100 million innocents would die. But it doesn't stop there. As more warheads plummet to the earth, millions more will perish. When the final nuclear blast occurs, who remains alive? How will she or he stay alive? And why would they want to?

"A nuclear war would have catastrophic consequences. It would thrust us into a decade-long nuclear winter. This is a profoundly serious matter. There are no winners. If we retain a thread of humanity, we have no choice but to choose life."

Adler looks out into the group and sees a few side glances but also notices that leaders nod in agreement. The Chinese President slouches in his chair, his legs spread wide. His defiant expression tells her that problems lie ahead.

"When you meet with your counterpart, think strategically about the needs of your people, and bring those needs to the discussion. The time has arrived to think more about the wellbeing of our people and less about how we might annihilate others. We need to share resources, not fight to acquire them.

"Keep in mind that if our thoughts are about eliminating our enemy, we are also eliminating the possibility of our enemy's resources when we use nuclear weapons. According to scientists, our stockpiles can cause an atomic Armageddon many times over. Ultimately, what do we gain if we lose everything, and our people die from a nuclear exchange?" No one speaks, but from the set jaws and stony silence, Adler knows there's work to be done.

"If there are no questions, let's reconvene at 18:00." Adler watches as the attendees push their chairs back and leave the conference room. Though pleased, their body language and furtive glances make her realize that she might be the only one to feel that way.

Adler follows the Russian President to a small meeting room and sits across the table from him. His eyes narrow. "We meet again."

Her thoughts race back more than a dozen years. She was still in the Army when called to testify at a hearing in D.C., at which President Smirnov was also in attendance.

"Different circumstances. Now, we're asked to work together."

The President smirks. "What is your country prepared to offer?"

"We're prepared to take deliberate, verifiable steps toward disarmament."

"And what, precisely, does that mean to you?"

"Precisely, it means that we're prepared to reduce our stockpile by half."

The Russian President's expression changes from irritation to surprise. He sits up and looks at Adler intently. "I didn't expect that reply. Do you speak for your President?"

"I do."

He stares at Adler while tapping his fingers on the table. Finally, he says, "We will match your commitment. But we insist that a team of our making verify each step."

"Absolutely agreed. Each of us must choose our representatives for an evaluating team."

"Equal number."

"Certainly."

"And after this first step?"

Adler straightens and states, "In two years, we evaluate the success of the denuclearization effort and, depending upon our findings, we reduce the stockpile by half yet again."

"Interesting. With all precautions in place, I could agree."

"We could use drones for aerial surveillance and have in-person veri-fications three times a year."

"Agreed. I like working with you, Adler. No nonsense—it's the only way." He smiles and pushes back his chair.

Down the hallway, raised voices indicate that another meeting has begun, but not as successfully.

# Chapter 16

————•————

*W*hen the world leaders return to the main conference room, the space fills with lighthearted banter. Margaret smiles and waits until everyone gets seated.

"Thank you, all. War may have shaped our histories, but given the joviality in this room, we are aware of the common humanity that we share.

"We all have stories, not of greatness, but of horror, not of friendships but of hate. Wars begun and ended, entire populations affected, winners few. Today, we create an alternative history. I invite President Smirnov to come forward." The Russian President adjusts his collar, clears his throat, offers a quick glance across the room, and walks with purpose to the front of the area.

Margaret, says, "Would you, please, explain what our two countries have decided?"

A slight smile forms on his lips, and he announces, "The United States and Russia have agreed to reduce our nuclear stockpile by fifty percent over the next two years."

No one speaks, and the shocked looks convey disbelief. Members listen intently as the President continues, "It is our hope that, after two years, we will reduce our stockpile again by another fifty percent."

Eyes dart and faces register astonishment. No one envisioned such a resolution. Silence spreads throughout the room.

Adler says, "We all know the consequence of nuclear war. Once begun, it will end only with full annihilation. President Smirnov and I love our countries, and we love our families. We want *life*. We have agreed to work together to ensure survival, and more than survival—abundance. The trade embargo between our countries will lift. We will use drones for surveillance and have three in-person investigations each year. We'll do all that we can to guarantee the success of this effort."

It's clear the two nations are serious. The French President stands and claps enthusiastically. The Prime Minister of the United Kingdom joins the applause. Then the remaining leaders stand. The acclaim soon becomes rhythmic, and the roar of sound sends waiters and other staff rushing into the room.

Adler smiles, turns to her counterpart, and extends her hand, which Smirnov grasps firmly. They shake and nod to one another. They have just created the impossible—a future.

President Zhang speaks loudly over the crowd, "Vice President Adler, may we take a fifteen-minute break? I don't think any of us expected this development, and we need time to meet with our assigned partners."

Adler looks at the eager faces. "Let's take a break. We'll resume in 30 minutes."

Teams gather—China with France, the United Kingdom with Pakistan, and India with Israel.

Within minutes, all eyes focus on the Chinese President. He yells and threatens. Security has moved closer to their table.

Adler calls out, "Gentlemen." They show no response. Again, she shouts, "GENTLEMEN!" and slams her fist on the table. "Is this a conversation that we should all hear?"

President Zhang sneers. "Why should we trust you?"

"Who trusts anyone? It is *time* that will create trust. Time and repetitive trustworthy actions. Tell me, do you suggest that China be part of the investigative team?"

"I … eh … I would like that."

"Excellent. Consider it done. Do we have any other volunteers for the investigating team?"

Not one person anticipated such a question. After a brief pause, both France and Israel raise their hands. Adler looks out over the membership. "Others?"

The United Kingdom and Pakistan raise their hands, and Adler acknowledges.

She turns to her Russian counterpart and nods. "I believe we have our investigating team." She notices the surprise on everyone's faces.

"If we're honest with ourselves, or anyone else, we'd admit freely that we don't trust, that we live in fear, and that we are always ready to impose a deadly strike. In fact, our power is measured by our ability to destroy. Isn't that right?

"No one suggests that we abandon our need to protect our country's boundaries and our people. Rather, today, we lay the foundation for an alternative way of relating. Shall we proceed?" Members glance one at another and nod their agreement.

For the next two hours, the leaders present and discuss their preliminary ideas for progressive nuclear disarmament. The Pakistani leader asks for a break, and Adler concurs.

"Let's reconvene in fifteen minutes," she says.

As chairs get pushed back, and people stand, Adler walks out onto the deck. A chilly breeze brushes her skin, which she welcomes. This is her first visit to Iceland, and she smiles. *What a perfect location.*

The Russian President interrupts her reveries when he stands by her side. "This is a day I could not have imagined, standing shoulder to shoulder with the Vice President of the United States, looking out on ..."

Adler smiles. "I couldn't have imagined it either. Here we are, the two most powerful countries in the world, nations who have hated one another for a century, marveling at natural beauty and a child playing with a kite. No, I couldn't have imagined."

President Smirnov gives a side glance and asks, "Where did it occur?"

Adler realizes that he's noticed her arm prosthesis. "Afghanistan."

"Ah, another reason to hate Russians."

"Don't we all have *reasons*? You wonder who holds the power—truly. Those of us who can destroy, or a child who plays innocently with her kite?"

An uproar of yelling sounds from inside, and Adler and Smirnov dash back indoors. The Chinese leader waggles his index finger at the French leader, warning him of Armageddon. Security has moved next to them—again.

Adler calls out, "Gentlemen!" Seeing no response, she shouts, "GENTLEMEN!"

They stop their arguing. The Chinese leader spits on the floor.

"Your disdain evokes my own," Adler states. "Now, bring your argument to the floor."

The French leader says, "He called me a fraud and said I was unscrupulous."

President Smirnov pushes forward. "ENOUGH OF THIS!" He looks directly at President Zhang. "Enough of the child's play. We came here to carve a different tomorrow. I'm intent on doing just that." He tosses a napkin at Zhang and stares intently.

The Chinese President starts to respond, and the Russian President moves closer to him. With their faces just inches apart, he declares, "I don't care about your reasons. We have a task to do and limited time."

The standoff between the two superpowers deadens the room. No one speaks, and no one moves. Finally, President Zhang motions to his staff, who rush to his side. One of his attendants takes the napkin to wipe the floor.

"Do we understand one another?" President Smirnov asks with contempt. His squinted eyes send stony daggers into the Chinese President.

President Zhang fastens a look of hate on Smirnov and holds his head high. "We do."

Adler hurries to the podium and calls the meeting to order. "Colleagues, over these last couple of days, we've forged a treaty and begun to establish the mechanisms for ensuring the treaty's success. We've talked about the lack of trust and have just witnessed an example of that deficit. Time alone will mitigate our doubts. Time alone will soften our hatreds. It cannot happen overnight.

"We must remember that as we choose alternatives to conflict, we choose life. For our countries, for our families. No matter who you are or what side of the conflict you are on, we need to admit that we could have done what our opponent has done. Depending upon the perspective, no one is innocent."

On edge, the crowd glances from one to the other.

"It is easy for us to point fingers and think in terms of enemies. But, with a little effort, can't we testify to the resilience and universality of the human spirit? Haven't we all heard stories of forgiveness that have left us breathless, even when revenge seemed justified? These restorative narratives offer hope that we can surmount the horrors of war. We aren't locked into hate if we can summon the courage to transform our pain.

"We can accept that we don't trust, but also accept that we can make it possible for trust to emerge."

Applause begins and grows.

Adler looks into the faces of her colleagues and fights the tears that well. "Esteemed leaders, we need to finish our work. Our countries depend upon us."

Adler and President Smirnov walk side-by-side to their assigned room. Grateful for his assistance throughout the summit, she reaches over and offers a hug. He recoils but not before she has embraced him. Margaret tries to hide her shock. She felt it. A knotty growth on his spine.

"How much longer?"

"A few months, maybe." He glances at the floor.

"Do your people know?"

"Only the doctors."

"Inoperable?"

"So they say."

"I will tell no one." Adler settles her hand on his.

"I appreciate that."

"You want a legacy?"

"I want life for my people."

"You love them, don't you?"

"They are my life. They may not realize it, but it is so."

"You want to preserve life?"

"Yes, and more than that. I want to *ensure* life for generations to come."

"Do you trust me?" Adler looks directly into the President's eyes.

"More than others."

"Strangely, I trust you as well."

"You've no reason to."

"You want life. That's reason enough for me." She smiles at him.

"You've lost a limb, partially because of Russian offensives."

"My life has changed because of Russian offensives, but they didn't take my life."

"So, you're willing to let it go?"

Margaret nods. "Revenge, hate, control? Yes, I did that long ago. How about you?"

"I want to take steps to ensure that my people prosper."

"We need to build alliances."

"What do you mean?"

"I'm not sure, but maybe convene our artists. Somehow, we need to lay a foundation of trust—something that will endure."

"Will you come to our country?" He looks at her imploringly.

"I could. Why?"

"I'd like you to meet my people, and there is someone I'd like to introduce to you."

"When are you thinking?"

"Soon, of course."

"Of course. I'd consider it an honor."

Adler returns to her room, exhausted by the day but proud of the progress they've made. She brings up the sleep app on her phone. It helps her tinnitus—another consequence of the mortar attack that took her arm and the lives of several soldiers. She sleeps as she always does with a small butterfly pin at her side. She fingers it and gives it a kiss. A gift from her fiancé, before he left for Afghanistan and never returned.

# Chapter 17

The following morning, Margaret steps up to the podium and congratulates the leaders on progress made. "A team of writers will present us with a document tomorrow. If you would like to join them, please do. We'll go over the document in the morning, line by line. The transcribers will make adjustments as we direct. We aim to leave here tomorrow by 17:00 with our treaty and all accompanying details. Questions?"

President Zhang responds first, "What if all of us don't agree?"

"Well, that choice can only bring suffering. How would your people respond to your unwillingness to cooperate?"

The President looks at her with scorn but holds his tongue. He doesn't like her and doesn't support the agreement, but he needs the alignment of other superpowers if his hope to disrupt the process is to prove successful.

Adler notices his eye movements and those of the Pakistani leader. She needs to plan for an insurrection. Smirnov's gaze tells her that he's aware of the situation.

Margaret says, "Since our Chinese collaborator has brought up a potential disagreement, let's discuss repercussions if anyone violates the treaty."

The Russian leader says, "We have each signed the treaty. Now, we simply need to articulate how the treaty will be followed. I don't see how any of us can sign and then disagree. If there is a breach—that is, if one of us breaches the commitment—I believe that country should suffer severe trade embargos."

"We agree," the U.K. Prime Minister says. "This isn't a football match. We're a collective, and the consequence of insurgency is death. Perhaps we need to spell out the penalties for a breach of contract."

Adler turns to President Zhang. "Would you like to address the group?"

President Smirnov raises his hand. "If I might, I'd like to speak before my colleague."

The Chinese President motions for him to proceed.

President Smirnov clears his throat and looks at each of the representatives. "It takes courage to hope. Even a coward can press a button that will send millions to their deaths. But hope, it takes courage.

"It's easy for me to hate, easy for me to plan offensives and send my soldiers to war. But, with these meetings, I've begun to hope. That is an emotion I've not permitted myself since I was a young man serving in Vietnam. It takes courage to hope because to do so means I must trust."

He turns to his Chinese counterpart. "We share a border. We've had our skirmishes, our disagreements, but we've created peace. How have we managed to do that? Through diplomatic agreements. I believe that what we are doing now is an extension of the *2001 Treaty of Good-Neighborliness and Friendly Cooperation* between our two countries. You and I set this in motion. You and I.

"What have we learned from our treaty? Speaking for myself, I've learned that we *can* work together for the greater good. Do we trust? No, we're realistic. We both want more. More oil, more commodities. What you have, I want. And so, we work it out. There's a give and take."

He looks directly at President Zhang. "What's the difference now?"

The Chinese President appears baffled. He looks around the room. All eyes are on him. He turns back to President Smirnov, and in a measured way, responds, "I see your point. It is similar, and I can proceed based on our mutual experience."

Adler takes a deep breath; the conflict is averted. She says, "We're discussing possible consequences for a breach of contract."

The French President says, "We need to be accountable to our people. One way to ensure this is to make our meetings and decisions public. We could invite the media to join us."

The United Kingdom leader says, "I could agree if we also had consequences for misrepresented information."

President Smirnov says, "They don't need to hear our discussions, maybe just our conclusions. So, could we invite them in—after we've finished our deliberations?"

Adler says, "That seems a wise approach. Are we in agreement?"

Everyone nods. "Okay, then, if or when we have challenges, we will meet to resolve our differences, and then invite the media to join us. Our populace will know if we're being faithful or not rather immediately.

"Esteemed leaders, we've achieved what we, initially, thought impossible. We're ready to send our treaty to the editors."

# Chapter 18

*O*n the other side of the world, at the Begert Air Force Base, military leaders tackle a different problem. They struggle to understand the trail of attacks. Admiral Parker thinks he might have figured it out and calls Taylor. "Can you meet with me? I've got information."

"I'll be there in five."

Then Parker calls Gruner. "Taylor and I are meeting in five minutes. Would you join us?"

"Absolutely. See you momentarily."

Parker makes steady improvements and walks short distances. He even manages to get in and out of bed with minimal discomfort. In preparation for the meeting, he moves slowly over to a chair by the windows.

Taylor and Gruner arrive at the same time, eager to hear what Parker says. They grab a seat next to the Admiral.

"Thanks for coming," Parker says. "Last night, Johnny and I stayed up late and went over each attack. To date, I've been targeted with three life-threatening assaults, and each one has been traced to China. But why me? I'm an old guy with little power. I think Johnny and I have figured out the reason.

"When the beautician held me captive, she said, 'the future is no longer yours.' I felt like I was an obstacle to whatever she or they are planning. What if we have, wrongly, attributed her comment and the previous attacks to the effort to create a One World Government? Or what if there are two separate but overlapping agendas in operation—China's agenda and that of the cabal? In terms of China, what if the beautician's statement meant that the future belongs to China?

"Her mention of the USS Gerald R. Ford puzzled me, and I've gone over that scene many times. Why would a beautician know anything about carriers, and why that *particular* ship?" Parker pauses and looks squarely at Taylor and Gruner.

He continues, "The USS Gerald R. Ford is our lead carrier. It has the capability of moving ordnance from deep within the ship to the flight deck with an agility that we don't have on any other warship. With six elevators, 200 jets, and nuclear weaponry, we can't be too careful. A software glitch would make it a floating time bomb.

"This is what I want to tell you. I designed the electronic system within the USS Gerald R. Ford. I know it better than, perhaps, anyone. Right now, it approaches the Gulf of Oman. I believe there will be an attempt to destroy that carrier. Its superior capabilities make it a threat, and I think China wants full control. Until now, I would've thought this an impossibility, but when Johnny and I talked last night, it struck me with a force that scared the hell out of me. The carrier's software is complicated and encoded, and I've always assumed it to be impenetrable. Why do I change my mind now, you might wonder? We purchased the software from China."

Taylor stares in disbelief. "If your assumptions are correct, we don't have much time. Everything on the ship is dependent upon software. If the anti-ballistic system gets deactivated, we've lost our defense."

"Exactly. What if China wants control of all the oil in the Persian Gulf? It's already aligned with Iran and Pakistan, so what will its next steps be?" Noticing the shocked expressions, Parker adds, "I think it's time to speak with the Chief of Naval Operations."

Taylor shakes his head. "Parker, you've nailed it. Let's go to my office to make the call. Gruner, given this new information, I'd like you to reexamine every detail related to these attacks and find out what you can about the mysterious cabal. We've got the makings of World War III."

"I'm on it, sir." Gruner hurries out the door.

Parker says, "You know, General, odd as it might sound, I felt relief when I finally understood why I became a target. I might be old, but I know ships, and as for the USS Gerald R. Ford, I know it inside and out."

"Understood. Now, old man, I'm going to get a wheelchair and give you a ride down the hallway to my driver. We've got work to do."

Within minutes, they sit in the General's office. Taylor asks his assistant to contact the Chief of Naval Operations and arrange a conference call about an urgent matter.

The two sit in front of a monitor and await the call, which comes in within minutes.

"Chief, thank you for responding so quickly."

"General, when someone of your rank says it's urgent, I trust that it is. I see Parker is with you, so I know something is going on. Let's get to it."

Parker takes the lead, "I wish this were a social call, but unfortunately, we've got serious matters to discuss." He proceeds to describe the attacks and concludes with his insight as to the reasons for the attempts on both his life and the President's. Then Parker focuses on the USS Gerald R. Ford.

As the Admiral describes the ship's vulnerability, the Chief sits motionless except for a narrowing of his eyes and a tightening of his lips. "What do you suggest, Parker?"

"There may be a plant on the carrier, but China can just as easily control the ship from afar. I've detailed a diagram of the ship's vulnerabilities, and where I suspect China may attack. If the Commander knows what to expect, he can better safeguard the system. But, bottom line, you need your brightest to re-engineer the software."

The Chief straightens, and without taking a breath, he says, "My thoughts, exactly. Please send the diagram now." He waits silently. "Okay, I've got it. If I have questions, I'll get back in touch. Feel free to call me anytime. This is my priority, and I best get attending to it. Thank you."

After he disconnects, Taylor turns to Parker. "He's certainly a no-non-sense kind of guy, isn't he?"

"Well, we've just given him a potential catastrophe, and time isn't on his side. He'll mobilize quickly. I wouldn't be surprised if he moves the carrier into the Arabian Sea."

"What about POTUS? Don't you think you should call him?"

"Yes. But before doing so, let's check in with Gruner. He may have an update."

The General calls Gruner, who tells them, "Only one thing, sir. Police got called to an explosion about 45 miles east of Modesto. When they arrived, they found a house engulfed in flames and discovered a body, along with an RPG and other toys. We may have found our assassin. A hazmat team is going through the charred debris right now. The fumes were such that the area had to be cleared."

"Thank you, Gruner. Excellent work. We'll talk later." Taylor runs his fingers through his hair and turns to Parker. "What about making that call to the President?"

# Chapter 19

*M*argaret is en route to Moscow. President Smirnov invited her to attend his public address about the denuclearization treaty. She's not sure what to expect, but President Williams encouraged her to attend.

"As long as Russia and the U.S. are aligned," he'd said, "China remains at a disadvantage. If the two are at odds, we've got a problem. My sense is that you can trust Smirnov. He loves his country and people. Ultimately, he'll choose the higher path if he sees it's better for Russia."

The flight itself proves uneventful, but the intense debriefing on Russian/U.S. affairs seems agonizing. Margaret massages her temples as she memorizes the names and positions of key Russian dignitaries. When the plane lands, she takes a deep breath and stands tall as she departs the craft. Two men and a color guard greet Margaret and her entourage of Secret Service and staff. In the distance, a man dressed in military attire approaches. He uses a forearm crutch, and an assistant walks at his side.

"Ms. Adler?"

She nods.

"I'm Ivan Smirnov. My father said I'm to meet with you."

"It's a pleasure meeting you, Ivan. Have we met before? You look familiar."

"I believe this is a first for me."

"Well, I'm happy to meet you. Your father said there was someone he wanted me to see. I didn't know he meant his son. May I ask, did you receive your injuries in Afghanistan?"

"No. My wounds came from you. I was in Afghanistan to arrange for the delivery of military equipment and helicopters when one of your mortars misfired and came too close. Now, do you understand why I have no interest in talking with you?"

Margaret ignores his cynicism. "Our countries took different positions with regard to Afghanistan, but that need not affect our work at hand."

Ivan gives her a hateful look. He tightens his lips and squints his eyes. "You don't know what you're talking about."

He quickens his pace as he leads the way, acknowledging the soldiers when he walks past them. Margaret does the same, and Ivan appears surprised. At their respective motorcades, Margaret continues the conversation.

"I understand your anger and hate. I lived with both after I lost my fiancé. But then . . ."

"But then what?" he spits out.

"But then I realized that my enemies were just like me. They were doing what they thought was right by following the directives of their leaders. They weren't inherently bad and thought they were doing good. But that thinking had serious consequences."

"Well, if you don't follow your Commander's directions, you'll have chaos and mutiny."

"Yes, that's why the nuclear powers met this week—the supreme leaders, not the enlisted soldiers."

Irritated, Ivan tells her, "I and my team will lead the way to the Kremlin." Then, without another word spoken, he gets into his limousine. When they reach the Kremlin, Ivan climbs out of the vehicle and walks toward the building, seemingly oblivious to Margaret. She lingers behind, spellbound by the iconic structures, the colors and shapes of the towers, and their golden rooftops. *Just like a storybook*, she thinks. *Absolutely beautiful.*

Ivan frowns and appears impatient with her distraction. "You must hurry." He increases his pace and reminds her, "My father expects us in the Senate building."

Once Margaret catches up, he asks, "Tell me, were you successful in reaching an agreement with the leaders? My father seems to think so. I don't, but I'd like to hear from you."

"We were successful in delineating a plan for progressive nuclear disarmament."

"Do you think you can trust anyone to follow through?"

"I believe I can trust most, and that trust extends to President Smirnov."

"Interesting. You imagine my father has a heart." He laughs mockingly and sneers, "My father only cares about his power."

"I don't think so, Ivan. He cares deeply about you and his people. He's taking this step for the generations that follow. Especially with his . . ."

"With his what?"

"With his advancing age … he wants to leave you and his people with the best opportunity of life."

"Well, that's a new development."

"Hmm, when your father and I talked, his focus was always the Russian people. Tell me, what has hate gained us? I lost the person I loved and a multitude of friends. And yet here we stand. An American and a Russian—miles of pain between us. Whatever horror I can bring up, I'm certain you can match. Our two countries are skilled in warfare. We can, literally, destroy the planet. What a horrific capability. It's absurd, don't you agree?"

Ivan studies her face. Then he looks at the office entrance. Margaret follows his gaze. President Smirnov stands next to the security detail. Ivan rubs his face. One side looks badly scarred, with the skin patched and rippled. The other side is untouched by the heinousness of burnt flesh.

Margaret asks, "Afghanistan, correct?"

"No, as I have already said." His irritation mounts.

"It's possible we were there at the same time. What do you remember? Maybe we were in the same locale."

"Are you serious? Really? Why would anyone willingly recall such bloodshed?" Ivan's eyes lower, and he glances to the side.

Margaret recognizes the expression on his face—he's experiencing flashbacks despite his hard words. She presses, "I keep thinking we've met. Would you humor me and think back with me?"

"I don't like such games." Ivan's response sounds gruff, and Margaret steps back as her agents step nearer. "Besides, I'm not sure what that would accomplish. This is one nightmare I choose not to recall. I was in the wrong place at the wrong time." He glares at her. Then he glances over at his father again, and he appears aggravated.

Margaret nods. "I understand, of course. But if we can travel back in time, perhaps we might decide if we can trust one another."

He shakes his head and scoffs, "I can't imagine that to be possible."

"Isn't it worth the effort to find out?"

Her persistence wears down his obstinacy, and begrudgingly, he agrees. Ivan stares off into the distance.

Adler notices his grimace and realizes he's gone back to the battle.

She lowers her voice and says, "A shell hits the building I'm in, and I rush outside. I can't see through the clouds of dust and debris. People scream. People run. I hate this place, and it hates me.

"I call to my men, 'Let's get out of here.' There's gunfire, and we're unsure which direction to run. I can smell the blood, the sweat, and the fear. It's musty and thick; it lingers and gags me. Sand and bodies lie beneath my feet. I stumble and recoil at the horror that I meet. I see a female soldier among the masses. She moans from the hit she received. I reach for her arm to pull her up, but the limb is all that follows me. I retch and call for my men."

"Pomoch' yey!" Ivan yells. "And my men help her. They put a tourniquet on her arm, and we move on."

Margaret holds back the shock that she feels and looks at Ivan. He keeps his eyes closed, and he appears to be caught in a battle.

Margaret says, "Another explosion. The shell lands close to me. My face is on fire, and I get thrown backward. I can't move."

Ivan reacts with a gasp and reaches for his face, now frozen and white and trembling.

Margaret says, "I'm being moved—my body dragged. The Afghan Northern Alliance is helping me."

Ivan's jaw clenches, and he holds his shoulders rounded and slumped. Resignation floats across his face.

Adler notices his instability. He teeters. She calls out, "Soldier, lean in. Lean in!"

Ivan leans toward Margaret, and she braces for his weight as she moves closer.

At the entrance, the President watches intently. His guards make a move to go to Ivan, but the President signals that they back off. The guards proceed in directing the guests to the next room. Soon, the office is empty except for Ivan and Margaret, the President, and the guards.

Ivan leans into Margaret. She wraps her arm around him, and time becomes fluid. Ivan chokes out tears, first in agonizing bursts, and then in sobs—loud and wrenching. Wails fill the air, and the security team looks at the President, ready to rescue him, but he motions *no*.

Margaret draws Ivan closer. They now stand cheek to cheek, tears blending. "Ivan," she says. "Ivan, what do you feel?"

He doesn't respond.

Again, she asks, "Ivan, what do you feel?"

His words are halting, "Failure. I could do nothing. I was only there to arrange for more armaments."

"All right, what else do you feel besides failure?"

He holds her tighter. "Useless. I'm barely a man now. My body has betrayed me; it is broken."

"There's more, Ivan. Tell me what else you feel."

"Sadness. So many are gone. My friends, my enemies. Gone. And for what?"

"The remorse of a soldier. I understand. There's more."

He flounders and struggles to regain composure.

"Ivan," Margaret says. "What more do you feel?"

He pulls her close and whispers, "I feel hope—hope that maybe the treaty will work. It has to. It must. Maybe the countries are serious about ending this horror. That is my hope."

Margaret nods. "You've identified your purpose."

Ivan clasps her left arm, and at the firm feel of the prosthesis, he jerks away.

He opens his eyes and looks into hers. "You're the one, aren't you? The one we stopped and helped."

"Yes. You saved my life."

His eyes fill, he fights the tears. Ivan sits in a chair and puts his head into his hands. "I saved one, but how many more have I killed?"

President Smirnov hurries to his son's side and waits for an acknowledgment.

"Father," Ivan says, haltingly. "I understand now."

"Will you help me, son? Help me to promote the treaty?"

"Yes. It's our only hope. My only hope. I will do what I can." He stands and embraces his father, and then he recoils. "How long have you had that lump on your spine?"

"Several months."

"Terminal?"

"Yes."

"Why didn't you tell me?"

"It wasn't the right time."

"Does anyone else know?"

"Other than your mother, only Margaret. She embraced me at the summit and felt it; otherwise, I would never have spoken about it."

"I'll help in any way I can."

"I'd like you to succeed me."

"I'm not ready for that."

"Yes, you are. You've made your peace. And as Prime Minister, the people trust you."

Ivan glances at Margaret. "My father is correct. You've helped me let go of the hate. Thank you."

"It was nothing. My years of therapy helped me guide you. I need to give you both some privacy." She turns to walk away, but the President calls to her.

"Margaret, please, join us. I have a favor to ask."

She takes a seat near the two men, and the President says, "I am to address my people tomorrow morning. I'd like to introduce you and have you explain the treaty to my people. After you do this, I will offer my summary and introduce Ivan as the transitional President."

"Father, how can you say that? The people know that I don't have your experience and will not accept me."

"No one knows better than you why we need this treaty. Assert your commitment and strength. The military will step in line, and the people will follow."

"Will you tell them of your health concerns?"

"No. However, I will explain that your mother needs care and that I'm stepping down to be with her. I'll work with you, but you will manage the daily demands with my guidance."

"I understand. But, Mama—she is healthy, correct?"

"Yes and no. She suffers from heart disease, which has left her in a weakened state. But that stays between us."

"Father, this is a lot to take in. Both of you in ill health and all."

"You can manage, son. I'll help you get situated. Of course, it will be the people who decide."

"Of course. Thank you for introducing Margaret to me, Father. I feel like I can breathe now." He gives Adler a shy glance. "It's like I have a heart again."

"I feel equally grateful," she says. "Your kindness saved my life. I lay near death when you found me."

Ivan nods. "I think I had died already. When I saw you, I responded to your moans mechanically, but then your arm came off into my hands, and I was shocked into a frightening realism."

As they talk, the President smiles.

Margaret senses an attraction between the two of them but pushes it to one side. She addresses Smirnov, "Are you sure it's wise for me to speak? Won't your people object?"

"They will follow my lead. Just be yourself, and you will be successful. Wear that beautiful red dress that you wore on the last night of the deliberations. You'll be an instant success."

Margaret blushes and smiles. "I'll do just that."

# Chapter 20

------·------

*V*ice President Margaret Adler climbs the steps to the ceremonial platform, which overlooks Red Square, and follows an entourage of Russian dignitaries led by President Smirnov. She takes up her assigned position, at the left side of the podium, and gazes out at the thousands of people gathered to hear their beloved President. St. Basil's Cathedral frames the regal event, and a large military band plays with patriotic enthusiasm.

President Smirnov strides with authority to the podium. When he nears the microphone, the synchronized applause of thousands drowns out the drums and cymbals, the trumpets and saxophones. His people love him greatly, and his response indicates that the affection is mutual. He offers a quick bow and waits until the crowd quiets.

Smirnov explains his work on a treaty, and his people cheer. He then states that he has a distinguished American guest. The joviality shifts, and the people become serious.

"Ms. Adler, please join me." Margaret walks up to the podium and stands at Smirnov's side. Her red dress catches the breeze and lifts while she walks. Around her neck hangs a white and blue scarf. She wears Russia's colors, and the people roar their acceptance.

The President takes her hand. "Ms. Adler is the Vice President of the United States. Their President is ill and could not participate in the final deliberations, so she managed alone. Her work was exemplary, and you will soon understand why. Ms. Adler, would you, please, address my people?"

"Thank you, President Smirnov. I feel honored to be your guest today. I would like to begin with a request. Could all who have served, or are currently serving, in the military please acknowledge by raising your hand?"

A rumble fills the gathering space when the men and women lift their arms. Among those responding, proudly attesting to their service, are the President and his son.

"Thank you all for your service. You know the worst and the best of life. You know what it is to risk everything for your country, your family, and your principles. It is possible we—you and I—supported opposing sides. We may have fought valiantly for different ideals. I want you to know that I respect your fearlessness and courage. We are soldiers. We have done what we were told to do faithfully. Thank you for your service." She begins to clap, and the assembly joins her.

Margaret waits for people to resettle. "Almost two decades ago, I served in the United States Army in Afghanistan. I suspect that many of you also served in that country in the 1980s." She looks around the audience. Some of the men nod.

"Afghanistan was my first and last deployment." Margaret pauses and removes her four-button cardigan to reveal her arm prosthesis. A gasp carries across the expanse.

"I lost my arm to a mortar attack and was near death when a Russian soldier on diplomatic business got caught in the same battle. It wasn't his battle to fight. It was mine. America was at war with Afghanistan because of the 9/11 attacks on the United States. This Russian soldier and his men tried to get out of harm's way, but there was no safe direction to turn. As he walked through the destruction, he heard my moans. The last thing I remember was his demand to his men, 'Pomoch' yey!' 'Help her!'

"His men put a tourniquet on my arm and went on their way. This one action saved my life. Yesterday, I met this soldier once again." She turns, looks at Ivan, and asks that he join her. As he walks to the stand, she extends her hand to him, and he grasps hers firmly. The people clap and stand. Adler returns to the microphone, and the people quiet. She puts her cardigan on and says, "We Americans and Russians have known much pain over the centuries. We take care about who we trust for good reason. We've lost loved ones, we've lost properties, and we've lost hope. Sometimes the reasons for our fighting has not been clear, but the fighting has been gruesome nonetheless.

"As time passed, our two countries became experts at destruction. We know how to inflict damage better than anyone. Our nuclear weapons are so powerful that they can destroy ALL life. One aberrant warhead, and the world we consider our home will no longer exist.

"The treaty we have signed directs us to progressively reduce our nuclear stockpiles. Your President and I have decided that our two countries will cut our holdings in half over the next two years. Even with this notable reduction, we can still destroy the planet. We will monitor our progress continually, and within the next two years, we will meet again to, hopefully, cut the stockpile in half once more.

"We are not naive. Much can change in two years, including our leadership. To ensure that we keep our promises, we will use drone surveillance and arrange for multiple investigative visits each year.

"Trust does not happen overnight. It takes time for confidence to emerge, and that is a burden that any leadership must bear. We are creating a new frontier—one that we travel together. We will not stockpile more weapons. Rather, we will learn to depend upon each other through trade and negotiations.

"We have been successful in eliminating or deactivating intermediate-range and short-range ground-launched ballistic and cruise missiles. So, we have proven that we can do this. Now we take the next step.

"I trust your President. I trust his son. And I trust the inherent goodness of the Russian people. We can do this. We, you and I, can create a future for our children founded on mutual understanding—on peace."

The President and Ivan stand and applaud. The entire assembly follows their lead. The response becomes thunderous, and Margaret walks in front of the microphones and to the edge of the stage. There, she extends a slow, respectful bow to the people. She then returns to her position between the President and Ivan.

Smirnov eases up to the podium. "As Vice President Adler has explained, we are creating our destiny. I invite my son to come forward to describe this new prospect."

Ivan positions his forearm crutch and walks to the podium. Father and son shake hands, and then Ivan turns to the people.

He explains the mechanics of denuclearization, shares how released funds would be used for the people, and identifies trade possibilities between the two countries. His words then take a personal turn.

"Like many of you, I've seen the worst of war. I know what it is to lose family and friends. I know what it is to suffer the consequences of battle. I regret nothing and would do it all again for my country and its people. But, now, we have a choice. A life-giving choice. At such a juncture, how can we not hope for a different way of relating to our enemies?

"To meet Vice President Adler came as an unexpected jolt from the past. I did not recognize her from the battlefield, because blood covered her when I saw her almost two decades ago. Her blond hair lay matted against her head and barely distinguishable from the sand that surrounded her. It was her whimper that drew me to her and then her young face.

"I never knew what had happened to that woman, though the memory stayed alive in me. I tried to move the wounded soldier and grabbed one of her arms. It came off in my hands. Shocked and appalled, I held her arm, detached from her body, and the horror of it all overcame me. That is when I called out to my men to help her.

"It has been an extraordinary gift meeting Vice President Adler. I am heartened that something good came out of that grisly battle. For through our re-encounter, there has been much healing.

"War is impersonal. We kill, not knowing whom we kill. It must be that way; otherwise, we could not do what is expected of us. But in situations like this, it becomes personal. We see our victims, and like us, they suffer, bleed, and are alone and afraid.

"When I learned of the Russian and American negotiations for nuclear peace, initially I thought it foolish and impossible. How could we ever trust a country that has levied so much destruction? How could we work with them, collaborating for an undefined future?

"Then I met Vice President Adler. She has given me a reason to hope for such a future, one built on mutual understanding. I am confident that with the safeguards in place, we can and will move forward. And, I am committed to making this treaty a reality for all of us.

"Let me show you why this is critical. Please, look at the screen. This simulation captures what will occur from any nuclear activity." While the video plays, a chill settles on the crowd, and evident fright fills their hearts. Ivan says, "Within a few hours, not only is our country destroyed but the entire world as well. Survivors will not stay alive for long. Earth will become a dead planet.

"We must, diligently, move toward nuclear disarmament. This means we must learn the art of negotiation and build understanding across our differences by listening to one another. This is the work of peace. We've proven our might, and now we must prove our wisdom."

The audience erupts into applause. Ivan turns to Adler and nods. Then he walks to his father and gives him a shoulder-to-shoulder embrace. The two proceed to the podium and thank the attendees. Then they turn and thank Vice President Adler. All the while, the people applaud enthusiastically.

# Chapter 21

President Smirnov leads the way off the platform and thanks Margaret for speaking to his people. "My family and I would be honored if you could join us for dinner tonight."

Margaret glances at Ivan and notices his smile. "It would be my pleasure."

Margaret and her Secret Service detail return to the hotel, but since she has several hours to spare before dinner, she wants to walk around the area. After some misgivings, the Secret Service team accepts her request and accompanies Margaret to the Red Square. The team watches for anyone who might try to harm the Vice President.

A young man approaches, and the team surrounds Margaret. The guy nods to the detail and says to Margaret, "Thank you for visiting our country. You give me hope that, maybe, we can coexist peacefully."

"Our hope needs to be our commitment," Margaret says. "We've suffered enough, don't you think?"

"I couldn't agree more. I need the treaty to succeed. It's time for us to lay down our arms."

A woman approaches, and in broken English, she thanks Margaret for visiting. "My son served in Afghanistan and did not return. My only other child died at birth. Now, I am widow and feel sad."

Margaret hugs the woman. "I, too, lost a loved one in the war. I'm alone as well."

More strangers approach—each with a story of a lost or harmed loved one. The Secret Service team moves in close to Margaret. She tries to walk away from the crowd, but the people follow. Then Ivan appears at her side. He speaks in Russian to the crowd, and the people leave.

Margaret asks, "What did you say?"

"You have traveled a long distance and feel tired. They needed to give you some peace."

"Thank you. I hope they didn't think me rude, but truly, I felt overwhelmed. Is it time for us to go?"

"Just about. Do you need to collect anything from the hotel?"

"I'd like to pick up a warmer jacket and a few other things."

"Okay, then, I'll walk with you and your team and wait for you in the lobby."

Once at the hotel, Margaret takes the elevator up to her room. Grateful for the time alone, she flops onto the bed. The day has exhausted her, but she can't allow herself to fall asleep just yet. She reminds herself that she needs to tell President Smirnov her concerns about the Chinese President.

Her phone rings, and Margaret jumps.

"Vice President Adler, this is Ivan speaking."

"Am I late? I'm sorry."

"Not at all. I wondered if you'd like to join me for a drink before we go to my parents' home."

"What a great idea. I'll be down in a second." Margaret looks in the mirror and decides she's presentable. She runs a comb through her hair, puts on a little perfume, and dabs on a bit of lipstick. Before heading to the lobby, Margaret remembers the gift for Mrs. Smirnov. Her staff had suggested she bring one, just in case. She grabs the small box from her suitcase and heads out the door.

Ivan stands by the elevator as the doors open. Upon seeing his broad smile, she can't help but smile in return. "How about a short tour of the city?" he asks.

"I would love it. Apart from the Red Square, I haven't seen anything but this hotel and the conference room."

"Okay, a celebrative drink, and we're on our way."

They go to the bar, where Ivan orders two Belugas. "I feel pretty certain you haven't had this drink, and you can't appreciate Russia without trying at least one shooter."

The bartender brings the vodkas and a plate of pickles. Margaret watches Ivan and follows his motions. "To love, health, and luck," he says. Margaret repeats the toast and drinks the cold vodka.

"It warms the soul, don't you think?"

"This is a first for me, but it definitely makes me feel warm inside."

"Okay, now we go for a tour. Your limo can follow mine, and as we travel, I'll point out the attractions via our cell phones."

Ivan calls for his Security Service driver and instructs him to take them to the usual places of interest. Margaret's detail follows closely. When they approach the Red Square and St. Basil's Cathedral, Margaret asks if they could stop and look inside.

Ivan instructs his driver to halt, and Margaret does likewise. As they walk to the holy site, Ivan offers a brief explanation for the unique architecture and explains that the cathedral consists of nine churches. Once inside, Margaret pauses to try to absorb it all. Inlaid gold and icons of the saints cover the walls and soaring ceiling. Like a labyrinth connecting centuries of hopes and sorrows, the cathedral testifies to the human and the divine throughout time.

"This is breathtakingly beautiful," Margaret murmurs. "One could spend all day here."

Ivan looks pleased to see how affected she is by the artistry and solemnity. At an altar crowded with candles, she pauses. "I need to pray just a moment." Ivan watches as Margaret kneels and lowers her head. When they leave, Ivan asks her about her prayers.

"I prayed for the healing of our people, and for peace between our countries. I also prayed that I might be of service."

Ivan turns and faces her. Gazing into her eyes, he says, "I think your prayer is being answered. For certain, you are an answer to mine." His tenderness causes Margaret to blush, and she wonders what's developing between them. She never thought she'd love again, and yet that's the emotion she feels. When Margaret stares into Ivan's eyes, she sees his yearning and feels her own. It's been a long while since she tasted desire. Though she neither expected nor looked for love, it's surprised her in this most unlikely setting. And from such a short acquaintance.

From the cathedral, it takes only a few minutes to reach the Smirnov family home. Like many in Moscow, a wall surrounds the residence. The Security Service pulls up to the gate, and Ivan enters a code. The driver takes them to the front of the house, and Margaret's team parks near the entrance.

As the two walk up to the door, Ivan confides, "I wish you weren't leaving tomorrow. I'd like to get to know you better."

Margaret doesn't know what to say. She wants to tell him what's in her heart, but she hesitates and, instead, says, "And I with you, but my President is ill, and I must step in and help until he recovers. Perhaps we will see each other when we begin the disarmament checks."

"Maybe before." Ivan smiles playfully, and Margaret reddens. He opens the front door and calls out, "Mama, Papa, we're here."

# Chapter 22

───── ·── ─────

Koshka, the family's Russian Blue cat, greets the two at the door. She purrs and rubs against Ivan while he removes his shoes and dons slippers. Margaret follows Ivan's example and takes off her outdoor footwear. At the same time, Ivan takes a pair of slippers from the shoe cabinet and gives them to her. Koshka moves to Margaret's feet and rubs against her legs.

"This is a good sign." Ivan chuckles. "She likes you."

Margaret picks up the cat and cuddles her. "Hello, Koshka. It's so good to meet you."

"Do you have a cat?"

"I used to, but since I've worked in this position, I don't have any pets. I travel too much. It wouldn't be fair to them."

"Well, Koshka is special. She's almost human. She's trained to sit and eat on command. Can you believe that?"

Ivan's grandmother rushes to the entrance and joins the two. "Hello, hello, my dears. Please, come in and make yourself comfortable."

Ivan says, "My babushka raised me, which is typical for most families." He gives her a big hug and a kiss on each cheek. Margaret also kisses her on the cheeks and extends her hand. The grandmother's firm grip surprises Margaret.

"You must be starving," the grandmother says. "But first, a drink. What can I get for you, my dear?"

Margaret isn't sure of the protocol, so she says, "I'll have whatever the family is having."

Ivan laughs. "You're too trusting. Would you like a beer, or some wine, perhaps?"

Margaret looks at the grandmother and smiles. "I'd like a glass of dry white wine."

Ivan smiles and motions to his babushka that he'd like a beer.

"Welcome," President Smirnov calls out, as he and his wife walk down the hall to greet Margaret and Ivan.

"We're so happy you could join us," Mrs. Smirnov says.

"I'm greatly honored to be here." Margaret exchanges the customary kisses.

Smirnov says, "Let's go into the living room where we can be more comfortable."

When they walk down the hall, Margaret notices the family photos on either side of them. One picture catches her attention. It shows a family of five on horseback. The three children, two boys and a girl, look like young adolescents. She turns to Ivan. "Is this your family?"

"Yes, my sister lives in St. Petersburg with her husband and baby. My older brother died in the war in Chechnya in 1999."

"I'm so sorry . . ."

"When I got injured, it was especially hard for my mother because she had lost a son already."

"She must have felt terrified at the prospect of losing you."

"She did. She's lived with a lot of suffering."

The hallway takes them to the living room. Margaret pauses at the entrance and looks in all directions. The Persian rug on the wooden floor captivates her, as does the intricately tiled fireplace, the beautiful brocade couch and matching sitting chairs, the large wall bookcase, and the chandelier in the center of the room. Margaret glances over at Ivan and smiles. "Beautiful," she whispers.

Ivan's chest swells, and he responds proudly, "I'm glad you like it."

"Come join us, Margaret." The mother motions. She has prepared appetizers to accompany the drinks. "I've looked forward to meeting you."

"And me, you. Your home is so lovely."

The President straightens with pride. "Let's toast to the success of the treaty." Everyone raises their glasses. "To its success." The buzz of the President's cell phone interrupts the joviality. While he excuses himself to answer the call, Mrs. Smirnov asks Margaret about her family.

"My parents live in North Carolina. They're retired now and enjoy a quiet life. I have a sister, who's married with four children. The young ones bring all of us much joy."

"But what about you? Are you married?"

Margaret grows shy and realizes that all mothers think similarly. She looks over at Ivan and sees his diverted gaze and slight smile. "No, I was engaged, but my fiancé died in Afghanistan."

"And here you are now. Life is amazing, isn't it?"

"Yes, I've thought the same many times."

The President returns to the room but seems distracted. He looks at his wife and asks for forgiveness, but he must bring up business matters. Mrs. Smirnov grows visibly frustrated but shrugs for him to proceed.

Smirnov clenches his jaw and then says, "The call was from our intelligence team in Beijing. The Chinese have launched a long-range intercontinental ballistic missile that can carry multiple warheads. Thankfully, it wasn't loaded, because the launch was successful."

Margaret frowns. "President Smirnov, before I left Washington, President Williams asked that I convey a message to you, which now seems a good time to do so. My apologies to Mrs. Smirnov for bringing business to this lovely evening."

"Goodness, please don't be concerned, Margaret. I'm accustomed to the political dramas of the day."

"Well—" Margaret looks down and then back at the President. "— the CIA has evidence that the mid-air assassination attempt on President Williams was orchestrated from a Chinese cell located near the base. One of the terrorists' phones shows multiple calls to Beijing. President Williams asked that I give this number to you. The CIA believes that the attempts on Admiral Parker's life also originated from this same Chinese cell. President Williams asked me to warn you about the duplicity of China's President."

"Please thank President Williams. In terms of the duplicity, he's verified what I have assumed all along about my neighbor. We can't choose who lives next to us, but we can certainly choose how we respond to their behavior."

The President signals for Ivan to come to his side. They speak privately, and then Ivan nods and explains that he'll return in just a few minutes. As he walks away, Margaret notices that Ivan holds the paper that she gave to President Smirnov, which has the phone number used by the terrorists.

"May I call you Margaret?" the President asks.

"Please do. I'm not accustomed to formality."

"I want to congratulate you on your work on the treaty. It was truly exceptional." He looks over at his wife and says, "Margaret hadn't planned to attend and didn't have the proper preparation. Yet, she managed some of the most difficult leaders on the planet with unsurpassed professionalism."

Margaret demurs, "Thank you for your kind words, but I didn't do anything special."

"Your strength was and is that you believe in the greater good. Your integrity evokes respect, just as your vision encompassed all of us. You are a rare leader."

Margaret's cheeks grow warm. "President Smirnov, you're too kind. Your support throughout the meetings set the tone for our negotiations. I couldn't have done it without you, and I remain deeply grateful. When I spoke with my President and told him of your help, he said he expected that would be the case."

Smirnov bows his head and smiles. "Friends help friends. There may have been times when our two countries have fought on opposite sides of a battle, but Williams and I think similarly, and we are committed to forging a new future. It's our responsibility, after all."

Ivan returns and whispers to his father, who smiles knowingly at Ivan's news. "Thank you, son."

Mrs. Smirnov invites everyone to dinner. She motions for Margaret to sit beside Ivan.

"A toast is needed," President Smirnov says. "To a new future."

Unsure what's expected, Margaret raises her glass and repeats the toast.

The grandmother excuses herself and brings out the food with the assistance of kitchen staff. The dinner begins with Borscht, a rich beet soup, followed by beef stroganoff, Pelmeni dumplings filled with minced meat, and potato salad. After the main course, the grandmother brings out Paskha, a cheesecake dessert.

The evening fills with much levity until another phone call to President Smirnov interrupts the family gathering. He stands, excuses himself, and says, "I must take this call."

Margaret watches as he walks to the next room and closes the door. Smirnov's voice rises and falls, but Margaret can't understand a word. She glances at Ivan and realizes that he sits listening to the one-sided conversation. His eyes appear dark and far away, and he sits with his jaw set.

When the President returns to the table, he apologizes. "The Chinese President was in a one-car accident as he left Sheremetyevo International Airport. His driver didn't survive, but the President's injuries may not be serious, though he is unconscious."

Margaret catches her breath and glances over at Ivan. His eyes focus on the Paskha, and he refuses to look up or respond to his father in any way.

President Smirnov mentions the unfortunateness of the accident and expresses his hopes that the Chinese President will soon recover.

Margaret doesn't know what to say, and an uneasy chill runs down her spine. After a second or so, she says, "I don't know him well, but he's challenging to work with. If a replacement is needed, I hope the new person shares our vision."

"That will not be a problem." Smirnov takes another bite of the cheesecake. "His people want peace. He wants power. If a successor is necessary, I suspect that he would be more in line with the people's wishes."

Mrs. Smirnov gives her husband a playful shove. "Oh, let's not talk about this anymore. I'm getting indigestion. Margaret, dear, I didn't have a chance to thank you for the beautiful Tiffany Grapevine scarf. How thoughtful of you. Won't you tell me more about your parents? They must be lovely."

Over the next hour, Margaret shares her experience of growing up on the outskirts of Raleigh, North Carolina. They laugh about her childhood antics, and the Smirnovs provide stories of Ivan's growing years. All the while, more drinks get poured, and toasts offered. When the time comes to leave, Margaret embraces Mrs. Smirnov as though she were her own mother. She thanks President Smirnov and walks outside with Ivan.

"Thank you for everything. This has been a lovely evening."

Ivan takes Margaret's hand and holds it tenderly. "I don't want to say goodbye. Surely, we'll meet again soon." He embraces her and whispers, "This has been a memorable evening for me. Thank you, dear Margaret." He waits for her to get in the car and watches as she leaves.

Back in her hotel room, Margaret sits deep in thought about the evening. One question troubles her the most: *Did Ivan order the car accident involving China's President when he took the phone number and made that call?* She paces the room and waits for daybreak, unable to sleep.

Air Force Two's scheduled departure time of 08:00, the ten-hour flight, and the seven-hour time difference, mean that Margaret will arrive late morning in Washington D.C. She sends a note to her secretary to explain that she'll meet with President Williams later and bring her questions to him then. She shuffles the papers in her lap and decides she must focus and write up her report. Still, the fateful phone call at the Smirnov's home haunts her.

A knock at her hotel door stops her speculation. She looks through the peephole and sees Ivan, standing alone with a book in his hands.

"Good morning. I'm surprised to see you."

"I couldn't let you leave without another goodbye. Besides, I don't want you to think I'm a monster because of what occurred last night."

"Well, I do have questions."

"It's your possible answers to those questions that trouble me. Let me say that I relayed a message, and the message had nothing to do with the accident. I simply repeated what you'd indicated and offered the phone number. Sometimes, accidents truly are accidents."

"Did you find out to whom the number belongs?"

"This morning, the Foreign Intelligence Service confirmed that the number leads to China's government headquarters. Which office, I don't know. But they'll find out soon enough."

"And you'll let me know?"

Ivan smiles mischievously. "It's not a secret I'd keep. Yes, of course, I'll let you know."

"My apologies." Margaret steps to one side. "Won't you, please, come in. I can offer you coffee or tea."

"How could I pass up an offer like that?" Ivan chuckles. "One cup of coffee, and I'll head off. I know you have a plane to catch." As Margaret fills his cup, he says, "Tell me what you enjoyed most about your visit."

Without missing a beat, Margaret says, "St. Basil's Cathedral."

"Ahh, I thought that might be your response. I brought this book for you. It's a pictorial history of the cathedral and the architects who worked on it through the decades."

Margaret lights up. "I can't wait to read it. This is so thoughtful of you." She sees his tenderness and can feel her cheeks reddening. "When I return to Moscow, maybe we could walk through the cathedral with the book?"

"I'm always ready for an adventure, especially one with you." Ivan rises and walks to the door. "A quick hug?" Margaret moves closer, and he wraps his arms around her and pulls her near. Margaret sinks into his embrace, and her head drops onto his shoulder, where it rests. As though time itself has paused, neither wants to let go.

Ivan gives her a gentle kiss on the cheek. "We'll see each other soon." Margaret watches as he disappears down the hallway with his entourage of staff and catches the hint of a grin from one of her Secret Service. Quickly, she gathers her belongings and walks out to join her team.

They drive the seventeen miles to the airport, each lost in the whirlwind of the last two days, and board Air Force Two. Margaret sits alone, where she can stretch out and rest. She glances down at Ivan's gift and turns its pages. Her thoughts travel back to their parting embrace—his heart beating next to hers, the warmth of his touch, and the smell of clove. *Can it be that I'm falling in love with a Russian?*

She receives a text from Ivan: *China's President has regained consciousness and is doing well. Safe travels.* She smiles. Ivan knew she'd want this information. Now she can work on her report for the President.

# Chapter 23

*A*t Begert Air Force Base, Sergeant Gruner focuses on his assignment: an in-depth explanation as to why five luxury jets—two Bombardiers BD-700, two Gulfstreams, and a Falcon 7x—landed in Lofoten, Norway, the week prior. The General expects Gruner to uncover possible links to the recent assassination attempts.

As a first step, Gruner contacts his counterpart at the Royal Norwegian Air Force station in Evenes. He explains the reason for his call and sends the digital photographs in question.

The Norwegian Airman says, "Well, I know that a week ago, Madam Edel Berven contacted us to explain she'd invited guests to her husband's seventieth-birthday party. Since her guests needed to fly into Evenes, she asked for landing clearance at the Harstad/Narvik Airport and explained that her private helicopter would take the guests to their mountain estate. We approved and thought no more of it. Now you suggest there may be something nefarious involved?"

"I have nothing concrete, but it's an unusual gathering, don't you think?"

"Maybe, maybe not."

"I trust your Commander implicitly. Has he raised any concerns or particular events that he wants you and your team to watch out for?"

"He mentioned that the Americans believe that some rich people might have formed a cabal."

Gruner smiles with relief. "Right. We think they might be responsible for a bunch of assassinations and attempted killings."

The Airman gasps. "It's hard to believe that Madame Berven would be involved in such a thing. She's a leading supporter of the arts in our area. Highly respected. Nevertheless, I'll request the flight plans for the jets. Perhaps points of origin will help resolve this mystery. Give me two hours."

"Perfect. Call me at this number when you're ready."

"Ha det bra. Goodbye!"

True to his word, the Norwegian Airman returns the call within the hour. "Billionaires associated with the Federal Reserve, the European Central Bank, the pharmaceutical industry, and technology, own the jets in question. Mr. Berven is a wealthy man. It's entirely possible that this gathering was, indeed, a birthday party. But, then again …"

Gruner asks, "What are you thinking?"

"Don't birthday parties usually include family members and the spouses of guests? There were none—the Berven children didn't attend, and the owners of those jets didn't bring their partners. To add fuel to the fire, I checked our files, and Mr. Berven was born in December, not March."

Gruner gasps. "You're serious? So, if Berven blew out candles, it wasn't on a cake? This changes everything."

The Airman sounds alarmed, "There's more. Two days before the arrival of Berven's guests, a Gulfstream landed. It departed at the same time as the others. We're looking into its ownership, but we know one thing—the point of origin for this flight to Lofoten was Beijing."

"Now I feel more concerned. Can you keep me posted about anything that might bear any relation to this case? I'll do the same for you. We *have* to get to the bottom of this."

"Copy that. I'll stay in touch."

Gruner says his goodbyes and stares at his computer screen. *What are those powerful people planning? What do they have in common?* His thoughts take him back to the earlier conjecture of a One World Government. *But didn't we rule that out?*

Gruner turns around, gives his team the names of the five men, and asks each Airman to focus on a different person. "Find out everything you can about your individual—who he associates with, his political and religious beliefs, his international contacts, recent travel, and—especially—if there were any new work-related developments this past week.

"Tomorrow morning, we'll meet at 10:00. Bring your findings. This is top priority, and we need answers."

Gruner texts General Taylor: *Sir, Berven was born in December, not March. His guests appear to be tied to the global economy. My team has mobilized.*

The General responds: *I'm headed to my quarters. I'll stop by.*

Gruner stands and faces his team, "Snap to, everyone. The General will arrive momentarily."

Seconds later, Taylor walks through the doors of the OPS center, recognizes the Airmen standing at attention, and goes directly to Gruner. "You've certainly got my attention. Tell me how Berven and his guests are tied to the global economy."

"Sir, here's the list of owners and their affiliation or company."

General Taylor's lips tighten as he reads through the list. "I can see why you concluded *global economy*. One way or another, these tycoons control our lives."

"There's something more, sir."

Impatient, Taylor taps his fingers on the desktop while Gruner explains the arrival of the mystery person two days before the others. "That person flew in from Beijing, sir."

Taylor's face hardens, and his hand stops moving. "Make this an *urgent* priority."

# Chapter 24

*O*ver the next several weeks, Gruner's team uncovers additional evidence of wrongdoing associated with the mysterious gathering in Lofoten. General Taylor contacts President Williams and informs him of their concerns. Shortly thereafter, the CIA and Norwegian Intelligence Service begin their investigations. All this while the White House prepares for the first nuclear site visit.

Nine countries signed the Denuclearization Treaty of 2021. Each country committed to reducing its stockpile of nuclear warheads to half of its existing strength. The United States volunteered to host the first oversight visit at Kirtland Air Force Base Nuclear Weapons Complex in Albuquerque, New Mexico. In consultation with the Joint Chiefs of Staff, President Williams decided that since the base claims, perhaps, the largest repository of nuclear weapons in the world, it would make the ideal place to launch the denuclearization effort. He asked Vice President Adler to act in his stead at Kirtland AFB because he still doesn't feel strong enough for travel.

Margaret and her entourage of experts arrive in Albuquerque several days in advance of the planned inspection. They must ensure that all arrangements are in place and manage the last-minute details. She, her staff, and the entire team of international dignitaries stay in Santa Fe at a boutique hotel an hour from the base—reserved exclusively for the officials and their associates. The private location makes it easier for the security forces to monitor. To further provide for everyone's safety, Airmen from the base also stand guard.

Two days before the visiting team's arrival, Margaret walks alone near the fenced perimeter of the hotel property, unaware that Ivan and his support crew have just arrived. Deep in thought, his approach startles her.

"Margaret, my dear friend, you look as though the weight of the world rests on your shoulders."

She turns and lights up. "Oh, Ivan. It's so wonderful to see you." She offers him a brief hug. "It's just that I have this gnawing feeling that something bad is about to happen. China has sent me one demand after another. I don't understand the aggressiveness in their communiqués, but it's coming from somewhere. I've tried to figure it out, but nothing is clear."

Ivan reaches for her hand as they walk. "You're not alone in your apprehension. I always feel on guard whenever I deal with China, so I understand. They arrive in two days, right?"

"Yes. I've arranged for a military transport, not just for the Chinese, but for each team flying in for the inspection."

"President Zhang will be reticent to try something if I'm beside you. I'll make sure I'm always near you. He needs Russia's support."

"I'd appreciate that."

"I have a proposal. You're busy with logistics, and I'm here ahead of my father to learn from you and help if I can, but let's find time tomorrow to see Santa Fe. You need a break. Want to?"

Margaret looks down at the path and then over at Ivan. "I'd love to."

Later that evening, after dinner, the Russians and Americans congregate around the giant fireplace in the center of the hotel lounge. Ivan calls out to his team in Russian, and they chuckle and nod. One of the men connects his cell phone to the audio system, and soon, the music to the folk song *Kalinka* sounds throughout the room. Several of the Russians stand and begin dancing. The joviality lifts everyone's spirits, and the Americans join their Russian counterparts in the playful dancing around the room.

Margaret laughs as she watches the antics.

Ivan asks, "Would you consider joining me for a glass of wine somewhere quieter? My room, perhaps? From my balcony, I have a beautiful view of the desert landscape, and from there, we can watch the sunset."

Margaret smiles. "How could I turn down such an invitation? Besides, a glass of wine sounds rather refreshing."

The two leave the festivity, and their security detail walks behind. Once at Ivan's room, the bodyguards position themselves near the door. Their side-glances and restrained smiles expose an awareness of which they cannot speak. One shrugs, another nods, but no words are exchanged.

Ivan and Margaret spend the next hour sipping wine and sharing stories. Afterward, Margaret returns to her room, afresh with hopes and dreams.

Before falling asleep, Margaret picks up the television remote and finds a *60 Minute* episode on Syria. Members of the International Rescue Committee visit an orphanage in Turkey. She watches intently while the cameras move from one child to the next. Big-eyed babies stare silently from their cribs while older children sit on the floor. Margaret feels a surge of maternal urgency as the sea of little faces engulfs her and calls out for help. A little girl stands to the side, alone. She has only one arm and limps when she walks. According to the IRC narrator, Amira got hit with shrapnel from a bomb. When the visitors approach, the child scurries away and hides behind a half-opened door. Little fingers hold tight to the doorframe, but otherwise, she stands invisible to the cameras. Margaret grabs a notepad and writes down information about the orphanage. This is a child she must help. A child she must meet.

# Chapter 25

————— • —————

*T*hree days later, while storm-clouds gather, the leaders from the nuclear nations board an armored military transport and travel to the designated visitation site. An Air Force engineer greets them and explains how the investigation will proceed. He describes the disarmament process and points out the care that is taken for storing the disarmed warheads. Margaret stands to his side and listens intently as he discloses the intricate steps required. The engineer then leads the team to a viewing room, where members can look out upon the collection of deactivated warheads.

After the technical questions get answered, the team returns to the hotel. They proceed to the conference room to discuss their experience and plan for the next steps. If they'd expected a leisurely working-lunch, events soon disabuse them of that notion. As the attendees take their seats, a scuffle breaks out among the Chinese delegation. A member of their team points a semi-automatic weapon at his President and yells, "Zhang subverts Mao's principles and lives by his own!" Then he shouts something in Chinese and opens fire.

The Chinese President falls to the ground. Screams erupt and chairs topple as people scramble out of the way of the assassin. Several rush to the door in a panic. Chaos ensues.

Stunned, Margaret stands and stares, mouth agape, and heart thumping. The shooter points the weapon directly at the Vice President. "This charade will end today."

Margaret keeps her eyes on the assailant and edges away from the group. Those still seated take cover beneath the table, and those standing take a few steps back. TV crews capture everything. Though nauseous from fear, Margaret confronts the man in quiet tones, "Sir, this is not the way to handle a disagreement. Innocent people surround you. Move to the open area, as I have done."

President Smirnov hurries forward and steps in front of Margaret. Meanwhile, soldiers work their way through the crowd and hold their assault weapons drawn on their target. Smirnov tries to talk the militant shooter into laying down his gun, but he will have nothing to do with the Russian President's directive. Instead, he aims and fires upon him. Immediately, a barrage of automatic shots discharges and kills the assailant.

Margaret can't help but scream. She covers her mouth with her hand and blinks in shock. Time seems to stand still, and then the roar of pandemonium and fear hits her. At last, she finds that she can move.

Ivan and Margaret rush to Smirnov's side. Hit in the chest, he bleeds profusely. He coughs blood and struggles to breathe. Smirnov tries to speak, but words fail to emerge. Ivan cradles his father's head. "I love you."

With tears pouring down her face, Margaret holds Smirnov's hand. An Air Force medical team dashes into the room and to the downed President's side. Smirnov's eyes are barely open, but he looks at Ivan and then Margaret and sputters one audible word—*family*. His eyes close. The Russian President takes his final breath.

Overcome by sorrow, Margaret chokes back her tears. As though in a dream, she stands. Smirnov's blood covers her hands and suit. She summons strength and raises her voice, "We have just beheld the courage of a true leader. He has made the ultimate sacrifice."

Margaret's voice breaks, and she takes a deep breath while she struggles for words. "Over these last months, President Smirnov became my friend. He was someone I trusted. Someone I could depend upon. Today, he has proven himself a hero. He died for all of us because he died that we might have life through this denuclearization process. We must move forward as he would have wanted."

She pauses and looks at the assembly. "You've seen our stockpiles. We've deactivated 950 warheads, and we plan to do more. Are there any questions you might have for me?"

Through red-rimmed eyes, she looks at the faces of the team. Shock and sorrow reflect back at her. Nobody voices any questions. Margaret nods. "Let us continue the work that President Smirnov would have us do and offer our respects to our fallen comrade."

Margaret motions to the guards, who come to her side. She directs them to cover the bodies and arrange for their removal. "Please, contact the base Commander. He will want an investigation and may place the base on alert."

Margaret goes to Ivan and embraces him. They stand in silence as their tears fall. Several team members gather at their side. Margaret steps away from Ivan so that the members might offer him their condolences. Others leave the room.

Patiently, reporters wait for the opportunity to speak with Margaret or Ivan. After a minute, Margaret walks over and thanks them for respecting the bereaved.

"We don't want to interfere, but we've been on the air since this began. Everyone wants to know what's happening. Can you please speak with us?"

Margaret decides she should. "For a few minutes, and then I must handle …"

"How do you feel?" one reporter asks.

"I'm not sure I can assimilate right now. I'm still in shock. My heart feels locked in a terrible dark prison that I cannot escape. I'm numbed by sorrow."

Another reporter asks, "What about the treaty? Is it broken because of this?"

"Not at all. I'm confident the treaty will become even stronger. Today's actions show us why it's critical that we move forward in peace."

"We saw you speaking with President Smirnov. Did he say anything that you can share with us?"

"Because of his injuries, he couldn't speak. He managed one word: *family*."

"What's that mean?"

"We're all family. We aren't simply Russians or Americans or Chinese. We're humans—part of one family. His position was that we need to protect one another and live as family."

The reporters nod in understanding.

"Gentlemen, Ladies, I truly appreciate your desire to interview us, but I need to end this now. I must attend to President Smirnov. Thank you for respecting the circumstances."

Margaret turns away and walks over to the Airmen assisting with the removal of the bodies. "Airmen, President Smirnov took the bullet meant for me. He's a hero, and we will honor him as such."

The first Airman salutes. "We'll prepare the body for shipment and treat him as one of our own, Madam Vice President."

"Thank you. Let me know if you need anything."

Margaret closes the distance to Ivan. "I'm so sorry, my friend. Your father was like my own, and my heart aches for you and all of us."

Ivan looks into Margaret's eyes, and with tears in his, says, "He spoke of you as his daughter. I don't think of you as my sister, but you have, most definitely, become part of my beloved family."

They embrace and hold each other longer than friends might. Margaret says, "Have you called your mother?"

Ivan straightens and shakes his head. "No, but I'm sure she's aware."

With tenderness, Margaret says, "But she needs to hear from you."

Ivan stares at Margaret for a few minutes and replies, "You're right. I'll call her now. Please, can you stay with me today?"

"Of course."

# Chapter 26

News of the two murders spreads quickly. The reporters at the scene contact all the networks and provide the assassination story, along with video footage of the initial heated exchange. The world population may have been unaware of the nuclear leaders gathering, but they're all too aware now. Even while Smirnov's violent death appalls the world, the budding partnership between Russia and the United States rivets them and offers a glimmer of hope.

All of which Ivan had assumed would happen. And, of course, his mother had heard of her husband's death. When he makes the call home, gratitude toward Margaret fills him. Just as she'd said, his mother needed to hear from him. Mrs. Smirnov breaks into heart-broken sobs as soon as she hears her son's voice. "Did he suffer?" she asks.

"He didn't. Papa died almost instantly. After he got shot, he couldn't talk, but he mouthed 'Family.'"

His mother sniffles and clears her throat. "What do you think he meant?"

"I'm not sure, but just before, he looked at me and then Margaret. I think he referred to her and I being family. Then again, he could have meant the global family."

"Both possibilities seem right to me," Mrs. Smirnov says. "Your father hoped the two of you would get together. And, of course, he thought of the world's population as one big family."

"Maybe. I guess we'll never know." He lowers his head, feeling the weight of sadness.

"But you do, Ivan. You do know. Will you come home soon, son?"

"Yes, they're preparing the body now, and I'll return with Papa and his belongings this evening."

"Thank you." His mother coughs and sniffles. "As much as I feel devastated, I also feel so proud of your father. He died a hero—as I always knew him to be." She sobs brokenly.

"Mama, I'll come home soon. I'll notify the appropriate government officials so that they can make preparations for the funeral. Please, don't worry about anything. Just rest. I love you so much."

Once the call concludes, Ivan looks over at Margaret. He holds back his tears and reaches for her. She moves into his embrace, and Ivan exhales the torture of his grief. He'd thought he had more time. More room to say he was sorry. And more space to ask for forgiveness. Above all, he wanted more time to laugh. Just … more … time. But death stole such luxury and left him barren, except for his memories.

"Can we go somewhere more private?" Ivan asks.

"I need to address the investigators, and then I can leave. Shall I meet you in your room? I appreciate that you'll need to pack."

"Thank you. I'll wait for you there." Ivan picks up his notebook and glances at the crowd as he walks out of the room.

\*    \*    \*

Margaret turns to the dignitaries. "Colleagues, out of respect for the departed, and with respect to each of you, I want to close our meeting. President Smirnov's courage and leadership will guide us in the months ahead. If you have lingering questions, please send them to me, and I'll respond as soon as I can. Our next visitation will occur in three months. We're scheduled to meet in Moscow. Unless you have pressing questions, I thank you for your dedication, hard work, and steadfast efforts to help the human family. Safe travels, my friends."

As she readies to leave, a Chinese diplomat walks up to her. "May I, please, speak?" His eyes appear red-rimmed, and he holds his lips taut. "Please?"

Margaret sees his pain and nods her agreement. "Colleagues, one of our Chinese associates has asked to speak. Please offer him your attention."

Yong Li walks to the front of the room, and everyone becomes silent.

"The Chinese nation extends its heartfelt condolences. We strongly support global denuclearization. The traitor who shot our President and the Russian President doesn't speak for our country. We condemn his behavior and ask for your forgiveness. I assure you that we will do all in our power to achieve world peace. Thank you." He bows slowly and holds the bow. Raucous applause greets Mr. Li.

Margaret walks to the diplomat and thanks him, and then she turns to the gathering. "Colleagues, this is a day we will never forget. Two of our colleagues died in our midst. Besides the horrors of senseless bloodshed, we witnessed the consequence of hate. I think that each of us needs time to process our pain. I'll stay for a few more days, and if you intend to remain too, let's find time to meet. If you plan to leave soon, then I extend my heartfelt wishes for a safe journey. Whatever your circumstances, thank you for the sacrifices you're making to achieve real peace."

One-by-one, Margaret greets the dignitaries and offers condolences. Her assistant stands nearby in case logistical concerns arise that she can resolve. Once the room has cleared, Margaret tells her assistant that she needs to say farewell to Ivan Smirnov.

Up on the residential floor, Margaret knocks on Ivan's door, and he ushers her inside. Two packed bags wait by the doorway. His reddened lids show her Ivan's deep grief. Margaret reaches to embrace him, and when she does, he wraps his arms around her. Ivan composes himself and says, "I just need to hold you one more time before I leave. Things will change for me when I return. Because I'm the Prime Minister, I must step in as Acting president." He takes a deep breath and lets his head rest next to hers. Then he whispers, "You'll come to the funeral?"

"Yes, of course."

Ivan looks into her eyes with longing and pulls her even closer. He cradles her face, kisses her softly on the lips, and then just holds her.

A knock at the door interrupts them. An aide enters. "Sir, it is time."

# Chapter 27

The Cathedral of Christ the Savior in Moscow hosts the funeral for President Smirnov. A hearse, covered in flowers, carries the deceased President to the church. Crowds of mourners line the street and wait for the departed's arrival. Broken-hearted, the people wish to offer their condolences.

When the hearse arrives, bearers remove the casket. The people wail and cry out. The pallbearers move slowly and deliberately into the cathedral. With synchronized steps, they take the President to the altar, where he lays reposed in a half-couch casket.

The Orthodox patriarch begins the ceremony with the sign of the cross and deep-throated exhortations to prayer. As he swings the censor, incense rises, and the monks sing *Let my prayer arise*. Their voices draw the mourners deeper into their sorrow.

Ivan wraps his arm around his mother and holds his sister's hand. He clenches his jaw and tries to keep his sadness at bay. *I must stay strong for my family and my people.* Ivan wonders when he last came to a service while he watches the patriarch. *Was it graduation from high school? Maybe confirmation?* He can't remember. Then he notices that his mother follows the priest and responds to the words of his prayers. He hadn't known that she held such a strong belief.

At the conclusion of the solemn Orthodox service, with ethereal chanting and fogs of incense, Mrs. Smirnov moves to her husband's side and touches his face lightly. She leans over the body, whispers to her dead lover, and kisses him on each cheek and then his lips. The widow grasps his folded hands for a few minutes, and tears flow down her cheeks. She turns to go back to her seat, but the Orthodox patriarch walks over to her and takes her hand. He offers his condolences and then leads her to her pew. With the family seated, he offers a final blessing, bends to kiss the President's head, and closes the coffin.

Ivan rises to thank all those who came to honor his father. "My father chose to use his remaining days in service, protecting the innocent, whom he loved. His courageous act was a culmination of all his decisions and actions. In that defining moment, he taught us about the purpose of life, its preciousness, and its mandate. His final and only word was Family. It was his belief that we are family. The rich and the poor, the light-skinned and the dark-skinned, the Americans and the Russians. Yes, we're all family. May we each take steps to follow my father's example and ensure that this, our family, is protected."

The procession to the cemetery begins with much sovereign grandeur. The Deputy Prime Minister leads the procession. He carries a large, framed photograph of President Smirnov. The immediate family walks behind the coffin, followed by visiting dignitaries and State officials. Margaret walks among the dignitaries. After the heads of state, soldiers march in unison.

Once the procession comes in sight of the cemetery, a choir standing by the gravesite sings the State Anthem of the Soviet Union, and many of the mourners join in. The bearers lower President Smirnov into the grave during a 21-gun salute.

Ivan catches Margaret's eye. He longs to hold her. Across the sea of people, they meet in their thoughts. He feels her love and allows himself to let go into dreams of tomorrow. He doesn't know how such an unlikely romance could develop, but he leaves those worries and, instead, turns to his father's grave. *Thank you, Papa, for bringing Margaret into my life. Help us find a way to love, even though we live in different countries.*

Ivan looks for Margaret, but she isn't there. His eyes search the crowd, but he cannot find her. And then a hand slips into his. Margaret. Overcome by emotion, he lowers his head. Ivan wants to bring her close and feel her softness next to him. He leans toward her and whispers, "May I visit you tonight?"

Margaret returns his whisper, "Please." Then she tugs on Ivan's hand, and he bends to her. "I'll go now and wait for you tonight. I'm staying at the Azimut Hotel on Smolenskaya."

Familiar with the hotel, Ivan smiles and whispers, "Let's meet at 19:00. I know a good spot for dinner, so be hungry."

Margaret squeezes his hand and then lets it go. She walks over to Mrs. Smirnov and expresses her condolences again. To her surprise, Mrs. Smirnov returns her simple gesture with a hug and double kisses. She grasps Margaret's hand, and while patting it lovingly, says, "Family, we are family."

Tears rise as Margaret looks into Mrs. Smirnov's eyes. Her kindness tells Margaret that she's accepted and loved.

# Chapter 28

Not a minute late, Ivan arrives at Margaret's hotel room, holding a small gift box. When she opens the door, he greets her with a loving smile and arms that wrap around her. Margaret ushers him inside the room, where Ivan again draws her to him. The warmth of his body against hers awakens passions long dormant. The expression "swept off her feet" comes to mind, for she feels as if gravity has lost its pull. Margaret rests against Ivan's chest and wonders . . . wonders about touching him.

"I've brought you a little something Russian," he says and then hands Margaret the gift box. She opens it and finds a pendant necklace with a hand-enameled Russian blue egg. Before she can say anything, Ivan tells her, "Miniature enameled eggs are given to a person you love, along with three kisses and a wish." He proceeds to kiss her on each cheek and then focuses on her lips. "Here's to good health and a friendship that grows ever deeper."

Margaret cradles Ivan's face and presses up against him. The next kiss lingers, and his tongue reaches hers. When his hands travel up her back and then down her sides, her desire mounts. And when he pauses at her breasts and holds them with tenderness, her arousal grows even more substantial. She wants him. Margaret runs her hand down his back and to his hips.

Ivan brushes her golden locks aside, kisses her neck, and nibbles her earlobe. He whispers, "Dearest, shall we proceed? I long to make love with you, but only if you would desire it as well." Margaret reaches to kiss him again and nips at his bottom lip while slipping her hand beneath the waistband of his pants to touch his erection. Her wish is clear.

Slowly, Ivan unbuttons Margaret's blouse, and when it falls to the floor, he unfastens her bra. "You are magnificent, my love." With his fingertips, he brushes her nipples and then fondles her breasts. Waves of pleasure roll over her. She works to remove her slacks and panties. Ivan helps her and then, hurriedly, shirks off his pants and yanks his shirt over his head. Margaret moves her hand across his scarred chest. War has taken a part of each of them, but battle is what brought them together.

They hold each other and climb onto the bed. On his side, Ivan moves his hand slowly across her body and kisses her breasts, her stomach, and her sweetness. He breathes deep of the smell of her and murmurs, "I've missed the scent and touch of a woman. Especially a woman I love." Ivan looks into her eyes, and she into his. The world disappears, and only the two of them exist.

Uninhibited by circumstance, Ivan enters Margaret, and together, they move as only true lovers can. Each kiss draws them deeper into the fervor of the moment. Two soldiers, now lovers, let go of the past and sense a future. In the throes of love's pleasure, as their bodies contort and envelop, they experience the emergence of hope. They glisten in the evening shadows, and the world of death and struggle, of politics and threat, becomes no more.

Later while they rest in each other's arms, Ivan speaks in low, measured tones, "I love you, my darling. I've loved you since the day you took my memories back to Afghanistan. I don't know what lies ahead for us, but somehow, I think we'll stay together. I can't imagine it otherwise. For now, though, I feel grateful for every moment we spend together. I don't want to be apart from you." He kisses her. "You've given me a second life, and I want to share that life with you."

Ivan's innocent admission brings tears to Margaret's eyes. She hadn't known whether or not any man would want her after she lost her arm. But, with Ivan, she feels whole and a desirous woman once more.

She whispers back, "I feel the same, my love. When I lie in your arms, I feel safe and at home, as though it were meant to be."

Ivan draws her closer. "Your softness has reached into all the desolate areas of my soul and uncovered my long-buried joy."

Margaret looks into his red-rimmed eyes. "What will happen to us?"

Ivan looks down and hesitates.

Margaret asks, "What is it? Please, talk to me."

Ivan glances at Margaret and then lowers his head. "I can't bear to think of leaving you," he whispers.

"But, surely, we'll meet again soon, right? There's much we need to do with the disarmament."

"And then it's goodbye again ..."

"What're you saying?"

"I'm in love with you, and I can't bear our separation. You're Life to me, and being apart feels worse than death. I want to marry you, and yet, we both have obligations to our country. I don't know what to do." Tears well in his eyes.

Margaret wipes a salty droplet from his cheek and kisses him tenderly. "I'm in love with you as well, my dear, dear Ivan. There's nothing I'd like more than to awaken each day in your arms. Can't we figure out a way to love each other through the complexity of distance, time, and heritage? We won't always be in our current roles. At least, I won't. Then . . . then we could stay together permanently."

Ivan's sad eyes brighten. He gets up and retrieves something from his slacks. Then he kneels by the side of the bed, and Margaret sits up at its edge.

After taking her hand, he says, "Dearest Margaret, would you honor me by becoming my wife, for better or worse, through distance and time? Would you bless me with a quiet private ceremony at which I can attest my love for you before God, and vow to remain faithful to you until the end of our earthly lives?"

"Yes, my love, I do. Though we'll make our vows in secret, this will be the happiest day of my life. Someday, in the not so distant future, when we're free to live together as husband and wife, we can have a public ceremony. Then, we can begin and end all our days together. Until that's possible, I'll seek out opportunities to come to you—be that Russia, America, or elsewhere."

Ivan shows Margaret a ring with a red stone. "Would you accept this ring as a symbol of our promise? It belonged to my grandmother and then my mother."

Margaret struggles to hold back tears and inhales deeply. She slides the ring onto her ring finger. It fits a little too loosely, so she moves it to her middle finger, where it sits snuggly. "Our promise, our hope, symbolized."

Ivan gives her a smothering hug. "At our next tryst, we'll meet secretively with a priest and say our vows. Shall I tell my mother? She'll keep it confidential."

"Of course, my dear."

"Ask anything of me, please. I want you to understand the depths of my love."

"Anything?"

"Yes, anything."

Margaret lowers her gaze and then brings her focus back to Ivan. She studies his face and says, "I ask that the situation in Syria get resolved so that its people can return home."

Ivan gasps. "You've chosen the most difficult challenge I can imagine. You surprise me, my dear. Most betrothed would ask for riches, but you ask for nothing for yourself." He takes her hand, brings it to his lips, then states with resolve, "It shall be done."

✳   ✳   ✳

Across the city, Mrs. Smirnov lies in her bed alone. She looks around the room as though seeing it for the first time. She shudders at the chill and pulls the covers up higher. In the distance, the Sapsan high-speed train zooms past. She listens to its rumbling and whistles and is taken back to her trips to St. Petersburg, where her daughter lives. She loved traveling that route with her husband because he always made it special for her. "No work today," he'd declare, and though he'd acknowledge fellow travelers, his staff made sure no one bothered them. It was her exclusive time with him.

They would sit in the restaurant car and have their coffee and breakfast. Husband and wife would talk about simple things and laugh a lot. *He was such a jokester.* She smiles. He'd always bring a gift for her. She chuckles, thinking about the huge Cossack hat that he gave her with the raccoon tail. He insisted, playfully, that she wear it, and she did. Then there was the butterfly brooch. She didn't need any pushing to pin it to her jacket. Mrs. Smirnov loves it still and wears it almost every day.

On the train, she felt like a young woman, riding with her lover. They'd watch the towns pass, the farms and the stretches of land, and they'd talk of family and their dreams for the future. Distressed, she tightens her jaw as sadness replaces her momentary joy.

She stretches her arm across the bed to the vacant space that once held her husband of more than fifty years. Mrs. Smirnov chokes down her cries then notices the time on the bedside clock. Ivan hasn't returned home. With any luck, he remains with Margaret. The thought pleases her.

At the funeral, Mrs. Smirnov had noticed her son's distraction and looked to see its source. Upon seeing Margaret, she'd smiled through her tears. Mrs. Smirnov has waited for Ivan to fall in love and prayed for him to find someone with whom he could share his sorrows and joys. Never had she expected her son would fall for an American, but now she thinks, *how fitting.* She dabs at her tears. Her sorrow morphs into gratitude and joy for prayers answered.

"My dear husband, our son has found love, and tonight, he's rediscovered his manhood." Mrs. Smirnov smiles and thinks back through time. Then she continues her conversation with her deceased husband, "Remember when we were first together? We were so young. Our parents thought us *too* young, but you were persistent." She chuckles. "I think they finally just gave up." Through a poignant mind's-eye, she looks through the distance of time. "I thought you were the most handsome man alive. And in your uniform . . . well, you had me mesmerized." She pulls the covers up higher as memories crowd for attention. "Remember the night I conceived Ivan? You'd come home on leave. We didn't have much time, but we made the best of it, didn't we?" She giggles softly. "Those were good years. Yes, those were very good years." Tears form while she reminisces. Mrs. Smirnov reaches for her husband's pillow and holds it next to her cheek. The linen retains the scent of his aftershave—notes of amber, citrus, and cinnamon bring him near, and she holds the pillow as though her life depended upon it. "I'll be with you soon, my love. I'll be with you soon."

# Chapter 29

*M*argaret awakens to the sound of someone rolling a cart into the room. Ivan has ordered breakfast for the two of them. She peeks over her covers and watches the waiter exchange a few comments with Ivan and then leave. The aroma of espresso coffee makes her smile and sit up.

Ivan teases, "Coffee or me, which woke you?"

"Neither, I heard the cart." Margaret chuckles.

"I wanted to get a little something for my princess." Ivan climbs onto the bed and offers a wet, meandering kiss. Playfully, Margaret pulls him under the covers with her, which arouses more than just their appetites. The feel of his body next to hers sends quivering waves of desire throughout her body. "You make it rather difficult for me to return home. Ecstasy, or a desk job? That's not a fair choice."

Amused, Ivan grins. "We should plan another trip soon."

"Don't we need to visit more nuclear storage facilities? Let's plan for another rendezvous in a month." Margaret pauses and shakes her head. "A year ago, I couldn't have imagined getting excited about visiting nuclear sites."

"Nor I, but I'm grateful we have to make this journey together. We can visit three sites northwest of Moscow—more if time permits. When you get home, check your calendar, and let me know some dates. I'll get everything arranged."

"I'm plotting already. Hey, my flight isn't until three this afternoon—do you have any free time?"

"Unfortunately, I promised to help my mother this morning. She needs to go through my father's papers and feels overwhelmed."

"Of course. I would never want you to ignore those responsibilities. I thought maybe I could visit St. Basil's this morning and then go to the airport."

"Excellent plan. Just know, though, you might have admirers approach you."

"I'll put on a scarf so that no one will know it's me."

"Come on. You're a movie star now, and everyone will recognize you. I'll see what I can do to help you out."

✳    ✳    ✳

Margaret stands outside St. Basil's Cathedral, gazing in awe at the multicolored domes. A hunched woman approaches and reaches for her hand. Margaret feels perplexed, but when the tearful woman pulls a worn photo of a young man in uniform from her purse, she understands. As her own tears fall, the Vice President embraces the woman. At that moment, the barriers of language and nationality disappear. They are simply two women sharing sorrow, with no translator needed. Soon, another woman joins them and pulls a framed picture from her bag—again of a young man wearing his military uniform. The woman cries, and Margaret wraps an arm around her.

A crowd forms, all women, and the Secret Service stand guard. Deeply moved by the collective sadness, Margaret chokes back sobs. A uniformed man approaches and says something in gruff tones. The women look at Margaret, nod to her, and then turn and leave.

"Please, come with me," the man says in perfect English. He takes her to the side door of the cathedral. Another fellow greets them there. "I am a docent and wish to offer you a private tour."

Margaret suspects that Ivan arranged the tour. While they walk the worn stone floors and travel through the artistry of the centuries, the docent explains why and how the cathedral became secular. His voice echoes through the chilly expanse of richly decorated chapels. Though silent now, Margaret glimpses the ages-old fervor of worshippers. Intricate images of the Divine cover the walls and ceilings. The docent notices her distraction waits for her to return to the present. When she does, he says, "This may be a museum, Ms. Adler, but we still perform limited religious services. You were wondering, correct?"

"Yes, thank you. I wish I could come here for a service."

"Ah, your next trip, perhaps?"

Margaret smiles. "Absolutely. I will surely return."

Time blurs by as they walk the hallowed halls. When the docent mentions the hour, Margaret realizes she needs to leave. Her Secret Service detail acknowledges the lateness of the hour. The guide leads them to a side exit, where her limousine waits.

Occupied with thoughts of the last several days, Margaret travels to Sheremetyevo Airport. It's been a whirlwind of sorrows and joy. At the airport, a three piece-band plays folk songs in the terminal. She pauses to listen, and the lead singer stops and invites her to join them.

"There was a time when I would play guitar and sing my heart's desires. I miss that so much, for there's a song that plays in my heart. *This Is My Song* by Lloyd Stone. But, alas, it's not possible. I had to give up my guitar ..."

"We know song and will play for lady." Tall and heavily tattooed, the twenty-something young man introduces himself as Dimitri. "We go on tour. On way New York."

"Nice to meet you, Dimitri. I'm Margaret."

The guy nods. "Vice President Margaret Adler from United States, yes?"

She smiles ruefully. "That's me."

"I following your work. Let's do this." He makes an announcement in Russian and garners the attention of the people in the lobby.

Margaret looks over to her Security detail and nods.

Dimitri plucks a few notes, and Margaret realizes he does know the song.

"You'll join me, right?" she asks.

Dimitri smiles and rocks his head mischievously. Margaret clears her throat and waits until he's ready. Her new companion nods, and as he plays, she joins in. It's been a long while since she's sung publicly. And yet, in an airport on the outskirts of Moscow, she lets her heart speak.

*"This is my song, Oh, God of all the nations, a song of peace for lands afar and mine."*

Passersby pause and then draw closer. Many applaud, and Margaret feels emboldened enough to continue. Some of the passengers take out their smartphones and record the performance.

*"My country's skies are bluer than the ocean, and sunlight beams on cloverleaf and pine.*

*But other lands have sunlight too, and clover, and skies are everywhere as blue as mine. Oh, hear my song, oh God of all the nations, a song of peace for their land and for mine."*

Her passion and grace fill the lobby. As she belts out the final words, the people shout, "Bravo. Bravo" in a multitude of languages.

Margaret bows, turns to the guitarist, and gives him a hug. "I couldn't have done this without you, my friend. Thank you. For a while, I forgot I couldn't play because you were in step with me."

"Was easy to do. I have honor to have played for distinguished Margaret Adler."

Margaret places money into the donation basket and then accompanies the Secret Service team to the plane. As she climbs the boarding stairs, the flight attendant greets her, "Good afternoon, Ms. Adler. I hope you had a good trip?"

"I couldn't have hoped for anything better. Thank you."

Margaret finds her seat and stares out toward the airport lobby. She sends a quick text to Ivan: *I'm leaving now and miss you already. I love you, my dearest. Forever.*

Immediately, Ivan responds: *Forever and ever, Amen. I saw you singing … marvelous. I'm stunned.*

With a smile, Margaret sighs and wraps a blanket around herself. Then she faces the window and ignores the activity on board. Teary, she closes her eyes, and the hum of the 747 silences her sobs.

# Chapter 30

"We will land in 30 minutes," the pilot announces.

Margaret rouses from her nap and looks outside. The daunting demands of her position, the President's failing health, and the expectations of the upcoming elections all overshadow her magical week with her lover. She grimaces as she thinks of what lies ahead. Margaret fingers the ring Ivan gave her, and her mind transports back to the promises they made. *I must stay strong.*

The pilot starts his descent, and Margaret watches as D.C. comes into sight. When Air Force Two hits the tarmac at Joint Base Andrews, Margaret takes her phones off airplane mode and notices a text message from Ivan on her personal cell. *We will be together soon, my love. When things heat up, remember our promise and know I'm with you. Send dates for the next visit. Forever, Ivan.*

A Secret Service agent interrupts her reverie, "Ma'am, will you be going to your residence or the White House?"

"The President texted that he'll see me in the morning, so I'd like to go home."

"We'll be ready when you are, ma'am." He pauses and smiles. "You have a beautiful voice, ma'am."

Margaret had forgotten about the airport trio and her accompaniment until that moment. *What was I thinking?* She blushes and says, "That's kind of you to say. I have no idea why I joined in, but it seems the world knows about my misstep now."

"Misstep, ma'am? Not at all. You sounded amazing."

Margaret smiles and shrugs. "It was fun being a kid for a bit."

The passengers disembark, and Margaret heads home to a white 19th-century dwelling, located on the grounds of the United States Naval Observatory, and about two and a half miles from the White House. Tucked back from the street, it feels worlds away from the political drama of Washington D.C. Margaret's home provides a peaceful retreat, and she needs that right now.

At the front door, her staff greets her, and then she turns and thanks her Secret Service team. The staff takes her luggage, and she walks into the den.

"Can I get anything for you, ma'am?" Stephen, her fatherly attendant asks.

"Thank you so much. Won't you join me for a glass of cabernet sauvignon? Some nibbles would be good right now as well." She collapses on the overstuffed couch and looks around the room. This is the one space she decorated with family treasures and personal photos. In here, she feels at home.

Stephen brings a tray of cold cuts, various cheeses, and a bottle of Napa Valley Cab. He opens the bottle and pours a glass for each of them. "Shall we toast, ma'am? To the success that lies ahead with disarmament."

"Ah, you've been watching the news."

"Of course, ma'am. And I've enjoyed listening to YouTube as well." He smiles mischievously.

"Oh, gosh. I feel embarrassed by that."

"You shouldn't. You have an incredible voice, ma'am. Staffers have had to field calls for the past eight hours. The networks want to interview you. We'll show you the list in the morning."

Margaret drifts off and rouses a little when Stephen asks, "Would you like to go to your room, ma'am?"

"I guess I should. Otherwise, I'll surely fall asleep here."

Stephen accompanies Margaret to her room and then says goodnight. She thanks him and walks into the suite. Spacious and opulent, the area gives a daily reminder of the disparities of life. Even after several years, she feels like a guest in this room. Margaret checks her watch and realizes that Ivan is probably asleep. She'd so like to talk with him but decides to call in the morning.

Just as she drifts into sleep, a phone call startles her into wakefulness. She sighs with relief when she realizes it's Ivan.

"My goodness, I thought you would be sleeping, that's why I didn't call when I got home."

"How could I sleep when Russia's latest singing sensation has taken over social media?"

"You're kidding, right?"

"About this? Heavens, no. Type in your name and watch what comes up."

Margaret does a quick Google search on her laptop, and the results stun her.

"Oh, my gosh. I didn't expect this."

"Of course not, but you need to take time to read the comments. It just might warm your heart."

"I'll do that later. Right now, I'm just so happy to hear your voice. How are you?"

"Well, other than missing my betrothed, I'm fine."

"I know what you mean. I feel lost without you near."

"We need to plan for our next rendezvous—longer this time."

"My thoughts exactly. I have an idea. As well as visiting nuclear sites, could we visit a Syrian orphanage in Turkey? I watched an exposé while we were in Albuquerque that broke my heart."

"And you want to adopt them all."

"Ivan. How could I adopt all of them? Maybe one or two."

"I knew it." He laughs good-heartedly. "Before you get too emotionally involved, just know that adopting a Muslim child is complicated if not impossible for non-Muslims."

"But, there's a thread of hope, right?"

"I'll look into it. It *has* been done, but rarely. Do you have a back story that you've not shared yet?"

"I saw a child, an amputee. She looked alone and terrified. I want to hold her, Ivan. I want her to see that she'll be okay. And I want her to feel protected. And yes, I'd like to adopt her."

"I'll investigate, but try not to get too hopeful."

# Chapter 31

———·———

*M*orning sneaks up on Margaret. She tossed and turned most of the night. "The worst part of travel," she mutters. She'd prefer to lounge but has a meeting with the President in two hours and must go over a list of items—not the least of which is the progress she's made with denuclearization.

A knock sounds at the door, and she gets out of bed. "Yes?"

"Ma'am, just checking to make sure you're up. Would you like your usual?"

"That would be perfect. I'll come down in fifteen minutes."

When Margaret reaches the first floor, her coffee and toasted bagel sit waiting. She smiles and thanks the staff. "You're the best. I missed you all."

Stephen flashes a smile and hands Margaret the *Washington Post* and *The Hill*. "Ma'am, you might want to look at the folded page in the *Post*."

Margaret flips through the paper and comes to the marked page. She freezes momentarily when she sees a photo of herself, singing with the trio in the Moscow airport lounge. "You'll enjoy the story, ma'am. I promise. The writer compares you to Joni Mitchell."

"I, eh, I don't know what came over me to sing with them. Years ago, I had a guitar and would sing at gatherings—just for fun, of course.

Those musicians took me back to those years, and for some reason, I didn't think—I just joined them."

After breakfast, Margaret grabs her briefcase and heads for the door. The Secret Service waits outside, and they drive directly to the portico of the West Wing of the White House. Then the team accompanies her while she walks to her meeting with the President. Margaret takes a deep breath when she enters the colonnade. The smiles from senators, representatives, and staff haven't gone unnoticed, and the reactions make her anxious about facing the President. She pauses at his door and waits to get announced. A side-glance tells her that the secretary's seen the video. *What possessed me to act like a teenager again?* She clenches her jaw, imagines the worst, and strides into the Oval Office.

"Bravo, Ms. Mitchell," the President calls out. "Come in, come in."

"Sir, my apologies, I . . ."

"Nonsense. You did more for international diplomacy than any politician. Of course, we'll need an encore." His smile lets Margaret know that he's pleased.

"Sir, it was just a spur-of-the-moment decision. And I don't know why I did it."

"Well, I'm glad you did. Instead of the daily hateful analyses from the networks, you've become the center of attention. Who knew I had a Joni Mitchell clone on my team?"

Margaret reddens and glances at the floor, at a loss for words.

"Okay, I'll stop embarrassing you, but this isn't the end of our discussion about your singing career." He chuckles good-naturedly. "Let's go over the denuclearization progress."

Margaret sighs with relief. Prepared for this discussion, she offers the President an outline of steps taken. He listens intently and then stands. Margaret watches as he paces slowly, deep in thought.

"Love is a powerful force, Adler. It demands sacrifice, but the rewards far exceed those demands. We love our spouse, our children, and our families. We'd do most anything for them. We love our country, and soldiers like you show us what that can mean. But, another love exists. It's rarer and transcends the confines of family or the perimeters of country. The love of which I speak is a love for humanity. It recognizes the value of life, not skin color or nationality, or gender or anything else that might narrow it to a descriptive. Humanity—the old and the young, those here at home, and those across the planet.

"You see humanity as an ultimate value and respond accordingly. That's your strength. That's why you're loved. And that's why you must become the next President."

Margaret stumbles for words. Though prepared to discuss denuclear- ization, even the disruptions and murders, she'd never expected this. She blinks away the tears that blur her vision and looks into Williams's eyes. Both fierceness and kindness greet her. "Sir, I'm at a loss for words. But if I were called upon to serve, I would do so to the best of my ability."

"I anticipated that response, Adler. When the time comes, I want you to declare your intention to run. Over the months ahead, keep this conversation at the forefront of your thoughts. Party politics will divide and derail, but you need to stay the course. Listen to your heart, and don't allow private interests to confuse you as they have so many others. I'll help you in all the ways I can."

"Sir, I'm deeply grateful for your endorsement. You know me better than almost anyone, so you'll understand when I say that I'm not a pol- itician. On the contrary, I'm a foot soldier who sees what many cannot, are afraid to, or simply refuse. I'm the eyes of these people. And I enjoy being your back-up. As for becoming the person always in the spotlight … well, I cringe at the thought."

"And yet you didn't mind singing your heart away at an airport."

"True, but that was a fluke."

"Then, I guess you'll have to imagine each day of your presidency as 'a fluke,' because you're needed."

# Chapter 32

*W*hile finalizing her report on the denuclearization investigation, Margaret's cell phone rings. A quick glance tells her the call is from Ivan.

"Oh, my goodness, it's so good to hear from you. Is everything okay?"

"Not really. I'm lying on top of my bed—alone. I don't like that." He chuckles.

"Ahh, we need a tryst." She stands and walks to the window. "You're more creative than me. Can you come up with a reason to travel?"

"Hmm, I've been thinking Syria."

"What? Seriously?"

"Yep. I've spoken with an Imam in Turkey. He's granted a visit to an orphanage near the Syrian border—the one you saw on *60 Minutes*. His approval comes with several stipulations, though."

"Like what?"

"Well, he wants a member of the International Rescue Committee to accompany us. Seems he trusts that organization. I believe the IRC is headquartered in New York, so could you speak with them?"

"I'm on it. This is awesome. I can't believe you've accomplished so much in such a brief time."

"The Imam insists that the visit completes before Ramadan and suggests we stay at the Incirlik Air Base in Turkey, where we'll have both

American and Turkish military support. He made it clear, though, that he can't guarantee our safety. The man has a few choice words for insurgents. Otherwise, simple things like dressing modestly, staying reserved and respectful in social settings—all things you do naturally."

"Before Ramadan? That doesn't give us much time. I'll speak with President Williams today."

"Do you think he'll object?"

"I don't think so, but I'll find out soon enough."

"On my end, I'll call President Ozdemir and ask about an overnight stay at the base. These last years, my father worked closely with Turkey, developing a long-needed accord. I'm hopeful he'll be receptive. If you get a thumbs-up, and if Ozdemir approves us staying at the base, maybe we could meet up in Moscow and fly together."

"Absolutely. I don't want to fly alone to that area. I'll contact the IRC this afternoon and come up with potential dates." She takes a deep breath. "Wow, Ivan, this is unexpected, and I'm soaring inside."

Ivan laughs. "I look forward to lying next to my bride, and perhaps engaging in a different kind of soaring."

"You're such a tease, but I love that image."

After they say their goodbyes, Margaret checks her calendar and considers possible dates for the trip. *First things first*, she tells herself. *I need the President's blessing.*

She asks for her assistant to join her. Together, they go through the President's agenda.

"I don't see anything out of the ordinary, do you?" Margaret asks.

"In terms of today's meeting, I think the agenda is straightforward. But you've had several calls from talk-show hosts who'd like to interview you, and network news is always demanding time."

Margaret moans. "I'd rather not deal with any of them, but I'll let the President know and follow his lead. Anything else?"

"Not that I'm aware of."

"All right, thank you. I've finished the denuclearization report, so could you make two copies? I need to give one to the President."

"I'll have it ready in a minute."

Margaret walks over to the Oval Office with the report, the agenda, and her hopes of visiting the orphanage. When she arrives, the President stands at the window, lost in thought. Without turning, he asks her to join him.

"Few people ever see this view. Standing here between the flag of our great nation and the flag of The President of the United States is a rare privilege and a weighty responsibility."

Margaret walks behind the desk and stands by Williams's side. "I agree, sir."

He turns and smiles, "I know you do, and I also know you're ready to assume the role. Let's take a seat. There's something I need to tell you."

Margaret nods and follows President Williams to one of the Oval Office couches.

"With my last kidney flare up, the doctors ordered a CT scan of my torso. This morning, I got the results. I have metastatic gastric cancer."

Margaret's jaw drops, and she takes a deep breath.

"The oncologist explained that I have maybe two months to live."

"Sir, I'm so sorry. I don't know what to say." Margaret wipes away tears.

"I had hoped to walk with you through the election process, but that's impossible now. My days are numbered, and they aren't many. I hope to remain in the Office for another month to finish what I can, but then I'll relinquish the responsibility to you."

"Sir, please depend upon me to help in any way."

"For now, I'm sharing this information only with you and my wife. In two weeks, I'll talk with my staff, and at the end of the month, I'll make a formal public announcement. We'll get you sworn in then."

"This is a lot to take in, sir. When will you talk with the Speaker and the Senate Majority Leader?"

Williams inhales slowly and looks across the expanse of the room before answering. "After my staff has prepared, and you're ready for the onslaught, I'll tell them. Most likely, this will happen a day or two before I address the public."

In the ensuing silence, the room feels as if it's turned cold. They both sit lost in the gravity of the situation.

The President breaks the silence, "Do you have anything pressing for me, Margaret?"

"Only one thing, sir, and surely it can wait."

"What is it?"

"Russia's Acting President has invited me to accompany him to a Syrian orphanage in southern Turkey. It's a trip that we must complete before Ramadan, so next week, most likely."

"This is Smirnov's son?"

Margaret nods.

"I've heard he's taken a fancy to you."

Margaret blushes and attempts a stammered response.

The President chuckles, "Oh, come on, do you really think we don't know such things? You and Ivan have done more for diplomacy between our two countries than anyone in modern history. Hell, yes. Go."

"Really, sir? But …"

"No buts. I suspect there's a little Syrian girl who needs you."

Margaret's eyes widen. "How do you know about her, sir?"

"For folks like us, a phone call is never just between two people. And when the Vice President talks about travel with the Acting President of Russia, I will certainly hear about it."

"Did I misstep, sir?"

"No, I just found out before you had a chance to tell me." He stands and offers Margaret a hug. "If that little girl becomes yours, what a life she will have living in the White House. I want you to take Air Force One to Moscow. It has more space and conveniences, which makes it ideal for long trips. If Ivan agrees, take it to the Incirlik Air Base in Turkey. We have about five thousand Airmen stationed there, part of the 39th Air Base Wing. They'll take good care of you. This trip isn't just for the child, nor is it just for you. It's for all of us. I suspect your visit will change the fate of that devastated country. Go with my blessing."

# Chapter 33

*M*argaret flies to Moscow with Rebecca Grimes of the International Rescue Committee. They've taken an overnight flight on the President's Boeing 747. Margaret and Rebecca sit in the Presidential quarters and talk through the next few days. They'll spend a night in Moscow and then journey to Turkey's southern border, where they'll visit the orphanage. Several months ago, Rebecca made the journey with IRC, which qualifies her to accompany the U.S. Vice President.

"This may be the largest orphanage in the world," Rebecca says. "It houses about a thousand children of all ages—many of whom have psychological and physical scars. A walk among these innocents steals your breath and shatters all notions of decency. These children have seen the worst of life. Many are victims of chemical weapons. Others sustained injuries from shrapnel or shells. Most of the children have lived in this make-shift community for years. They don't know that another world exists."

As Rebecca describes the scene, Margaret listens intently and travels back to the *60 Minutes* segment she'd seen. Big brown eyes had stared at her from across the miles and pleaded for her help. She interrupts Rebecca with a question, "I saw a little girl on the IRC Special that I'd like to meet. Is that possible?"

"It might be. Can you describe her?"

"She looks to be about three or four-years-old and has one arm. Though I don't know for sure, I believe her face is disfigured. She hid from the cameras, so it's hard to say. For most of the footage, she peeked around a doorway. I believe one of the IRC representatives referred to her as Amira."

"Ahh, I know her. The Syrian forces killed the girl's entire extended family. She's one of the few survivors pulled from that grizzly rubble. Her face and much of her torso got badly burned."

Margaret reaches for her neck. Sorrow lodges in her throat. She wants to scream but cannot. She wipes her eyes and says, "War is a horror that often takes more victims than it saves. But this, this is unthinkable. For the Syrian government to use chemical weapons against its own people is a crime we can't ignore."

Rebecca nods. "You'll see the results of that crime as you walk through the orphanage. Most of the children, including Amira, suffer from PTSD from all the bombing and brutality. They feel wary of strangers, or any sudden movement, noise, or unidentified object like a camera. When they see that they can trust you, then you'll see their playfulness."

"When I saw Amira on the television special, it broke my heart. Such a little thing to have suffered so much."

"Well, prepare yourself. Your heart will break over and over again at this orphanage. Amira is one of many disfigured and disabled."

"Will I be able to speak with her?"

"I'll do my best. The caretakers are open to visitors because their financial support comes through outside agencies like IRC. But Amira will be afraid to meet you. You'll need to find a way to communicate that you're a safe person. If she's pushed, she'll probably run and hide."

"Thank you. I know what to do. On a separate note, is there anything I should know about the area?"

"Have you read much about Turkey and their refugee problem?"

"A summary report is all."

Rebecca stares blankly and then looks to the side, shakes her head, and her jaw tightens. "You need to be aware that Turkey has nearly four-million Syrian refugees—the largest number in the world. Imagine the impact on labor, housing, and health care. It's unprecedented, and many residents resent it. The tension is profound. Crime, such as sex trafficking, is very real. As heinous as that is, the fact of the matter is, social services and police are overtaxed and can't respond as they should."

Margaret takes a deep breath and looks far into the distance. "It's an atrocity that this civil war has gone on as long as it has."

"I agree. It's a crime, and in terms of Turkey, it's a time bomb. It wouldn't take much for the Turkish people to revolt against the refugees. Imagine what would happen in the U.S. if we had a similar number of displaced persons. What if we had to find living quarters for over fifteen-million people? We're four times the population of Turkey, and fifteen million is our equivalent number of refugees."

Margaret becomes very still, and her face contorts. She looks down the aisle at her team, to the cockpit's closed door, and into the heavens that lead them. Finally, she says, "The Syrian people must return home to their country. It's the only solution. Russia has a stake in Syria. I'll work with their Acting President, Ivan Smirnov."

"I appreciate your optimism, ma'am, but this horror has been ongoing for ten years."

"Yes, but now Russia and the United States will join with the European Union to stop it."

"Your confidence is encouraging, ma'am, but others have tried . . . sort of."

"*Sort of* only flames the violence. No. The action must be swift and definitive."

The Vice President's stance catches Rebecca off-guard, and Margaret notes the woman's surprise. "You think me a naive idealist, don't you? I understand that, but know this, the genesis of this war is political and sectarian—always, there is a winner and a loser. The challenge is to resolve the underlying dynamics. That's what I intend to do. We need multiple *winners*."

Margaret shuffles a stack of papers before continuing. "The State Department has provided me with a report on Syria and the various factions vying for a piece of that country. I need to study it, but I have a favor to ask. I'd like to hear your candid assessment of what could help resolve the problems that currently divide the country. Perhaps in another hour?"

"Of course, ma'am. I'm ready when you are."

Rebecca stands to leave when Margaret adds, "One more thing. We'll travel with the Acting President of Russia and his assistants. I'd like your perspective on what Russia *wants* from Syria. Why has it been willing to lose men for this civil war?"

"I look forward to talking with you, ma'am."

"Thank you. I promise, once I have the answers to the *whats* and *whys*, I'll find a way to craft a workable solution. This war must end. And, Rebecca …"

"Yes, ma'am?"

"Find time to sleep."

✳    ✳    ✳

At mid-afternoon, the Boeing 747 touches down at Sheremetyevo International Airport in Moscow. The United States Ambassador to the Russian Federation awaits the Vice President, as does the Russian Military Guard. A black Cortege limousine approaches on the runway, and Acting President Ivan Smirnov gets out of the car and walks over to the entourage. Margaret watches through her window and smiles. She stands and calls her team together.

"President Smirnov has asked to meet with me. The Secret Service and I will follow him to the Kremlin, and from there, go to the hotel. Rebecca, please travel with the staff. They'll take you to your room. If you need anything, anything at all, just let them know. We'll be in touch later."

Rebecca nods.

"Tomorrow, we'll board this same plane at 07:00, along with President Smirnov and his team. If I don't see you this evening, we'll meet aboard Air Force One. Please, make sure we have a detailed map of the Middle East in the conference room before we depart. Enjoy the day."

Margaret steps out of the plane and walks down the boarding stairs. She greets the Ambassador, salutes the military, and offers a respectful bow to the President. "It's wonderful to see you, Mr. President."

"And you, Vice President Adler. Will you be my guest?"

"My time is yours."

# Chapter 34

———————

*E*arly the next morning, Air Force One purrs as it climbs and reaches elevation. Margaret and Ivan sit in the forward compartment, opposite each other. Their teams occupy the back of the aircraft. As morning light floods the cabin, a waiter serves breakfast. Over coffee, Margaret and Ivan exchange smiles and sneak leg embraces. Several hours before they boarded, they took vows before a priest and Ivan's mother.

"Your mom called me 'daughter' last night. Did you hear her?"

Ivan smiles. "Oh, yes, I was quite aware. She's considered you a daughter since my father passed."

"Really? I didn't know. Well, I'm honored."

"You should be. My mother chooses her words carefully, though it might seem otherwise. Don't be surprised if she invites herself for a visit." Ivan's chuckle lets her know that he's teasing—maybe.

Margaret smiles. "When we finish breakfast, shall we …"

"Talk Syria?"

"Yes, Syria."

"I've expected and even dreaded this conversation. If it were not such an entangled mess, I wouldn't mind, but Syria is a challenge."

"I know, but we're the only hope for its people."

"That sounds a bit grandiose, but you may be right."

With the last sip of coffee, Margaret leads the way to Air Force One's conference room. Her team has affixed a map of the Russian Federation and the surrounding Middle Eastern countries to the table's surface. They stare at the expanse of history and turmoil.

Ivan murmurs, "This isn't the honeymoon I'd hoped for."

"I know, but between the two of us, maybe we can figure out what we can do to mitigate this bloodbath."

"We'll need miracles to solve this mess."

"How about we just talk possibilities—*what ifs*?"

"All right … I confess, I'm not optimistic, but I'm willing."

Margaret offers a flirtatious smile and then clears her throat. "We start with the basics. The war in Syria must stop. Agreed?"

Ivan's shoulders drop, and begrudgingly, he says, "Yep, I'm with you."

"So, let's brainstorm. The Syrian President must go. He's a monster. Under his leadership, cities have been demolished, 500,000 people have died, and 40,000 political prisoners endure unthinkable torture. What should be parks have become massive graveyards."

"It's complicated, but I agree. The situation is horrendous."

Margaret nods. "Our first challenge is to remove the Syrian President. Germany has enacted universal jurisdiction. They want to prosecute President Hassan for crimes against humanity."

"Yes and no. Hassan needs to go, but when action is taken, we need to have leadership ready to step in, or we'll end up with even bigger problems. Multiple factions vie for control, and the sects hate each other."

Margaret stares at the map and thinks of the toll, of the thousands of U.S. soldiers who lost their lives in Iraq, Afghanistan, Pakistan, and Iran. "I understand," she mutters.

They both sit silently until, finally, Margaret says, "What if we developed a two-year interim government reflective of the country's diversity? A four or five-member council of people recognized by their civilian factions as leaders? If the United States and Russia backed this entity, wouldn't other countries follow our lead?"

"You believe this coalition would spearhead the rebuilding of Syria?"

"It's a thought."

"Interesting. For other countries to follow our lead, we'll need to convey strong solidarity for the Muslim world to trust us. Each of us has allies, but we also have enemies. My allies hate your allies and vice versa. When Syria's President gets delivered to Germany, we must be prepared for the worst."

Margaret's eyes grow wider. "Does Iran have nuclear weapons?"

"It claims not. The country has uranium, but supposedly, no bombs. That said, Iran has the most powerful military force in the Middle East, and it will use that force."

"What, or who, could convince Iran not to engage?"

Ivan sits lost in thought. Then he shakes his head. "I don't know, but the only deterrent I can imagine is if Iran believes it'll fail. It doesn't take kindly to humiliation."

He leans back in his chair and looks intently at Margaret. "I knew we'd have to talk about this, and I've spent hours thinking and preparing. But this conversation has gone in ways I never expected. We're discussing normalizing the Middle East, and I've never even considered that a possibility. This is a game-changer."

Margaret bites her lower lip. "Yes, but isn't it worth considering?"

Ivan takes a deep breath and cracks a half-smile, "Well, I don't think you know what you're getting into, but I'm game."

"If I'm not mistaken, Russia needs Syria for its naval facility at Tartus. What would help the new government accept Russia's continued presence?"

"Russia would make an invaluable neighbor. It could offer training to the Syrian forces, and defense if needed. It could also rent the space; it need not be free as it is at present."

"In that case, you have my complete support."

"What would President Williams say?"

Margaret smiles and leans forward. "He'd support me." She speaks her next words at a near whisper. "You should know that President Williams will step down in two weeks. Before I left, he told me he has terminal cancer. He hasn't announced anything yet, but he intends to let his staff know in a few days. The following week, he'll address the nation. Shortly after, I'll get sworn in."

"The poor man. So, it really is the two of us." Ivan intertwines his fingers. "We both thought it might come to this."

Ivan looks back at the map. "I want to say yes to your idea. And I want to let go of the past and start afresh. But I need to think about this. You're talking of a renaissance. An extension of the Arab Spring. Our partnership could help facilitate this, but I need to consider the ramifications."

Margaret purses her lips. "Soooo, back to the practical. Once we've facilitated President Hassan's removal, and an interim coalition government gets installed, we rebuild."

Ivan nods. "Yes, to all points. Russia will assume responsibility for removing the current incumbent. We'll identify a statesman both knowledgeable and respected to serve on an oversight team, and Russia will assist with Syria's rebuilding."

"When people see that we're serious, other countries will come forward and help. They want the Syrian people to return to their country as much as we do."

Ivan grunts his agreement. "The Syrian men will return en masse to do their part."

Margaret fills with hope. "This is the culmination of all we've worked for. Afghanistan may have introduced us, but hope brought us together. I can't imagine a more perfect honeymoon. Can you?"

# Chapter 35

*U*nexpected turbulence awakens Margaret. She grabs her armrest and looks over at Ivan.

"Wow, I usually don't sleep during a flight."

Ivan smiles. "I would have cuddled with you, but that might have raised more than a few eyebrows and maybe a visit from your Secret Service. You have quite the team, by the way."

"I know, they're good guys, and I'm pleased they take their job seriously, but ..."

The pilot makes an announcement over the audio system, "Buckle up. We're crossing the Taurus mountain range. It will stay bumpy for a few more minutes. We've begun our descent and will reach the ground shortly."

"My goodness, I didn't realize we were so near Adana. The trip went fast, didn't it?"

"Hmm, let's see. We spent several hours solving centuries of conflict in the Middle East, then had a leisurely lunch with our teams, at which Rebecca gave us a briefing on tensions within Turkey, and somewhere over Kazakhstan, you fell asleep. So, yeah, you could say that the trip went fast." Ivan grins mischievously.

"Okay, okay. At least we didn't get bored." Margaret throws back her hair and laughs playfully. Then she reaches into her briefcase for the itinerary. "It looks like we'll have time to settle into our quarters before meeting with Colonel Longfield, the American troop Commander, at 15:00."

"He's aware that I'm part of this expedition?"

"Of course. You're the leading dignitary."

"Then he won't be surprised that I must meet with Col. Aydin, the Incirlik Air Base Commander. He expects me. There's also the possibility that Turkey's leader, President Ozdemir, will come here to meet with me. I contacted him last week about this trip."

Margaret notes his serious expression. "Do you feel apprehensive?"

"No, but I'm obligated to show my respect. We need Turkey as an ally."

Margaret frowns. "What's this about?"

"I didn't want to mention it this morning because we've made good progress. But, in brief, Turkish and American trust has hit an all-time low. This is dangerous because your government houses fifty nuclear warheads on the air base. At the same time, Turkey's established a tenuous relationship with Russia by purchasing an S-400 missile defense system. That happened prior to my presidency. Trust me when I say that they're no one's friend."

"Why do you need to meet with Aydin?"

"Turkey wants to assert its power. It wants control, and it wants definitive action against the Kurds. It wants blood. I have to tell Aydin to back off because Russia needs more time."

"Do you think he'll listen?"

"My offer's better than the alternative."

Air Force One touches down at Incirlik Air Base. As the plane approaches the terminal, Airmen in dress attire line up and stand at attention. To the side, another troop approaches. The Turkish Air Force march in formation toward the aircraft.

Margaret nudges Ivan. "Look through your window."

Just behind the Turkish troops, a black Mercedes with Turkey's flag displayed above the front tires draws near.

Ivan's expression turns stony. He looks down, sets his jaw, and takes a deep breath. "I expected this." He sends a text message, and his security team rushes to his side.

"Gentlemen, we'll greet the Americans and then leave the task force to confer with President Ozdemir. Make sure precautions are in place." They offer a salute and return to the rear of the plane.

"I'm sorry about this, Margaret. I need to meet with President Ozdemir alone. It shouldn't be a long meeting."

"Are you safe?"

"Turkey is no one's friend. It's foolish to think otherwise. But Russia has what Turkey wants, so I *am* safe." He pauses to squeeze Margaret's hand. "When we begin our work with Syria, does Turkey have a place at the negotiating table?"

"They're neighbors and a threat, so they must be at the table."

"My thoughts precisely. I'll communicate that to Ozdemir."

An announcement sounds over the speaker system and breaks their somber mood. "It's been a pleasure serving you today. We will depart Incirlik Air Base tomorrow at 16:00. I hope your visit is a productive one. Stay safe and save a piece of Baklava for your pilot."

# Chapter 36

The next morning at 06:00, the team reconvenes for the three-hour trip to the orphanage in the troubled Hatay province. Col. Longfield has arranged for an armored bus to transport them and assigned guards to accompany them. Additionally, when Ivan met with President Ozdemir, he asked that military operations in that area cease until the expedition returns to base safely. The President agreed and added that his people would offer protection.

Margaret and Ivan find seats at the back of the bus, where they can talk more freely. An incoming text from President Williams alarms Margaret. *Be wary of Ozdemir. Operatives report there will be an attempt on your life. Accept no packages—from anyone.*

Margaret hands Ivan her phone. "Look at this text."

His face contorts when he reads the message. "I told you that we can't trust him. He'll try something while we're at the orphanage, so he can blame the Syrians."

Margaret shakes her head. "What is it with these people?"

"Centuries of hate. They carry it with them like a bottle of baby formula. It's their lifeline and what feeds their insanity."

"I wish I could wrap up in your arms right now."

"I want nothing more than to hold you."

Margaret leans back into her chair and extends her legs to his. He rests his hand on her knee and looks at her lovingly. "I won't let anyone hurt you."

"I'll forward the text to my team. They need to stay alert." She taps in a message and sends it. Immediately, her agents turn and look back at her and nod.

"When you met with Ozdemir, did anything alarm you?"

Ivan frowns. "Yes and no. I've rehashed that meeting, looking for clues, and the only thing that made me uneasy was his demeanor. He seemed unusually indulgent. Whatever I would say, he'd support. You would have thought that we were best friends and not uneasy competitors. When I walked out of the room, he shook my hand, and the hairs on the back of my neck stood up. Whatever he plans, it isn't good."

"Why did he come to the base?"

"He claims this was a calendared visit. With tensions running high, he's become more engaged with operations."

By late morning, the bus arrives at the guarded entrance to the orphanage. The convoy waits as passports, visas, and entry permissions get reviewed and approved. An armed guard enters the bus and moves from person to person, checking for explosives and contraband. When the soldier reaches the last row, he sees Ivan and stops.

"Welcome to Reyhanli, Mr. President." He stands alert and offers a formal salute.

"Thank you. I need to speak with you privately, soldier. May we move outside?"

"Certainly."

As Ivan follows the guard out of the bus, his armed escorts walk in step behind him. Margaret and the rest of the envoy watch and listen from their open windows.

Ivan says, "My intelligence has notified me of an imminent attack."

The guard stomps on the ground as if insulted. "That is not possible, Mr. President. You are misinformed."

Undeterred by the soldier's theatrics, Ivan says, "I'm told that a package will be used in an assassination attempt."

The soldier remains defiant. "Your information is wrong. We sort and check the mail with great care every day."

"Did the base grant entry to any trucks this morning?"

"We had one—a food delivery truck."

Ivan clenches his jaw. "Did you check the contents?"

The soldier scowls. "Yes, the truck held common goods such as apples and rice. The only thing different today was a cake for your reception."

"A cake? Big enough to hold explosives?"

Panic races across the guard's once-stoic expression. He grabs his radio and, seconds later, a siren sends children running to their rooms. Then the soldier orders the bus to drive away to a safe distance and wait. A while later, a bomb squad rushes to the orphanage and re-emerges minutes later with the cake. A robot takes the dessert to an isolated area of the grounds and detonates the bombs inside.

C-4 encased with ball bearings. The sizeable explosion would have killed anyone nearby.

The military police swarm the kitchen, searching for staff who could have been complicit. Guards handcuff three employees, all recently hired, and all with ties to Syria. Four soldiers march the prisoners into the courtyard, where local police wait. When one of the prisoners yells out profanities against Turkey, a guard knocks him to the ground and beats him. The police secure the three detainees in an armored van and drive past the checkpoint, where Ivan stands.

The driver pulls the bus up to the entrance once more.

The soldier salutes Ivan. "Mr. President, the building is secured. You may enter."

"Thank you. We'll follow your lead."

Ivan exchanges a quick salute with the guard and returns to the bus. He holds tight to the railing as he climbs aboard the armored vehicle, and cheers and applause greet him.

The guards slide the gates open, and the bus inches forward, escorted by sentries. The vehicle stops in front of a three-story building with a towering arched entrance. The emissaries follow orphanage staff into a large dining room, where they're offered seats next to the wall and asked to wait.

A bell rings, and a group of children fills the space with laughter as they run to their pre-assigned tables. Big brown eyes glance shyly to the guests, and one-by-one, the children wave for the adults to join them. Margaret finds a table and squeezes in between two boys. She looks back at her companions and urges them to do the same.

Ivan sits at a table next to Margaret. He's positioned himself so that he can see her and act quickly if need be. His agents stand nearby, alert to any problem that might arise. Margaret gets lost in the moment, and her heart fills with joy. She catches Ivan's adoring gaze and winks, and he responds with a proud smile.

Rebecca sits across from Margaret and Ivan. Playfully, she snuggles with the children, which sends giggles throughout the room. She's visited the orphanage twice before, and the children's innocence moves her deeply.

The kitchen staff brings out steaming dishes of traditional Turkish dumplings, and the children squeal in delight.

Rebecca smiles and tells Margaret, "This is their favorite dish."

The orphans bow their heads and offer a simple supplication, *In the name of Allah and with the blessings of Allah*. Then they eat with gusto.

While the children focus on their meal, Margaret scans the sea of little faces. She seeks Amira but doesn't see her.

Rebecca notices her distraction and goes to her side. "Disabled children eat in another room," she says. "Because they need assistance. When you're ready, I can take you there if you like."

Margaret stands and takes Rebecca's hand. "Thank you. This means a lot to me. Now would be good."

Ivan follows in their footsteps. His team brings up the rear.

Cribs and wheelchairs, crutches, and modified tables fill the special dining room. The children are quieter because most of them don't speak. Some of the orphans have lost limbs, and others are severely disfigured. Some cannot see, and all have experienced the worst of the Syrian war.

Margaret's gaze travels from table to table and stops at a make-shift highchair, where a small girl sits alone, facing the window. She has one arm.

"Could this be Amira?" Margaret whispers to Rebecca.

"I'll check." Rebecca talks to one of the nurses and then returns to Margaret. "Amira doesn't speak, but we can go see her."

Margaret approaches the child and stares through the window. Instead of addressing the girl, Margaret kneels, removes her sweater, and rolls up her shirt-sleeve to reveal her prosthesis. Then she stretches and moves the fingers of her artificial limb. Slowly, Margaret removes it and lays it on the floor.

After a few minutes, Amira climbs out of her chair and limps to the window. She paces and sneaks quick glances at the prosthetic. Finally, the child sits on the floor beside it. She runs her fingers across the artificial arm, and dares to speak, "Can I have one too?"

The nurse looks over at Rebecca and shrugs in disbelief. She whispers, "This is the first time Amira's spoken."

Margaret turns to the nurse, "She speaks English?"

The nurse says, "Amira's mother was a schoolteacher and taught all her children English."

Margaret focuses on Amira. Burn scars cover half of the girl's face, and one eye barely opens because of the disfigurement. Margaret reaches out her arm to Amira. "Maybe. I hope so."

To everyone's surprise, the child climbs onto Margaret's lap. "A bomb took my arm away."

"Mine too," Margaret says. "It took my arm and killed my friends."

Amira opens up about her family and her friends and finishes by saying, "I'm alone."

"You have friends here, right?"

"Eh, maybe. But I can't play like they do, because I only have one arm."

"We're alike, you and I. And I've discovered that I can do lots of things with one arm. My special arm helps too."

Ivan watches intently and smiles. Then he joins Margaret and Amira by the window.

"Hi, Amira. I'm a friend of Ms. Margaret. Can I show you something?"

The girl stares up at him. "Uh-huh."

"Just like Ms. Margaret, I have a special leg." Ivan rolls up his pants leg to his knee and shows Amira his brace.

"Did a bomb take your leg too?"

"Yes, the bomb was in the ground, and I stepped on it by accident. It took part of my lower leg."

"Did it take your family?"

"No, but it did take some of my friends."

Amira looks down. "Bombs are bad."

"I think I need a hug, Amira. Could I have a hug?"

She climbs out of Margaret's lap and goes to Ivan. He fights back the tears as she wraps her arm around him and gives him a kiss on his cheek. With a glance at Margaret, he signals, *yes*.

# Chapter 37

Turkish soldiers rush into the dining hall, and alarms blare. The children stop what they are doing and run to the designated safe areas.

"Mr. President," a soldier says, panting for air after dashing to Ivan. "The Syrian Army is approaching, and it isn't safe. You must leave now."

"Thank you, soldier." Ivan shouts in the direction of his companions, "Get on the bus now! Hurry!" He calls to his agents and directs them to make sure everyone is accounted for. Then he motions for Margaret to come with him.

In the near distance, explosions sound.

At each deep rumble, the ground shakes and sends tremors through the gathered men and women. For most, this is their first experience of imminent danger, but it feels all too familiar for Ivan and Margaret. Separately, they flash upon their traumas in the field, and time betrays them. They become lost in battle again.

Aboard the armored bus, their military escort explains the situation as they wait for the gate to open, "The Syrian Army is hitting Idlib hard, and we're within rocket range. So, we're in extreme danger right now. The military wants to eradicate the Kurdish freedom fighters who've retreated to Idlib. The locals are caught between an oppressive government and those trying to defend them.

"On the other side of the concrete border wall, thousands of refugees have crammed into tent camps. We have a severe humanitarian tragedy, and the people are trapped. They don't have the most basic supplies. They have nowhere to go, and Syria's troops advance."

"Incoming!" a soldier shouts. "Take cover."

An explosive hits the stone wall that surrounds the orphanage and sends debris in all directions. Particles crash against the side of the armored bus. No one gets injured, but all feel shaken. Uneasy murmurs and sobs fill the air.

"The Syrians have thrown a missile inside the Turkish border," the driver says. "The Turkish Army will retaliate soon. I must take a different route to the base. Buckle up. You'll be safe, but this may be a rough ride." The man puts the vehicle into high gear and speeds through the streets. In the distance, billows of black smoke hang and portend of the terror that lies ahead.

As the bus thunders toward the Incirlik Air Base, everyone sits in shocked silence. Margaret and Ivan jostle around at each bump in the road, deep in thought. For the first time, they feel the weight of opposing interests. Russia needs the Syrian government's support for its naval facility at Tartus. It is also dependent upon Syria's support for its pipelines, which are necessary for its oil and gas export. The United States, on the other hand, has backed out of the Syrian conflict. It wants a peaceful resolution to the strife, and for that to occur, it needs Iran out of Syria altogether.

Margaret says, "It falls to our two countries to do something."

"Not easy," Ivan says, his tone abrupt.

"If your naval base and the pipelines remain protected, would you consider possibilities?"

"What possibilities are you pondering?"

Margaret takes a deep breath and shifts in her seat. She pulls out a notebook and draws a rough map of the area. "What if the Syrian President travels to Europe, for whatever reason, and the Europeans detain and subsequently charge President Hassan with crimes against humanity?

The evidence of chemical weapons, mass murders, and crematoriums is overwhelming. If the United States and the Russian Federation support the necessity of such a judicial process, wouldn't other leaders follow? And, if the President gets indicted, wouldn't the prosecution need to hold him until the case resolves?"

"I see your point." Ivan grimaces and stares at the floor.

Margaret presses, "If that happened, wouldn't the key officials in his government also be charged? After all, Hassan hasn't acted alone. They're each complicit."

"I get where you're going. Their arrest would necessitate the installation of an interim government." His expression halts Margaret's brainstorming. With pointed resolve, he asks, "Is the United States prepared to act?"

"It will be."

"Prepared to commit soldiers, airpower, and funds for the rebuilding?"

"It will be."

"Will the United States honor the existing treaty, which permits Russia sovereign jurisdiction of the naval base at Tartus?"

Margaret purses her lips. "Earlier, you offered a solution, which I believe the Syrian people will support, and ultimately, they're the ones who have to make this decision. You mentioned paying rent for the use of the base, as well as offering training and defense. The United States will support the Syrian people."

"Can you make this assurance independent of President Williams?"

"In one week, I *am* the American President."

"Well, Madam President, we have a deal." Ivan's no-nonsense expression eases to a smile.

Margaret relaxes into her seat. "This may be our most difficult challenge, my love, but I know we can get through this."

"The whole thing will take considerable planning, but I agree with you. It's achievable."

"An Arab or two, a Kurd, an Armenian, or a Turk, could compose the interim governmental council. After two years, the people could hold an election."

Ivan studies Margaret. "You imagine that the country can be rebuilt during those two years."

"Yes, but I suspect we'll need foot soldiers along the Syrian borders to protect the country from neighboring interests."

"Not a problem. Once we have the current Syrian leadership under arrest, the European Union will commit soldiers and finances. They're incredibly vested because of the refugees." A mischievous smile lifts Ivan's features. "We've got work to do."

# Chapter 38

The driver announces, "We're almost at the Incirlik Air Base. Just a reminder: you're safe in the American sector, but please do not wander. Your flight leaves at 17:00. We'll board at 16:30."

Margaret notices that Ivan appears troubled. "What's the matter?"

"I'm wondering about talking with President Ozdemir. He might expect a call from me."

"Maybe Col. Aydin can arrange for an electronic meeting."

"Video conference—that's a good idea. I'll text him now to request the remote meeting with Ozdemir."

"Should I join you?"

Ivan smiles. "I hadn't thought of that. It might prove helpful. He may not trust either of us, but he'll understand that our two countries will work together to resolve the Syrian war. That will speak volumes, and he'll want to be part of the effort."

A return message arrives from Col. Aydin. *The President would like to meet with you at 15:00. A driver will bring you to my office.*

Ivan types back, *Thank you. Vice President Margaret Adler would like to attend. Please ask President Ozdemir if this is acceptable.*

Within moments, a reply arrives. Ivan smiles. "We're on. He wants to meet you."

When the armored bus pulls into the complex, Turkish guards stand next to a limousine. Ivan walks over to greet them, accompanied by his Secret Service. Margaret stays right behind them.

A window rolls down, and Col. Aydin asks them to join him in the vehicle. "I hope you had a good trip."

"It was remarkable in many ways," Ivan says. "To see so many children cared for so lovingly was impressive."

"I was sorry to hear about the attacks. Some things we can't control, but we did respond to the assault after you left."

Aydin ushers Ivan and Margaret into the military complex and to his office. The Colonel points to the chairs in front of his desk. "Take a seat. President Ozdemir will join us momentarily. We'll use the screen behind my desk."

"Welcome, welcome," President Ozdemir says. "It is good to see you both. I trust you had a good trip."

Ivan says, "Yes, thank you. An incoming shell interrupted the final hour, so we got a taste of the conflict as well."

"Our soldiers responded to that untimely intrusion. There's never a dull day in Reyhanli or any other place near the border."

"Mr. President," Margaret says. "This incursion prompted us to consider another future for Syria. For certain, what exists now is no future at all."

"Hmm, I couldn't agree more." The President motions to an unseen waiter to bring tea. "Tell me your thoughts, Ms. Margaret. I'd like to hear more."

Adler leans forward in her chair and says, "Russia and the United States have agreed to work together to end the Syrian war and return the country to its people."

The President smirks and stares at Ivan. "An interesting development." Then he returns his attention to Margaret. "Please, continue. Who are these people to whom you refer?"

Adler keeps her expression neutral and says, in firm tones, "The Syrian citizens, Mr. President. The Arabs, the Kurds, the Turkmen, the Assyrians, the Circassians, and the Armenians."

"Do you have a magic wand to wave?" The President's voice oozes sarcasm.

Ivan jumps in before Margaret can respond, "The only wand we will wave is mine. I will deliver the Syrian President to the European Union so that they can charge and try him for crimes against humanity. I'll ensure that he and his cohorts face a tribunal."

The President's expression changes. "You intend to install an interim government?"

"Correct. A council of four or five men, representative of the country's citizenry."

"What do you get out of this?"

"Our naval base in Tartus, our pipeline, and use of the Khmeimim military airbase."

"Ms. Margaret, what does the United States get out of this?"

"Peace, sir."

Ozdemir takes a long sip of his tea, looks down at his desk, and then returns his focus to his guests. "Ms. Margaret, are you sure there isn't anything more you want?"

"Well," she hesitates and glances at Ivan. "A disabled child lives at the orphanage we just visited, and I would love to adopt the girl. Like me, she has only one arm. She's also the victim of a chemical attack and is disfigured. However, I assure you, she forms no part of this operation. The girl is simply an impossible dream of mine."

The President taps his pen on his desk and considers what's been said.

"President Smirnov, if and when the Syrian President gets delivered to the EU, I will stand with you and commit Turkey's full military force to Syria's rebuilding. And, Ms. Margaret, I will make arrangements for your impossible dream to become a reality."

President Ozdemir stands. "It's always good to talk with you, Ivan. Your father was a friend. I hope we become confidants as well."

"I look forward to securing your trust, Mr. President, and making my father proud."

"Ms. Margaret, it's been a pleasure." He smiles and offers a nod. "Amira, it's a lovely name, don't you think?" The viewing screen goes dark.

# Chapter 39

At precisely 17:00, Air Force One departs from Incirlik Air Base and climbs high above Adana. Margaret and Ivan sit opposite each other and stare out of their windows while the base disappears through the clouds. Lost in their thoughts, each tries to understand the meeting with President Ozdemir.

After the plane reaches altitude and levels, Margaret says, "I don't understand how the President knew Amira's name. Nothing makes sense. Does it to you?"

"I've tried to figure it out, but the only thing I can come up with is that they must have planted a bug when I met with Ozdemir in person."

"What do you mean?"

"Just that. Somehow, they planted a mic on me. I've rehashed every step and can't see any other answer. He shook my hand, patted me on the shoulder, and ... and ..."

"What?"

"When he said goodbye, he offered me his fountain pen. He pulled it from his breast pocket and showed me the affixed presidential seal. He was clearly pleased by it. I accepted and put the pen into my jacket, and his guard walked me to the door. The pen. That must be it!"

"Are you wearing the same jacket you wore yesterday?"

Ivan's face drains of color as he checks his pockets and pulls out the pen. He motions to one of his agents, who approaches immediately. Ivan hands the agent the pen and directs him to search for a bug.

The agent opens the pen, empties the barrel, and shows Ivan the transmitter.

"Take care of it," Ivan orders. Then he turns to Margaret. "We've been played. I should have expected that. The video conference was just a test. He wanted to see if we could be trusted. The good thing is that he's decided we can be. But, while he knows our plans, we don't know his. That's why he mentioned Amira by name. He's made it clear that he's a force to be reckoned with."

Margaret bites her lower lip. "Does this mean we have to go back to the drawing board?"

"No, this is a reality check. He knew I'd look for the bug after that comment. He knew we'd have this conversation. Ozdemir has given us a pass—one we can't afford to ignore. We must work closely with Turkey because it's aligned with most of the Middle Eastern countries. We daren't proceed alone."

"He mentioned your father. Maybe he's helping us already."

"Perhaps." Ivan glances through his window and then back at Margaret. "But I believe Ozdemir mentioned my father because the two of them brokered deals. He expects me to do the same."

The seriousness of Ivan's tone makes Margaret shudder. "You think we're on the brink of war."

"The man will scrutinize our every move, and not just Turkey but also Iran, Iraq, Saudi Arabia, and the rest of the Middle Eastern nations. Turkey's support is critical."

Margaret holds Ivan's gaze. "Do you doubt we can do this?"

"No. But this will be a defining operation and not without great risk. We must succeed—we have no choice—and the first step falls on me."

"Have you thought about what you'll do?"

"That's all I've thought about since we first discussed toppling the current regime. Russia is adding a destroyer to its Mediterranean fleet, which will arrive in six weeks. They'll hold a celebration, and I'll invite President Hassan to be my guest on the platform. Afterward, I'll ask him to accompany me on the maiden voyage. Once we get out to sea, Special Forces can pick him up."

Margaret notices their waiter approach. "I think we both need a drink."

The waiter offers them a tray of appetizers and takes their order.

"Vodka," Ivan says. "Two shots."

Margaret says, "I'll have a Scotch and water, two ounces."

The two of them grin and laugh. "Well, our not-so-friendly friends are driving us to drink." Margaret gives Ivan a playful kick.

"Yeah, we've got a lot of work ahead of us. It'll be a busy six weeks. But now you have your Scotch, and I've got my Vodka. We need a toast. To our health, our dreams, Amira, and success in the Middle East."

Margaret raises her glass and takes a sip. "Johnny Walker Blue has a way of calming the soul." She exhales deeply and sits back. "I have a question, though. Can you trust Ozdemir to remain silent about our plans?"

"I've asked myself the same thing. He has me on a short leash, and he's assessing whether I'm worth the investment. I don't think he'll betray our plans because he gains nothing by doing so. Bottom line, he wants the Syrian President gone. He doesn't care how that's achieved. If I'm successful, he'll join us because he follows strength."

"So, you trust him?"

"Not trust, no. Let's just say, he'll partner with us if it serves his purposes. I need to make sure his purposes are supported."

"Got it. What will happen after we deliver Hassan to Germany? How will Iran, Iraq, Saudi Arabia, and the others react?"

Ivan sips his Vodka. "That's a big question. We need to prepare for the worst. Have our military ready to respond if needed. Once it's clear that Russia and the United States have aligned, the landscape changes in a powerful way. It will no longer be business as usual." He smiles at Margaret.

"Your allies will support the move because they want Hassan ousted, but they'll remain leery of Russia's involvement and for good reason. Why should they trust us? Our two Air Force bases in northern Syria are equipped with the S-400. As for my allies, we need to get ready for the worst. Iran is the most problematic. It could use its Russian weapon systems against us both. Though we've been allies, Russia's alignment with the United States will be judged a betrayal, and Iran will not sit quietly on the sidelines. We'll need to prepare for military engagement."

Ivan's forehead creases, and he sips at his drink. "Then there's Iraq. It makes an undependable ally at best. The country is in a bind because its neighbor is a bully. It's possible that Russia and America's partnership will offer some relief, but we'll need to provide Iraq with support. And, like Iran, we'll need to ensure that we protect their oil and gas."

He shakes his head. "Turkey could end up becoming an essential ally. Ozdemir wants the Syrian mess resolved by whatever means. With millions of impoverished refugees in his country, and millions more trying to get in, he wants the problem fixed and is willing to go to any extent to achieve that. Turkey's recent purchase of the Russian-made S-400 surface-to-air missile system tells me they're ready for war. Turkey has been your ally, but keep in mind that after the American Senate blamed it for the Armenian genocide in December 2019, that relationship eroded drastically."

Margaret twirls her glass in her hands. "But we have clear evidence of Turkey's wrongdoing."

"True, but it's also clear that U.S. militia slaughtered thousands upon thousands of native peoples. As an example, take a good look at California's history in the mid-1800s. No one's hands are clean, Margaret. Not yours and not mine. Russia has a horrendous history of massacres. For us to resolve the Syrian crisis, we need to shift gears and focus on the future rather than on our less-than-stellar pasts."

Margaret clenches her jaw and looks out of her window at the darkness. Nothing but the blackness is visible, not even a star. "What has war ever solved? We've fought each other since Adam and Eve. To me, war is an admission of failure. It's easier to send our troops into hell than sit across from each other and solve our problems diplomatically. We attack, and then there's a counterattack, and soon, we forget why we're fighting. We just know we hate whomever and will kill them or be killed. Do you think anyone in either of our nations can tell us why we fought in Afghanistan? What they know is that their sons and daughters died or got injured. It's the ordinary citizens who suffer the consequences for our failure." Margaret's passion erupts and attracts the Secret Service's attention, and they stare at the couple with hard expressions.

Ivan takes a deep breath. "We need another drink. After that, I'd like to revisit your map in the conference room. Can we go there?"

"Of course." Margaret signals to the waiter and asks him to take drinks to the conference room. When she stands, she realizes that all eyes have focused on the two of them. She reddens and apologizes. "All is well. I got too excited talking about war. President Smirnov and I are going to the conference room to continue our discussion."

Ivan lifts his shoulders in a playful shrug.

The map of the Middle East and the Russian Federation still covers the conference table. The two stand and stare at the expanse until the waiter brings their drinks.

"Now," Ivan says. "Before we do anything, I need to hold you." He wraps his arms around her and cradles her tightly. When she relaxes and rests against him, he steps back and smiles. "My dear, you always have my shoulder. You're never alone. Even when we can't be together, I want you to know that you can always trust I'm near."

Margaret's eyes tear up.

Ivan crooks a finger and wipes them away with a knuckle. "Come on now, we need a toast, no tears." Ivan raises his glass. "To all our tomorrows and the fathomless love that we share."

# Chapter 40

*A*ir Force One touches down in Moscow at 23:00. Ivan has secured the top floor of one of Moscow's finest hotels for Margaret and her team. Ivan explains, "Because it's so late, I'll stay here as well." His room is two doors down from Margaret's. Unlike the accommodations of the others, however, their rooms have inside doors which open to a large honeymoon suite. After everyone settles for the night, Ivan ambles through the gorgeous room to the door leading to Margaret's chamber. He knocks lightly, and she opens the door to find him holding three-dozen white roses.

"Come with me, my bride." He takes her hand and draws her into a dimly-lit room filled with flickering candles. Chilled champagne, delicious dark chocolates, and fresh strawberries sit on the table while soft romantic music plays. The scent of lavender permeates the air. Ivan pulls Margaret close and leads her into a slow waltz.

"We may not have our own home for a few years, but wherever you are is home for me," he whispers into her ear. "I love you, my dear. I love everything about you, even that wonderfully active mind of yours."

Margaret smiles and snuggles in close to rest her head on his shoulder. As she sways with the music, she relaxes.

Ivan raises a flute of champagne and offers one to Margaret. "To years of happiness, good health, and ever-present laughter." Then he gives her a lingering kiss, picks her up, and carries her to the matrimonial bed.

Slowly, Ivan unbuttons Margaret's blouse. Margaret divests him of his shirt. He bends over her naked softness, barely touching his chest against hers. His lips inch across her closed lids, brush lightly down her cheeks, and end up at her waiting lips. Ivan lingers at her mouth and savors hints of citrus. His hands move across her body and caress her ample breasts. Kissing her there, many times, he suckles and teases. When she moans her pleasure, and her back arches, he continues with renewed motivation, down her velvety body. He reaches for her hand and holds it tightly as he enters her. With thrusts intense, they move together. Sounds of passion echo softly through the chamber as their arousal soars.

✳    ✳    ✳

The next morning, Ivan awakens at the break of dawn and nips Margaret's earlobe playfully. "We've got to get back to our rooms, my dear. Our agents will knock on our doors to wake us soon."

Margaret turns to pull him to her and whispers, "But I need another kiss first." He offers several and then, begrudgingly, climbs out of bed.

Ivan hurries to the interior door, and after he walks through it, he closes it quietly. Margaret does the same on her side. Ivan dresses quickly and makes sure his bed looks used, and the room lived in. When the agents knock, he's ready.

"Good morning, gentlemen," Ivan says to the agents. "I've ordered a spread, which should arrive momentarily. Please, invite our guests for a light breakfast."

As if on cue, the elevator opens, and two servers push a cart laden with breakfast items. Ivan motions to the servers that he's ready for coffee.

He smiles at his protectors. "Thank you for all your help on this trip. It wasn't easy, but you were there beside me, and because of that, I always felt safe."

"It was an honor, sir. Ms. Adler's team surprised us. They're good people."

"Yes, they are."

Doors open and close in the hallway. The agents check on the commotion and indicate that the team should come to Ivan's room. There's just enough time for coffee and a quick bite, and then they must leave for the airport.

✳    ✳    ✳

Never have goodbyes seemed so difficult. Margaret smiles at Ivan's light-hearted interactions with the team and dreads the words that will soon separate the two for an unknown number of months. With coffee in hand, she walks over to the window and stares down at the Red Square. *What lies ahead? For us, for our countries, and for the world?*

Ivan follows her to the window. As if he's read her mind, he says, "Beautiful sight, isn't it? More than a thousand years lie before us. Years of wars and massacres ... not obvious now. Most of the world has seen brutality and destruction. The countries rebuild, the people forget and move on ... until the next war. It's the cycle we're trying to halt in Syria." He looks over at Margaret. Her tightened lips prompt him to say, "You and I know the battlefield. We know the horror of failed negotiations. This is why we can make a difference now."

Margaret turns to him, "Sometimes, I wonder if I'm just a foolish woman in love, blinded by passion, hungry for tenderness, and incapable of seeing objectively."

"You imagine the disarmament progress is unreal?"

"Of course not. We're making concrete advances."

"Hmm. Why the doubt, then?"

Margaret looks back out at the Red Square. "I don't want to say goodbye."

"Don't. Say 'I'll see you in a few weeks, my love.' After all, we have considerable planning to do."

A few minutes later, Ivan stands with his agents next to a limousine and watches as the team boards their aircraft. Margaret looks out of her window and offers him a salute. While she fights back the tears, Ivan returns the gesture, and under her breath, she repeats his words, "I'll see you in a few weeks, my love."

As the plane soars higher and higher above the Kremlin, Margaret reaches into her briefcase for her calendar. She discovers a small wrapped box with a note that reads, *Someday*. She opens the box. Tucked beneath folds of a crocheted cloth lies an antique Faberge picture frame that she'd admired at Ivan's home. The frame holds a photo of Amira, Margaret, and Ivan. The Secret Service had taken the picture at the orphanage when the three were together.

# Chapter 41

"Madam Vice President and guests—" the pilot announces. "—we will land within the hour. Skies are clear over the capital today. There's a good chance you'll be able to see the White House. On the ground, it's a warm 65 degrees. All's well."

Margaret unbuckles her seatbelt and walks to the team at the rear of the aircraft.

"This has been quite the trip, and I can't thank you enough. Each of you was extraordinary. We didn't expect to face mortar shells. We didn't expect an assassination attempt. I don't know how I would have managed without you. Truly. I especially want to thank Rebecca for her expert advice on Turkey and the orphanage. We would have gone in blind if not for her. So, thank you, Rebecca."

As the team applauds, Rebecca stands. "May I say something?"

"Of course."

Rebecca clears her throat and looks at each member of the team. "I've experienced bombings, a hotel kidnapping, and threats of all kinds, but I've never experienced working with such a supportive and skilled group. Politics has always been something I believed I had to endure. Now it means that people like you are trying to do their best. I'm so proud to be an American, and I'm deeply grateful for this opportunity to serve. Thank you, Madam Vice President."

Margaret reaches over and gives Rebecca a hug. "I'm sure we'll see more of each other. Have a safe flight back to New York."

A text from President Williams distracts Margaret. It sounds urgent. *Please see me as soon as you land.*

She replies immediately, *We'll be on the ground in a few minutes. Will see you ASAP.*

Once they land, Margaret has the agents take her directly to the White House then drop off her bags at her home. The message from the President concerns her. He wouldn't text unless something important needed her attention. *What could be so pressing? Health, international conflict, something else?* She hurries down the West Wing's main corridor to the Oval Office and braces herself for what she might find when she looks into the room. The National Security Council is gathered: the Secretary of State, the Secretary of Defense, the Chairman of the Joint Chiefs of Staff, the Director of National Intelligence, and others. Something major has occurred.

"Welcome, Margaret. Please, take a seat. We're just getting started. Team, I'll summarize our earlier conversation for Margaret's benefit." He turns to face Margaret, and as he does so, he grimaces with pain. Margaret wonders if anyone else sees what she does. "The Lebanese militant group Hezbollah fired rockets into Israel. Subsequently, the Israeli Army attacked targets in southern Lebanon. Right now, they're at a standoff, but it's tenuous at best."

Margaret asks, "Were there casualties, Mr. President?"

"Both sides claim none."

"That being the case, I would like to share my experience of the last few days."

"The floor is yours."

Margaret addresses the security council members, "I just returned from a humanitarian mission to Turkey, where I visited an orphanage of a thousand children. Russia's Acting President, Ivan Smirnov, and Rebecca Grimes of the International Rescue Committee also formed part of this mission. It proved an enlightening trip. An assassination attempt occurred, and it remains unclear whether Syria or Turkey is to blame.

Also, a Syrian missile attack struck the wall of the orphanage just a few feet from the armored bus that we traveled in. The shrapnel hit the bus but didn't hurt anyone. I felt like I was in a war zone again.

"Aside from the ever-present danger, we did forge two diplomatic bridges. First, President Smirnov and I established a comradeship that I believe will help transform the divisions within the Middle East. Second, both President Smirnov and I met with Turkey's President Ozdemir. I'm sure you're aware of the lack of trust between Turkey and the United States. Similar sentiments prevail between Turkey and Russia. That said, Smirnov and I spoke openly about our budding accord, and Ozdemir indicated support. I believe we can restore trust between our countries. Such alignment shifts the power base in the Middle East."

President Williams smiles. "Well, what did I say before you left? I told you that you might change the fate of Syria. Sometimes, I actually get it right."

"More often than not, sir. I'll have a full report ready for you tomorrow."

"Back to Hezbollah and Israel, with these developments—" the President says. "—I think we tread lightly. If things escalate, I'll talk to the Prime Minister. Questions?"

"We're going to need more information, sir."

"Absolutely. I suggest we reconvene tomorrow at 11:00 to review the Vice President's thoughts on how to proceed. Thank you, all." As everyone stands, Williams asks Margaret to stay behind.

"Tomorrow, we'll talk Syria. But today, I need to brief you about my personal situation. The doctors have warned me that I have less time than they'd hoped. Because of this, I'll speak to my staff this afternoon. I would appreciate it if you could join me for the discussion, as it won't be easy."

"Of course. I'll help in any way that I can."

"Thank you. I knew I could depend on you. When we meet in the morning, I'll tell my cabinet about my health and explain that my intention is to step down at the end of next week."

"This is a lot to take in, sir."

"You're ready, Margaret. You've handled difficult situations for months now. Plenty of presidents go into the position without any experience. You're prepared. Never forget that."

"The Senate and House, sir?"

"I'll ask my staff to schedule them, as well as the press."

Margaret nods. "And your friends, sir?"

"I'll begin today."

Margaret's head hangs low. "I'm so sorry, Mr. President."

"I know, and thanks. But I want you to understand that I'm not. Long ago, on a riverbank in Vietnam, I made my peace with death, and since then, I've lived each day as a gift. I've had a good life and am ready for this next adventure, as are you."

"I'm not sure of that, sir." Margaret looks away and wipes tears from her eyes.

"Thirty-five words, that's all."

Margaret nods, deep in thought. She remembers when President Williams took the Oath, how he articulated the thirty-five words.

"I don't have the time I thought I would, but I have enough to describe the political terrain, whom you can trust and depend upon, and who you cannot. After the cabinet meeting, we'll have lunch together and walk through the challenges as I see them."

"Thank you, sir. I'll do all that I can to complete the projects you've begun."

"Margaret, when we stand before our Creator, it isn't *projects* that are important. The culmination of our life involves our decisions and choices. Nothing more. Have we chosen for the greater good? Have we lived with integrity and generosity? Have we embraced life as the gift that it is?" He inhales and looks at her squarely. "I'm ready."

# Chapter 42

*M*argaret returns to her residence at One Observatory Circle, weighed down by the long flight, the emotional meetings with the President and his staff, and by the gravity of her approaching responsibilities. When her trusted attendant greets her at the door, she feels ready for a glass of wine and quiet music.

"Welcome home, ma'am." Stephen reaches for her hand. "It's been a full day, hasn't it?"

"I'm sorry it's that obvious, but you're right. It has been a complex day. I hope you and the staff are doing well."

"We've missed you, but we're fine. Because of the hour, I've put a glass of cabernet on your desk, ma'am. And the chef has prepared your favorite, macaroni and cheese. Shall I bring it to your room?" Stephen waits at the bottom of the stairs and watches for Margaret's response.

"Yes, that would be lovely," she says.

Margaret pauses at her bedroom door and wonders when she'll have to make the move and what the President's quarters are like. She shakes her head. *I guess I should ask. I'll add that to my list.* Upon opening the door, the delicious scent of narcissi greets her. Next to the arrangement sits a bowl of dark chocolates. She smiles and thinks back to all the times she's returned home to find flowers and chocolates waiting for her. *My staff knows me so well. I wonder if the team could move with me? I shall look into that possibility.*

Margaret scans the room. Her staff has laid her nightgown out on the bed and turned down her sheets. *The Washington Post* and *Stars and Stripes* sit on her desk next to her laptop and the glass of wine. She crosses to the drink, takes a sip, and then another, and looks out of the window. *It's all so manicured, so perfect, and not at all like the embattled area I just visited.* Her attendant brings dinner.

"You'll feel better soon, ma'am," he reassures as he sets the table for her. "Some things in life are beyond our control, and all we can do is choose our response."

"I apologize for being in a funk. It's been an extraordinarily difficult day."

"I understand, ma'am." Stephen pauses and then says, "I remember when Vice President Ford sat at this desk and struggled with what lay before him. He seemed distraught. The country was in turmoil, and he didn't know how he could mend the divides. Do you remember what he said after he took the Oath?"

She looks at him and wonders if he knows about the President's condition. "I was just a toddler during the Watergate fiasco, but over the years, my parents have talked about it."

Stephen straightens and, with pride, says, "Ford said, 'I assume the presidency under extraordinary circumstances. ... This is an hour of history that troubles our minds and hurts our hearts.' Does that sound familiar?"

*He must know. But how?* Margaret nods.

"There was no one better prepared than Ford to step into the President's role, and yet, he doubted himself. Who wouldn't, given the situation?"

Margaret sits in silence and shifts in her chair. She gazes at her trusted attendant. "Thank you for sharing Ford's story, Stephen."

"Whatever the challenges might be that you carry, I feel confident you'll decide with consideration of the greater good. You always have, and you always will." He smiles and gives her a nod as he leaves the room.

Margaret takes another sip of wine. She realizes that someone from the President's staff must have called him. "There's no other explanation," she mutters. "At least now, I know how speedily confidential information travels."

Margaret enjoys her meal and then focuses on her report. Just before midnight, she stretches and calls it quits. *Twenty-five pages and I've barely begun.* She rests her forehead in her hands and sighs. If these last hours have taught her anything, it's that the task she and Ivan have embarked upon is monumental. She looks at her desk clock and decides to call him.

"Ivan, dearest, I knew you'd be awake."

"Of course, but I don't have my love next to me, so I'm lying here feeling sorry for myself."

"Oh, come on, I suspect you've showered already and had your first cup of coffee, and you're reading the paper."

"Hmm, you know me too well, but you made a mistake. I've had two cups by now." Ivan chuckles and adds, "So, tell me, what's going on? I can hear the apprehension in your voice."

"Well, there's no easy way to say this, but when I arrived back in the U.S., President Williams met with me privately and explained that he will step down next week. His cancer has progressed to the point that doctors have given him a month to live."

"Oh, Margaret, I'm so sorry. Has he shared his prognosis widely?"

"He informed his staff today, and tomorrow, he'll talk with his cabinet and then other government officials. Given the way information travels around this place, I suspect the world will know by the end of the week."

"And you feel overwhelmed at what that means for you?"

"Exactly. The thing is, I knew this was coming, but I didn't expect it to happen so quickly. I don't know what I would have done differently if I'd had another two weeks, but at least I would have prepared emotionally."

"Maybe, but you'll never know. Margaret, dear, your situation is similar to mine. The circumstances are different, but overnight, I went from Prime Minister to Acting President. If anyone knows what you're going through, I do. And I also know you can do this."

"I hope so. I truly hope so ..."

"Margaret?"

"I'm sorry. There's something more the President said. He-he told me that the intelligence team at Begert uncovered evidence of a dangerous international cabal. Our CIA assists with the investigation."

"And its membership includes folks involved directly with the global economy, right?"

"Yes, it's a dangerous cluster."

Ivan says, "We've tracked them for the past two years. Though brilliant, they're fools. They've aligned with China and imagine themselves leaders of a One World Government. What they don't understand is that the CCP wants *everything* and will stop at *nothing* to get what they want."

Margaret's voice rises in pitch, "*You knew about this?*"

"Well, aren't you alert to developments in Mexico and Canada? Some neighbors demand our attention. Once you're sworn in, and after you've had a chance to settle into your new role, we'll talk about this cabal. For now, set it aside. You needn't worry about it. We'll face it together at a later date."

Margaret takes a deep breath. "I feel like I can breathe again. By the way, I finished my report on Syria tonight, and I sent you an email with it attached. I know there are probably details I've overlooked, so please make changes as needed."

"Who else will see the report?"

Margaret can hear the worry in his voice. "I'll meet with the President in the morning and give him a copy. Otherwise, I'll wait until I've taken the Oath before sharing it with the Joint Chiefs of Staff."

"Does the President need the paper report? Keep in mind that his staff will pack up his files and desk items. We can't be too careful."

"I hadn't thought about that, but you're absolutely correct. I won't bring the report with me. And I doubt the President will even ask me about it because he'll be preoccupied with saying goodbye to the different branches and their directors and officers."

"If Iran finds out what we intend, the entire Middle East will erupt. We'll have to deal with a conflagration like nothing either of us has experienced."

"I wish you could be here when I meet with the Joint Chiefs of Staff."

"I can, through a video conference. I suspect Ozdemir would also like to participate. The three of us, interacting together, will be convincing for the Joint Chiefs. Otherwise, they'll think you naive and will reject any notion of an agreement. My military leadership will react similarly. If they listen to the three of us talk through the plan, however, they'll get on board."

"I'll calendar a meeting as soon as I get into the office in the morning. Also, I'll contact Ozdemir. Will next Friday at 08:00 EDT—15:00 your time—work for you?"

"Let me check. Eh … yes, that works. A final note, I think the document needs both our signatures. I'll go over it today and will return it within eight hours."

Margaret nods and purses her lips. "Even though I feel overwhelmed, I'm also excited. I know we can do this."

"I know it too, but I'm looking at the clock and realizing that it's well past midnight for you. I need to let you sleep. I'll say good night and fantasize about you in your skimpy blue nightgown. You have a big day tomorrow, and all I want you to do is hold tight to three words: I LOVE YOU."

"You know that anxious feeling I told you about?"

"Yeah …"

"I don't have it anymore."

# Chapter 43

*M*argaret stands in front of her full-length mirror and stares blankly while she buttons the jacket of her new navy-blue suit. After taking a deep breath, she walks to the window next to the table that holds her now-cold breakfast. She doesn't have her usual appetite. Margaret focuses on the cherry tree in full bloom and wonders what she will see from her White House bedroom.

This is a day Margaret never expected. Even when asked to become the vice-presidential running mate, she never envisioned herself in the President's role. Margaret only agreed as a favor to Samuel Williams, a person she had admired throughout his political career. The noise of politics was abhorrent to her, and yet, today, she will get sworn in as President.

Her support staff gather at the base of the stairs and wait for her to emerge. As she makes her descent, they applaud. One reassures, "You'll be wonderful, Ms. Margaret."

"There's no one more capable than you," another says.

Margaret thanks them for their kindness and wishes it were as easy as they claim. Her limo idles at the curb, and after offering a salute to her team, she climbs into the vehicle. *There's no escaping now.*

She fumbles with her phone and rereads the text Ivan sent in the early morning. *Hold your head high, my dearest, and think about the millions you will help. Be happy. Be grateful for this opportunity to serve. Most importantly, remember that I love you.*

As she walks down the hallway to her new office, one person after another offers their congratulations and support. Margaret wishes she could feel it … the support. But every smile registers as a burden that further tightens the binds across her chest. *Can I do this?*

Margaret chats with her new secretary and then walks into the Oval Office. The morning sun glistens across the desk that will be hers in another hour. At the corner of the table, white roses sit regally in an antique enameled Russian vase. A smile forms across her lips. Ivan will have sent them. Another flower arrangement sits on the coffee table—a mixed bouquet of purple, blue, and yellow shades. An attached gift card reads, *From your home team.*

Lighthearted laughter erupts in the adjoining room, and Margaret turns to see her parents walking toward her. They wrap their arms around her and hold her tightly, as they had when she graduated with honors from West Point. "We're so proud of you," her father says, and she knows he means it. She takes a deep breath. *Now I'm ready.*

"I've a favor to ask," Margaret says. "Will you both walk me down the hall to the East Room?"

"Of course." Her dad stands tall with pride while her mom wipes away tears that flow too easily. "We'll stand at your side."

A knock at the door grabs their attention. "It's time, ma'am."

Margaret takes her parents' hands, gives them a quick squeeze, and proceeds to the door. As she steps into the hallway, with her mother and father close behind, spontaneous applause from well-wishers who line the way to the East Room meets her.

The Chief Justice asks Margaret to place her left hand on the Bible and raise her right. He instructs, "Please repeat these words after me:

"I, Margaret Bernice Adler, do solemnly swear."

With a dry mouth, she manages to repeat, "I, Margaret Bernice Adler, do solemnly swear."

"That I will faithfully execute

"the office of President of the United States,

"and will to the best of my ability,

"preserve, protect, and defend

"the Constitution of the United States.

"So help me God."

Margaret repeats, "So help me God."

The Chief Justice smiles. "Congratulations, Madam President."

The gathered people burst into applause. Margaret stands tall and walks to the podium.

"Honorable Chief Justice, family, friends, and fellow Americans, I accept this honor with a broken heart. President Williams is a dear friend and an invaluable mentor. I never expected to be sworn in as your President. I only agreed to become his vice-presidential running mate because of the respect I hold for him. Now, I am left trying to fill his shoes, which I assure you, are much bigger than mine.

"With your support, I commit to upholding the Constitution, establishing partnerships and alliances that will foster international peace, and strengthening our economic base.

"President Williams models a life well-lived. He's made it amply clear that our time on this planet is brief. With every precious moment that we're given, we need to ask ourselves, am I fostering life? Does this decision free hearts and minds? Does it bring healing?

"I promise to carry on President Williams's legacy and foster life in all the ways I can."

# Chapter 44

The following Friday at 08:00, Margaret meets with the Joint Chiefs of Staff in the Situation Room, located in the White House's West Wing basement. Designed for intelligence management, Presidents and their advisors use the room to handle complex crises in the United States and abroad. It has a secure communications system, which Margaret needs.

The invited members of the Joint Chiefs of Staff—the Chairman and Vice-Chairman, an Army Chief of Staff, the Naval Operations Chief of Staff, the Air Force Chief of Staff, and the Marine Corps Commandant—have arrived and await Margaret. When she walks in, she asks them to be seated.

"Gentlemen, I'm honored and humbled to stand before you as your President. Undoubtedly, you wonder why I've invited you here. Perhaps, why I've limited the membership of the meeting to the six of you. What we will discuss is highly classified. I cannot risk anyone outside this circle knowing what I will soon explain.

"As a backdrop, you've read my dossier. You know I proudly served in the Army. You'll discover shortly that I think strategically, and that's because you taught me to do so. I bring this to your attention because what I need to share will make you question my abilities. Please withhold judgment until I finish my presentation.

"I suspect you're aware that I traveled to Turkey for humanitarian reasons a couple of weeks ago. I spent the night at the Incirlik Air Base and visited an orphanage in the Hatay Province. The orphanage houses over a thousand children, and they appeared well cared for. This location sits just a few miles from the Syrian border. During our brief visit, somebody made a failed assassination attempt. I'm indebted to President Williams for alerting me of the impending danger via text just before we entered the complex. Either it was one of you or the CIA who saved my life and the lives of many that morning. Later in the day, an errant missile hit the orphanage's perimeter wall, sending shrapnel throughout the grounds and striking the armored bus I was in. It was a war zone, and I hadn't anticipated that.

"Accompanying me on this trip was President Ivan Smirnov. I can see by your glances that you are quite aware of who he is, but I hope by the end of this presentation, your judgments will have softened.

"Smirnov and I worked closely on the trip. We met with President Ozdemir and spoke of our growing concerns about refugees and more. Ozdemir is an interesting person, neither ally nor foe. I think you would agree. Smirnov and I shared a plan that could resolve the refugee problem in Turkey and other surrounding countries, and perhaps, bring peace to the Middle East. This is what I submit to you today.

"The EU has filed charges against President Hassan, the Syrian Commander in Chief. They claim crimes against humanity for Hassan's use of chemical weapons against his people, for his mass murders and crematoriums, and much more." Margaret walks around the table and hands a portfolio to each officer. "Included in this folder is a printout of the plan we will now discuss. You'll also find recent photo evidence of the carnage. When we complete our meeting, I ask that you leave your folders with me. I will lock them in my safe."

Margaret returns to her seat and says, "Smirnov promises to deliver Hassan to Germany for prosecution. The tentative date for this action is one month from now, just after Ramadan ends. Once we have Hassan under arrest, Turkey will move in and provide resources and military strength to restore Syria to its people.

"Gentlemen, I have asked Presidents Ozdemir and Smirnov to join us via satellite. Please turn now to the screen, and I will dial them in."

President Ozdemir appears first. "Good afternoon, Madam President, gentlemen. President Adler asked me to address you regarding the planned coup. I assume she has outlined the plan, so I will explain Turkey's involvement. When this is set in motion, we're prepared to act immediately. We will push back against Hassan's forces in strength and bring in notable humanitarian aid. We commit to helping to rebuild Syria. I'll have contractors deployed as soon as the country stabilizes. Why, you might ask? Turkey has over four-million Syrian refugees. Syria's crisis is Turkey's crisis, and it's taken a toll on our people and economy. We want a strong neighbor we can depend upon, not a menace who kills its own people."

Smirnov appears on an adjoining monitor. Ozdemir calls out to him, "Ah, President Smirnov. Good to see you again. Please, proceed. I've talked enough."

Smirnov clears his throat and says, "Madam President. Gentlemen. It's a pleasure to join you for this historic meeting. Much time has passed since WWII when our three countries worked together to defeat Hitler. My hope is that the Syrian coup will announce a powerful alliance of cooperation and trust. I commit to you today that Russia will deliver Hassan to Germany. I will also increase our military presence at our naval base in Tartus, will ready the S-400s for possible deployment, and will follow President Ozdemir's lead in engaging Hassan's military.

"There's much that needs to be done for this coup to be successful. Some of the preparation is military, some political. Concerning the latter, we will, together, establish an interim government, representative of the people. Together, we'll rebuild the infrastructure so that citizens can receive the assistance they so urgently need—hospitals, schools, mosques, and markets. From my vantage point, we must act upon this immediately. Without such prompt action, unimaginable suffering, and a very real risk of disease will occur." Smirnov continues with an outline of the plan and then turns the discussion over to Adler.

"Thank you, President Ozdemir and President Smirnov. Are there questions …?"

"President Smirnov," the Chairman says, "Everything is contingent on Hassan being delivered to the German police. Can you share how you intend to achieve this?"

"Of course. In four weeks, Russia's newest warship will dock at the Tartus Naval Base. At its commissioning celebration, President Hassan will speak. As part of the ceremonies, we will cruise the Eastern Mediterranean Sea. At an appointed time, we shall detain Hassan. Then a Blackhawk will land on the ship and take Hassan to the German officials."

Ozdemir's expression hardens, and he interrupts, "Smirnov! Turkey will pick up Hassan. He and his regime have hurt my country more than any other nation outside of his own. Turkey will, proudly, deliver him to the Germans."

The room grows silent. The attendees look from one to the other, and then the Chairman of the Joint Chiefs says, "Presidents Adler, Ozdemir, and Smirnov, the plan is workable. Now we must attend to the details. Be assured, we'll play our part. Diversionary activity will be needed in countries aligned with Hassan. We can provide that. Additionally, our carriers are in the theater. If threatened, they will respond with full air support."

"Thank you, General," Adler says. "I wouldn't have expected less." She then thanks Presidents Ozdemir and Smirnov, and adds, "Together, we face formidable challenges, and united, we'll be victorious, and this atrocity will end. Good day to you both." After turning off the screen, Margaret directs her attention to the Joint Chiefs of Staff.

"Gentlemen, I depend on your strategic experience to bring this plan to fruition. I'd like us to meet next week at this same time. For now, consider this information as highly classified. I won't speak with anyone else about this operation—not even the CIA. If our partnership with Russia and Turkey became public, and our intentions were to leak, it could only result in war and a great loss of life. Obviously, we don't want that. We move forward, respecting the War Powers Resolution Act, and we'll prepare carefully for what we hope won't materialize. Speak only to each other and to me. If you have no further questions, we're adjourned."

The Chairman collects the documents and places them in front of Margaret. He remains standing and raises his hand for a salute. All the Chiefs follow his lead.

"Madam President, it's a privilege to work with you."

# Chapter 45

Back in her office, Margaret calls President Williams.

"Madam President, this is a delightful surprise," the former President says. "To what do I owe this privilege?"

"I would love your advice about a few things. Could I stop by to see you today? Do you have a few minutes?"

"For the first time in years, I'm relaxing in my garden and have plenty of time. Come join me for a cup of coffee."

"I'll see you within the hour."

Margaret notifies her Secret Service that she needs to meet with President Williams at his house. Because he maintained his home throughout his presidency, they're familiar with Williams' property. It was his private escape. The agents contact the team and arrange for transport. Once they arrive, a couple of agents lead Margaret to the garden.

"Ah, Margaret, my dear friend, come, sit by me. I know you have questions to ask, and I'm ready for them."

Margaret stumbles through the White House happenings and then grows more serious.

"When I was in Turkey, you texted me about an attack and told me not to touch any package. Who gave you that information?"

Williams sits back in his chair.

"Sir?"

"I heard you. I just need to consider my answer. We have an operative on the Incirlik Air Base. A Turkish officer. At times, I would receive cryptic messages from him, and I've learned to take everything he writes seriously. I don't know if the explosive came from Syria or Turkey. It could be either."

Margaret chooses her next words. "You know about the plans for a coup in Syria, so you also know this is a dangerous operation. I'm working with the Joint Chiefs of Staff, but I've not spoken with the CIA or the Secretary of Defense, as I'm concerned about an information leak. Could you tell me who you trust, or don't, in the ranks?"

Williams nods. "I wondered when you might ask that. Tell as few people as you can. The Chiefs are solid. You'll find them to be no-nonsense, factual, and dependable. The CIA operates in a different world. I both trust them and don't. As for the Secretary of Defense, he's a good man, but he's also a politician. Your Chiefs follow a chain of command. They won't overstep. The Secretary of Defense knows who his boss is, but as I mentioned, he's enmeshed in politics. The CIA imagines themselves as independent of everyone. That can prove dangerous. In your shoes, I wouldn't reveal anything to them until you're ready to execute."

"I thought as much. In fact, any written materials related to the coup are in my office safe. Speaking of the office, how secure is it?"

"During my first week there, I brought in outside surveillance experts and had my office checked. It was clean. You might do the same, but I never had an incident that caused me to question its security."

"What about my secretary?"

"One of the best. That said, why would you share classified information with her?"

"Good point."

"There *is* someone you need to be very careful of, however."

"Oh?"

"The Speaker of the House. You'll soon discover that you're in the tabloids. He'll be the source. So, play him at his game. Use him. Fair is fair."

"Do you suggest I lead him through the thickets to nowhere?"

"You might need to, and as I said, fair is fair."

"On another point entirely, can you recommend anyone for the vice presidency?"

"Margaret, you worked with me for six years. You know the landscape. You know who you like and don't. This evening, when you go home, pour a glass of wine and go through your list of friends. You need a person who'll stand by you and support you. Someone you can trust. Do you know why I chose you?"

"Not really, sir."

"Your military training and experience impressed me. Also, I trusted you instinctively because you didn't like politics. You were like a fish out of water. You didn't fit into this D.C. cutthroat world." His voice lowers, "You reminded me of my sister—down to earth, truthful, and good. That's why I asked you to join my team."

"Thank you, sir. Very kind of you, sir."

"Now, back to that glass of wine. When considering your VP, ask yourself who you'd like to spend time with. I've always felt that time with you was time well spent."

"Thank you, I—" An urgent text from her secretary interrupts Margaret. "I need to say goodbye, sir. It seems some folks are waiting to see me."

President Williams chuckles. "That's one thing I'll never miss. Good luck, my friend."

Margaret motions to her Secret Service detail and returns to the White House. The Speaker of the House and the Senate President wait for her. Margaret sighs and thinks back to Williams's comment about her hating politics. *How true.*

# Chapter 46

*T*he Joint Chiefs of Staff have prepared the Situation Room for war deliberations with the President. Screens once blank fill with maps showing Asia and Europe, as well as Syria and Iran. In addition to the electronic atlas spread across the walls, each seat has a binder in front, containing classified information on the Middle East and surrounding countries.

When Margaret walks into the room, a smile stretches across her face. She studies each map and then nods to the Chiefs.

"Gentlemen, we're ready to begin. Chairman, the floor is yours."

"Thank you, Madam President. In front of you is a binder containing information related to the three areas we plan to discuss today. The first section covers our risk level in the Middle East. The next section provides an overview of our military strength. The final section addresses timing and suggests a calendar."

Margaret opens her folder, and a photo of her holding Amira meets her gaze. She bites her lower lip, darts a quizzical look over at the Chairman, and tries to hide her surprise.

"We'd like to call our plan, Operation Amira, Madam President."

Margaret fights back her tears, glances down for a few moments, and then turns to the Chiefs. "Amira, it is."

The Chairman pushes back his chair, stands, and walks over to the map of Asia. He begins with an overview of the current tensions within the Middle East. Then he provides an analysis of the Syrian conflict and moves to the principal threats. The Chairman points out how two unfriendly countries—Lebanon and Iraq—share the Syrian border. Along with two friendly nations—Jordan and Turkey. He offers an overview of the strengths and weaknesses of each of these countries and then shifts to the allies—Israel, Saudi Arabia, and the United Arab Emirates. Finally, he walks over to the map of the real threat—Iran.

"Before I go any further—" the Chairman says. "—I need to ask a few important questions."

Margaret says, "Proceed."

"You trust Russia?"

"Impeccably."

"Turkey?"

"I'm not as sure. I believe Ozdemir will stay true to his word and will deliver Hassan to the Germans. I also believe he will help rebuild Syria. Both actions meet Turkey's needs. After that, I don't know."

"You're aware he has the S-400 Triumph surface-to-air missile system?"

"Quite aware."

"Then you also know the danger?"

"Yes. I'm also aware of the existent tensions on the Incirlik Air Base. I only visited there briefly, but it gave me enough time to notice that our relationship with Turkey has degenerated notably. Our Airmen coexist with theirs, and neither side trusts the other. We have nuclear warheads. They have the S-400. All rather troubling. We must rebuild trust, and soon.

"When Smirnov and I met with Ozdemir via satellite in the base Commander's office, I was left with strong impressions of who the man is. Above all else, he's proud. In fact, he's established himself as almost a king. The Ottoman Empire courses through his veins. If a military operation serves his needs, or his country's, he'll support it. Outside of that criteria, it remains questionable. As I mentioned last week, I consider him neither friend nor foe."

"Concretely, then, what do you advise?"

"Ozdemir's willing to commit his military and provide aid to Syria because, ultimately, that will elevate him in the people's eyes, and it will free his country of a longstanding economic burden. I believe we can trust him that far. His citizens will herald him as a hero if he delivers Hassan to Germany. And when the refugees return to their home nations, Ozdemir will be revered. What better time to establish a solid alliance between our two countries?"

"Thank you, Madam President. It's clear you understand our reservations. We can now focus on a declared enemy."

The Chairman motions to the map of Iran, and all eyes follow. He provides an analysis of its military readiness, points out the key bases and missile silos, and circles areas with large numbers of troops.

"Iran has successfully exported its revolutionary ideology into Syria, Lebanon, Iraq, and Yemen. There may not be a lot of love between some of these countries, but they will support Iran over us any day."

"What does he gain by going to battle with us?" the President asks.

"Revenge. Control. Power. We're in his domain, and he believes we have no right to be there. We're infidels, which gives him a religious justification for an attack. Syria and Iran share a common hate, and that hate drives both leaders."

Margaret nods. "Doesn't Iran have the S-400 missile system?"

"They have its predecessor. Our intelligence tells us that they're launch ready. There've been many recent drone and cyber-attacks, but we feel convinced these assaults are just a smokescreen to distract us from the actual attack they plan."

"Imminent?"

"We believe anything could set them off. Operation Amira commences immediately after Ramadan. We should assume that, separately, Iran plans an attack at the same time. Our principal advantage is that they remain unaware of our intentions. We must keep it that way."

"Absolutely."

"Madam President, we will now offer an overview of our readiness and suggest a course of action that we believe would prove effective. You'll find classified information in your binder that substantiates our claims."

The Naval Operations Chief of Staff says, "Madam President, the amphibious assault ship USS Bataan is in the Persian Gulf, accompanied by warships that carry 5,000 Marines and soldiers. We also have two carrier groups in the area. The USS Gerald R. Ford is in the Gulf of Oman, and the USS Dwight D. Eisenhower will arrive in the Mediterranean Sea on Wednesday. These strike groups are prepared to respond to any offensive that Iran or any other combatant country might initiate. Between them, we have over 20,000 military personnel and about 200 aircraft waiting for the signal. All systems are a go."

"Has the problem with the software in the USS Gerald R. Ford been repaired?"

"It's been completely reengineered, ma'am. Our men worked tirelessly on the challenge and replaced the entire system. We're prepared."

"Good to hear, Admiral."

The Army Chief of Staff straightens in his seat. "Madam President, we have approximately 65,000 troops surrounding Iran. The largest contingents are in Afghanistan, Qatar, and Kuwait. Iran has stated explicitly that they have missiles aimed at thirty-five of our bases in the region, the closest being in Bahrain, which has over 7,000 American troops. It houses our warplanes, spy aircraft, and a Special Forces Operations Center. From this base, we and our allies launch retaliatory actions against the enemy. It's critical to our success.

"As the Chairman stated, Iran's strength lies in its missile arsenal. Our projections put the number above 2,000. Since the January attack against our bases in Iraq, we've increased our stockpile, and by joining forces with our allies, we're a formidable presence in that sphere. To counter a full attack successfully, however, we need Turkey's help. Their S-400 missile system can destroy cruise and ballistic missiles. Intelligence has identified four Iranian missile sites, one underground. If Turkey works with us, we can eliminate this stronghold."

"General, you want me to speak with President Ozdemir?"

"Yes, ma'am."

"Does your report include an analysis of why Turkey might resist helping us?"

"Yes, ma'am."

Margaret looks at the Air Force Chief of Staff. "How many troops do we have at the Incirlik Air Base?"

"6,078, ma'am."

"Could you accept a joint command of these Airmen during the operation so that Turkey shares in decisions regarding their deployments?"

"Respectfully, that would be unusual, ma'am."

"Yes, it's also unusual to request another country's S-400."

The General darts a glance at his colleagues and says, "Dual command it is. We'll make it work."

"Thank you, General. I shall contact President Ozdemir within the day. If I don't need this bargaining chip, I won't use it."

"Madam President," the Army Chief says. "We have a substantial presence in the theater, but I recommend that we deploy an additional 5,000 troops to Jordan, increase our numbers at Camp Arifjan, south of Kuwait City, and move our Patriot Advanced Capability missile interceptors into the Persian Gulf. They'll provide early warning and strategic launches.

"Our allies need to be brought into this operation as quickly as possible, because they need to prepare as well. Saudi Arabia will want to increase its presence at the Iraqi border. Israel will want to do the same at its border with Lebanon. Jordan needs to increase troops along the Syrian border. Turkey lies next to Syria, Iraq, and Iran, and it must be prepared to strike."

Margaret nods. "Gentlemen, at this point, no one is aware of our collaboration with Russia. We need to keep it that way for now. But, when I speak with Ozdemir, I believe it would be advantageous to ask him for a formal agreement between our two nations. We would end the embargoes, assist with the resettlement of the Syrian people, and begin the process of relocating our nuclear warheads. On his part, he would use the S-400 to destroy Iran's missile silos, and Turkey would help rebuild Syria. If Ozdemir concurs, and I believe he will, this partnership needs to be celebrated publicly. Tell me your reactions, please."

After some deliberation, the Chairman says, "Madam President, this would be a win-win. If you can arrange it, then go for it."

Margaret considers her options. "Gentlemen, it's 19:00 in Ankara. I may reach President Ozdemir now. Would you like to remain present for my call?"

The Chiefs all nod in the affirmative.

"Okay then, let's see if our techs can pull him up on the screen." She motions to the team in the next room, explains the need to talk with Turkey's President, and they begin the process. Within minutes, President Ozdemir appears on screen.

"Madam President, this is unexpected."

"Yes, and I apologize for the evening call. I'm sitting with the Joint Chiefs of Staff. We've just completed a lengthy meeting regarding our upcoming operation, and we have a request and an offer."

"Hmm, a proposal. That sounds interesting. Tell me more."

"Our two countries have been allies for more than seventy years. Over the past decade, we've had our ups and downs, which became especially evident after the United States Senate blamed Turkey for the Armenian genocide. I promise to address that overstep. The proposal I bring to you now, however, is an agreement whereby each of us takes actions that will restore trust.

"In terms of the United States, I'll make sure there are no embargoes. Secondly, I'll mandate the relocation of our nuclear warheads at the Incirlik Air Base and have that task completed within the year. Thirdly, I'll ensure that the United States will assist in the resettlement of the Syrian people by providing manpower to help with rebuilding."

"I like what you've told me thus far, so what is it you expect from Turkey?"

"Two things. The first you have already promised. Turkey will help rebuild Syria and assist with the establishment of a representative interim government. The second is more complex. Turkey will destroy Iran's missile silos with its S-400 system. Our intelligence has evidence that Iran is preparing for a major attack. China is involved and is supplying the armaments. We cannot risk World War III."

"Can you share the evidence?"

"Yes. Obviously, this is classified information that would be dangerous if it got into the wrong hands."

"Of course. Turkey is no friend of China. Its weaponry has been used against us. And Iran, well, it's a menace that I would personally like to eliminate. Where does Russia stand with all of this?"

"After the coup, our three countries will sign a pact that details our points of understanding. For the present, we must work clandestinely. No one can suspect that Russia works with us."

"All right. Give me the day to think about this, and I'll let you know."

"One final thought. When we initiate the coup, there must be coordination and cooperation between your men and ours at the Incirlik base. The two Commanders need to forge a plan that will ensure a united front when we engage the Syrian Army."

"Absolutely. And if there's a disagreement?"

"Turkey's Commander makes the final call. It's your border that we need to protect."

"Madam President, I like working with you. Consider this a done deal. Send me the intelligence information, and we'll ready the S-400."

After Margaret has said her goodbyes, and the connection drops, she lets out a shout. The Joint Chiefs clap.

The Chairman says, "Madam President, this is a major step forward politically and in terms of Operation Amira. We share your concern about the need to restore diplomatic relations with Turkey. I'll provide you with the intelligence information in the morning."

A rare smile stretches across the Chairman's stoic face, and Margaret returns the expression. "We have work to do, and I don't want to hold you up. However, I do have three questions or concerns. First, are you in touch with our operatives in the field?"

"Yes. They report to leadership at the Bahrain base."

"When we meet next week, I'd like an update on when and how you'll notify them, and if they can identify leaders within the communities they've infiltrated. We need to establish an interim government as soon as we have Hassan in custody.

"Additionally, our Special Forces must prepare to remove Hassan's cabinet and staff ensconced in his governmental palace. Key personnel needs detaining for possible arraignment. As you know so well, the Syrian Republican Guard can be fierce; therefore, this campaign must be orchestrated carefully. Please provide a report."

"Finally, our allies and the CIA need to be informed. I would like your counsel as to when we do so. We are three weeks away from launch."

The Chairman says, "On your last point, Madam President, you can assume the CIA is aware of private activity between our offices. They don't know what it means, but they'll begin to surmise once they realize we're increasing troops on our bases in the Middle East. You can wait until next week to tell them, but if you decide otherwise, you can expect that the Director will pay you a visit. Similarly, Syria and its allies will notice the buildup. There'll be chatter. With a good diversion, however, their focus could be guided elsewhere. Israel is uniquely positioned to offer an effective diversion."

Margaret looks at each of the Chiefs and gestures agreement. "You're right on both counts. I'll ask my assistant to arrange a meeting with the Director for the beginning of next week. As for Israel, I shall contact Prime Minister Fisher tomorrow."

# Chapter 47

The sun has set by the time Margaret closes her laptop and heads home. She wanders down the hall to her quarters, thinking how strange it is to live in the White House. Elegant and pristine, her new abode screams wealth and royalty, and neither appeals. She thinks of Amira and smiles. *It won't be long, and Amira will make this place a home.*

Margaret's assistant greets her at the door. Stephen notes her cheerfulness and tired eyes.

"Ma'am, did you have lunch today?"

"I didn't have time and forgot."

"You know we've talked about that. Please, go and sit by the fire. I'll bring you appetizers and have poured a glass of cabernet already. It's on the side table, waiting for you. Dinner will be served shortly."

"What would I do without you?" She reaches and gives Stephen a quick hug. He seems like a second father to her, and he knows her better than almost anyone.

"I'll snap to in a minute. I just need a few sips of wine." Margaret walks over to the fireplace and plops onto the couch. "You know, this couch isn't so bad. I need to find areas that I can call my own. You'll help me, right?"

"Of course, ma'am. You'll feel at home soon enough. Did you notice the flowers on the coffee table?"

"Yes, they're lovely."

While Margaret reaches for the gift card, her assistant stands to the side and pretends to sort the mail on the console table near the entrance. He watches as she reads the card. *I will call at 10 PM.* Margaret blushes and then jumps up and goes upstairs, singing to herself, wine glass in hand.

Within minutes of reaching the master suite, Margaret's assistant knocks and presents her with Chicken Alfredo—another of her favorite dishes. She eats alone, thinking of Ivan and their night together in the Honeymoon Suite. *If only we could announce our marriage to the world.*

She starts to undress, and just then, her phone rings. She looks at the clock: 22:00. It has to be Ivan.

"Hello, my beautiful wife. I hope you didn't have to deal with too much nonsense today. Are you getting ready for bed?"

"I'm almost there. Just need to get my nightgown on."

"Before you do, I want to see you. Can you FaceTime me?"

Margaret laughs and says, "See you in a minute."

The video call connects. Ivan says, "Perfect. Your beautiful blue eyes tell me you have the weight of the world on your shoulders. Tonight, I want to help you forget about your troubles."

"You don't want to hear the highlights?"

"Eh, no, not right now. Remember when we talked about bridging the distance between our homes until we can live together?"

"Yes, and I don't think we solved that problem."

"We didn't. But what if we use our imaginations? We wouldn't be together physically, but we could explore through our visualizations."

"I was kinda doing that before you called. I was thinking of our night together in the Honeymoon Suite."

"Perfect. Did it make you smile?"

"Of course."

"All right, my dear. Could you play the CD I gave you—the one with Adele's *Love Song?*"

Margaret plays the music at a low volume. "Can you hear it?"

"Yes."

*However far away, I will always love you.*

"Every word is mine. Whenever you hear it, I want you to imagine that I'm singing to you in my heart."

"You're such a romantic."

"Let's dance, my sweetheart. Just close your eyes, listen to Adele, and imagine us moving across the room. We hold each other as our feet lead the way. No distance exists between us. We're at home next to each other."

Margaret reclines on the bed. "Yes, at home …"

"Remember when we undressed each other, one button at a time, until our clothes fell to the floor? I lifted you up and laid you on the bed. Do you see it?"

"I do. I can feel your warm hands, how they moved down my sides, onto my hips, and how you caressed my breasts. I remember it all."

Ivan's voice sounds husky when he says, "Your softness made me crazy inside. Can you sense my passion, my longing?"

"I want to be with you."

"We are. Remember the flickering candlelight, and how its shadows danced on the walls while we made our own music?"

"Yes, you took my breath away."

"See the shadows now. Hear the music we created. Hold on to that, my dear. Soon, it will be more than our imaginations."

# Chapter 48

*M*argaret sits in her office at daybreak. A mug of coffee keeps her company while she sorts through the notes for her early morning meeting with Israel's Prime Minister. They will speak via satellite at 08:00. As she goes over the material, she decides not to reveal Russia's role in the coup. President Williams's warning still haunts her. She'll follow his guidance and not share key information. *Next week, maybe.*

"Mr. Prime Minister, thank you for meeting with me."

"My pleasure, I'm sure. Congratulations on your advancement, Madam President. Israel wishes you well."

"Thank you. I wish the circumstances were other than what they are, but life always seems to have surprises for us. I suspect you wonder why I asked to speak with you."

"The question has crossed my mind more than a few times."

"Of course. The matter I want to discuss is classified and dangerous, but I know I can trust you."

"Of course, Madam President."

"Immediately after Ramadan, the United States and Turkey will remove President Hassan and deliver him to German prosecutors. They will also detain his colleagues. I can't share the details of this coup right now, but next week, I promise to do so.

"I alert you to this plan for three reasons. You're an invaluable ally, and I want you aware of our actions in the Middle East. Also, we expect a strong reaction from Iran, and possibly its allies. This response could extend to Israel, and we want you able to prepare. And we need your help."

"I'm glad to hear of this development. Please, continue."

"Our carriers and strike groups are moving into position. Our troops and Special Forces stand alert and ready to engage. We're taking other steps too, but I shall wait until next week to explain. Turkey, however, has promised its military force and, significantly, it's committed the use of its S-400 against Iran's missile silos. This is a game-changer, as I'm sure you'll agree."

"Before I venture a response, I'd like to hear more."

"I mentioned needing your help. My hope is that Israel can offer a distraction so that we might more successfully position ourselves for the campaign."

The Prime Minister's eyes dart to either corner of the screen, and then he focuses on Margaret. "This is a timely discussion, Madam President. Israel will help in any way necessary. We have a new intermediate-range ballistic missile that needs testing. If we deploy it over the Mediterranean the day before you initiate, it will garner much attention and give you some cover. We can also order attacks on Hezbollah strongholds. No love lost there. I, too, have a request, and separately, a question."

"Your request?"

"Israel will partner with you. The Syrian war has devastated its people and all the countries nearby. So, next week, I would like to review your operational plan. For a successful coup, it's essential to have clarity about our roles. I know you understand. Israel needs to be ready to jump in where needed. You agree, of course?"

"Absolutely. At the right time, I'll go through the details of our plan and seek your counsel as needed. Your question?"

"Ah, yes. It's a simple one. Do you trust Turkey?"

Margaret looks directly at the Prime Minister. "My Joint Chiefs of Staff asked me the same thing. My answer is a qualified *yes*.

"In this instance, Turkey has much to gain from the coup. Once Hassan's regime is removed, rebuilding can begin. It follows that the millions of refugees who fled Syria into Turkey will return to their home. During the rebuilding of Syria, my intention is to work concertedly for a lasting alliance with Turkey—the nation is invaluable to the ongoing stability of that region."

"I agree with you on that point. We need Turkey's engagement if there is ever to be peace in the Middle East. Israel should form part of this endeavor. We must show a unified front to effectively halt the fighting before it destroys us all."

"Let's discuss this possibility in more depth next week when I share the details of the coup. Is there anything more you'd like to bring to my attention?"

"Yes. I commend your efforts with disarmament; however, nuclear weapons are only one piece of this deadly puzzle. Never forget chemical and biological weapons. The Syrian war is a living testament to the use, abuse, and stockpiling of these weapons of mass destruction."

"I've never been more aware of this nightmare, as I am now. You're correct. We must deal with this horror."

Margaret says her goodbyes and notices her secretary standing at the door.

"Ma'am, the Director of the Central Intelligence Agency has arrived for her appointment with you. Shall I send her in?"

Margaret looks down at her desk and then back at her secretary. The Director has arrived a few minutes early. She assesses what she needs to do.

"Yes. Please, send her in." Margaret stands and walks over to greet the Director.

After pleasantries, the Director says, "Please call me Jessie."

Margaret decides she wants to keep the meeting formal and doesn't invite Jessie to use her first name.

"Of course. How can I help you?"

"I'd like to speak candidly if I might. These last two weeks, we've seen notable activity between the Joint Chiefs of Staff and yourself.

Given your recent trips to Russia and Turkey, as well as your work on disarmament, I suspect these meetings have to do with an operation in the Middle East. If my assumption is on track, we need to talk."

Margaret's eyebrows raise, "Need to talk? Why would that be the case?"

"Our operatives are throughout the Middle East. If there will be any military engagement, I need to know."

"Jessie, just to be *candid*, you're asking to know about military activity because you have operatives on assignment. If I understand you correctly, wouldn't these operatives inform you of military activity?"

The Director tightens her jaw. "Just so we understand each other, I'm protective of my operatives."

"Just so you understand *me*, I'm protective of this country. I will do nothing to jeopardize the men and women who serve, nor will I jeopardize innocent people irrespective of their home country."

Jessie clears her throat. "I think we've gotten off on the wrong track, or more correctly, I've taken us down this route and … and I apologize." Her eyes travel around the room and then focus on Margaret. "I'd like to start over."

"Please do."

"I've received reports of activity between your office and the Joint Chiefs. I'm also aware of troop movement in and around Syria. The CIA can be of assistance and would like to help if there is an operation planned."

Margaret stares at the Director, long enough to make the woman shift in her seat.

"How do I know you're trustworthy? How do I know that information forthcoming won't leak into the field? One leak, one simple misplaced word, could cause World War III."

Margaret has yet to blink. She continues to stare intently.

"Did President Williams indicate that I wasn't to be trusted?"

"No, he said you operated in your own world, and that can prove dangerous."

"I understand."

"Well, I need to hear *why* I can trust you, and to be frank, nothing has convinced me thus far."

"Perhaps I need to share our activity in the field. Would you be willing to meet with me at Langley?"

"I would need to arrive early. Tomorrow at 07:00?"

Jessie grabs her cellphone and checks her calendar. "Perfect. We'll meet then. I look forward to introducing you to our work, Madam President."

A few minutes later, Margaret's secretary comes in smiling and offers a thumbs up. "I don't know what you did, ma'am, but the Director left here in a hurry."

# Chapter 49

*M*argaret arrives five minutes early at CIA Headquarters. The Secret Service walks on all sides of her, as though the Langley campus is a hostile country. As Adler walks through the entrance doors, the staff ushers her into an elevator, which takes her to a conference room on the top floor.

The Director of National Intelligence walks over to her and introduces himself, "George O'Neil, Madam President. I serve as Director, and before that, I proudly served our country as Lieutenant General in the United States Army."

Margaret smiles. "You know how to brighten my morning, Director. It's good to meet you in person. I was unaware of your previous service, and given the conversation we'll have in a few minutes, your background is invaluable."

Jessie arrives, and Margaret turns to greet her.

After offering coffee, George points to a table and chairs at the east end of the room, next to a wall of windows that overlook the campus.

O'Neil says, "Madam President, please take the lead."

Margaret sips her coffee, looks at each of the Directors, and says, "Yesterday, Jessie invited me to see your operation, particularly the sector focused on the Middle East. Her invitation was extended because of our conversational impasse regarding possible operations in that conflicted area. I'm cautious of whom I trust because I'm protective of our country. Frankly, I fear a simple conversation could put us at great risk. You want to know what I know, and I want to know what you know. To bridge this divide, we need to establish trust. So, my question to you, Director O'Neil, is why should I trust you, Jessie, and the CIA as a whole?"

George nods. "That's a fair question. Let's take a walk. I'd like to provide a context for what I'll explain. Shall we?" He points toward the elevators.

The three go through a maze of hallways to a large office complex focused on the Middle East. As they walk, O'Neil tells of his service in Iraq. He explains his charge, his losses, and what he learned. "When I left the field, I knew I wanted to continue my work with intelligence, which is why I sought an assignment with the CIA. I've never regretted that decision."

Margaret looks around the room and at the men and women focused on their computers, listening to intelligence through headphones, and then notices the large monitors against the south wall. Each displays real-time footage of enemy military installations.

Upon seeing her interest, George says, "We know of activity before anyone else. The center screen shows a base in Mazandaran province in Iran. Those tanks weren't present a week ago. Now, look at the top left. That monitor focuses on a Pakistani airbase outside Karachi. Notice the transport trucks and the heavy artillery getting loaded. As of yesterday, this is new. Whatever's going on, something big is planned, something far graver than a simple border dispute."

Margaret looks at George intently. "Let's find a place to talk." She turns to Jessie, "I need to speak with Director O'Neil alone. I leave it to him to share information as needed. I hope you understand."

"Madam President, I respect your role and your decision. It's been a pleasure."

As Jessie walks away, the Director leads Margaret to his office. "Anything you say to me in this room is secure."

Margaret nods, takes a seat, and says, "I trust you, George, and because of that, I'll share our operational plans with you."

She sets the stage by pointing out who's involved, names the Joint Chiefs, and then explains that Russia, Turkey, and Israel act as equal partners. As she continues, George shifts in his chair and his gaze becomes laser-focused.

Margaret summarizes Operation Amira and concludes, "As you now appreciate, this operation involves much of the Middle East, in addition to the United States and Russia. The overall intention is to end the tyranny of the Hassan reign, and eventually establish an interim government of four or five men, representative of the communities within Syria. Then we begin rebuilding the country so the Syrian people can return home."

Margaret pauses and sits back in her chair.

George appears lost in thought. Finally, he says, "Madam President, this is a mission in which our department can assist in multiple ways. We have an operative among the Syrian guards at Hassan's palace and one who works for Hassan's wife. Moreover, we follow troop movements throughout the area. This information could prove invaluable to the Joint Chiefs."

Margaret's eyes narrow. "Director O'Neil, Tuesday at 08:00, the Joint Chiefs and I will meet to go over the plan in detail. Would you like to attend?"

"Yes, but I respectfully ask to meet with the Chairman as soon as possible—today."

"Please explain."

"I have intelligence related to the Syrian debacle and the associated Middle Eastern conflicts crucial to this operation. You saw the Iranian tanks and the Pakistani transport trucks. From the field reports, Iran is preparing for war. It's built up its troops along the western border with Iraq. That, coupled with the caravans of tanks and military transports around the Strait of Hormuz, tells us that an attack is imminent. Additionally, our intelligence has picked up Chinese involvement.

"A final comment. We have an operative close to the General of the Syrian Army. The operative reports that the war has become personal to the General because he lost family in Aleppo. He doesn't respect Hassan but cannot leave his post because such a move would mean death to his entire family. If you're looking for a leader, this is your man. He has the respect of thousands."

Margaret gives the proposal some thought. "The troops will stand down if he so directs?"

"Yes."

Margaret makes a call on her cell. "We need to meet as soon as possible. Yes, in one hour, the Sit Room. Yes, bring the Chiefs. George O'Neil will accompany me." Margaret ends the call, stands, and takes a deep breath. "We have work to do, Director. You may have singlehandedly prevented World War III."

# Chapter 50

The President, the Joint Chiefs of Staff, and Director George O'Neil gather in the Situation Room. They huddle over a large map of the Middle East on which O'Neil points to recent Iranian troop movements. He indicates key silo locations. His information corroborates that of the Chiefs, except that they were unaware of the troop movement to the Strait of Hormuz. This information brings a disconcerting development because the Strait is vital to the U.S. Navy and oil transportation. If it closed, one-fifth of the world's daily source of oil would disappear.

"I need to explain something more," O'Neil says. "We've discovered that the Chinese Army has troops in Pakistan and appears to be headed to the Gulf of Oman. We surmise they're preparing to strike the USS Gerald R. Ford."

The Chiefs look at each other and then at the President.

"Director," Margaret says. "I believe the time has come for you to tell us about the Syrian General."

"Certainly. General Abadi doesn't support Hassan's regime. He's under much scrutiny, and his life—and that of his family—is at risk. Our informant believes that, given the opportunity, he would turn against the Syrian President."

"You're certain about this?" the Chairman asks.

"I am. The General's a bit of a folk hero because he treats people with respect, even though there have been atrocities tied to his forces. Recently, he lost family members to Hassan's brutality, and thus the war has become personal."

The Chairman says, "Do you have a reliable contact who can reach the General?"

"I do."

Margaret notes that the Chiefs are ready to brainstorm. "Gentlemen, I leave you to your deliberations. I must return to my office. I have a satellite meeting with Saudi Arabia and, later, with Germany. I'd like to hear your report tomorrow. Let's meet at 14:00."

After returning to her office, Margaret asks her secretary to clear her schedule for the next afternoon.

"What about your meeting with the Secretary of Homeland Security?"

"Could you try to arrange a meeting with him for some time today?"

"How about 11:00? You have time after your meetings with the Crown Prince of Saudi Arabia, and then the Director of the European Center for Constitutional and Human Rights."

"That works perfectly. Thank you."

A few minutes later, Margaret speaks on the phone with the Prince.

"Your Royal Highness, thank you for meeting with me. My sincere apologies for interrupting during Ramadan, but I have pressing issues to discuss."

"Madam President, please always feel free to call me. Your issues?"

"At the end of Ramadan, several countries are banding together to remove Hassan from Syria and deliver him to Germany for prosecution. Turkey will transport him, but I cannot share just yet the full details of the operation. I wanted you to know so that you can take precautions within your country."

"Who will step in after Hassan's detainment?"

"I believe there will be an interim military leadership. Ultimately, though, a leadership council representative of the constituents of the country will be installed."

"You've aligned yourselves with the military against Hassan?"

"I understand your concern, but the man we have in mind is a folk hero, beloved by many. This is a temporary step. I can't say more than this until next week when I'll present you with the plan."

"Will Russia participate?"

"I cannot say more."

"Hmm, so Russia *is* involved. This changes everything. When you said 'precautions,' you were thinking of Yemen and Iran."

"And, perhaps, the Chinese. It appears they're headed for the Strait of Hormuz."

"They're interested in your carrier."

"I suspect so."

"Well, this is will be interesting. We'll be ready if you need our assistance. And we're only too happy to get rid of Hassan. May Allah reward you with all good."

Margaret's next call will be to the Director of the European Center for Constitutional and Human Rights. She stands and walks over to the window, deep in thought. With a grimace, she shakes her head. She knows what she must do. Rather than risk telling him about Hassan and his associates, she'll fabricate a story about Nazi criminals. She needs the ECCHR Director to get ready to receive the criminals. Margaret returns to her desk and makes the call.

"Director, is it possible to speak with you confidentially?"

"There's no one in the room, and nor can anyone hear our conversation. Because of the sensitivity of our mission, we're confidential. How can I help you?"

"Thank you. U.S. intelligence has identified four Nazi war criminals. These individuals will be apprehended next week. Once they're in custody, I shall release a statement to the public, and soon thereafter, they'll get flown to Berlin for prosecution by the ECCHR. Because of the charges, we can expect outrage against the prisoners and their families. For this reason, we must proceed with the utmost caution and delay public scrutiny as long as possible."

"Madam President, I'll inform my team about the sensitivity of your operation, and we'll prepare for their arrival."

"Thank you, Director. Please send directives as to where we should deliver the criminals."

Margaret says her goodbyes and sits back in her chair. *I wonder how long it'll take for the information to reach the press.* A tap at her office door startles her.

"Madam President, the Secretary of Homeland Security is here to see you."

Margaret walks over to greet the Secretary, a forty-something man with dark black hair, and offers him a seat. "I'm glad we're meeting today. I hope all is going well for you."

"Thank you, Madam President. All is well, but I have much to report." He offers her a folder, within which she sees diagrams, maps, and a report.

"This appears serious, Secretary. Please, walk me through your information."

"Two days ago, we noted an inordinate influx of Chinese citizens. If you look at the first sheet in your folder, you'll see a chart of the number of Chinese visitors over the last four years. Note the final column, which shows the numbers for Saturday."

"I see what you mean. The figures nearly equal the total number of Chinese visitors each year. This is rather strange."

"Correct, which is why this anomaly has us concerned."

"After they arrive, where do they go?"

"That's just it—each group travels to a singular location within the target city and then disburses to tourist sites."

"Such as? Give me an indication."

"Okay, the group that went to New York visited the Empire State Building and the Top of the Rock Observation Deck. Pretty ordinary stuff."

"What about the other cities?"

"The same story—popular tourist sites. The baffling fact is that they visited these locations at the end of each day, and all of the groups flew back to China the next morning. Furthermore, the new Chinese cruise ship, *The Emperor*, docks in Seattle next week. It will bring 2,000 passengers with it. This is its maiden voyage."

"What do we know about the ship?"

"Their marketing materials claim advanced technical capabilities and otherwise echo the cruise industry propaganda of comfort and pleasure."

"Did any Chinese tourists visit the west coast?"

"Oddly, no. You'll find the list on the next graphic in your folder. Other than New York, the groups visited Atlanta, Denver, Chicago, and Dallas."

"What's their purpose for docking in Seattle?"

"The Confucius Institute has sponsored its first conference, which the University of Washington will host."

"Have you spoken with George O'Neil?"

"Not yet, ma'am."

Margaret's face hardens, and her eyes narrow. She looks past the Secretary of Homeland Security to an invisible aggressor and then stands and crosses to the door. She tells her assistant to call the Director of National Intelligence and the Chairman of the Joint Chiefs of Staff and ask them to come to the Oval Office ASAP. She also hands her the folder and explains that she needs three more copies.

The Secretary of Homeland Security watches Margaret and wrings his hands. He flips through the report again, searching for answers. When she returns, he risks one question, "What's going on, ma'am?"

Margaret's jaw clenches. "Act immediately to close all the sites that the Chinese visited. Turn off all cameras within the locations and anything that might provide intelligence. Send in hazmat teams and search for whatever the tourists left behind. Identify the airplanes they used, cancel all planned flights associated with those crafts, and have hazmat go over every inch of the interior areas. Report back to me with your findings. China may have just declared war."

The Secretary of Homeland Security rushes out. Once he has everything in motion, he returns to the Oval Office and joins Margaret's meeting with the Director of National Intelligence and the Chairman of the Joint Chiefs of Staff. The group listens as the Secretary presents the recent developments involving the Chinese. The Director and the Chairman exchange furtive glances and then bring their attention back to the President. All present reach the same conclusion—China is preparing to attack.

"Gentlemen, it appears we're on the same page. Mr. Secretary, please ensure that all surveillance related to our Chinese visitors gets scrutinized. We must identify the terrorist cells in these cities and recover whatever they left behind. We don't have much time. After this meeting, I'll speak with the individual governors to ask them to assist you as needed with the National Guard. Thank you for bringing this forward. Excellent work."

"Thank you, Madam President." The Secretary shakes everyone's hands and walks to the door.

Margaret resumes the meeting, "The cruise ship—do we have intelligence?"

O'Neil says, "The CCP protects its airspace fiercely, Madam President, so we don't have a visual. That said, I believe we have an informant who works at the building site. I'll find out what I can."

"This is critical, gentlemen. I suspect the ship is equipped with technology that can paralyze communications in the western United States and missiles that can destroy Joint Base Lewis-McCord and others. All this as their troops move toward the Strait of Hormuz."

The Chairman says, "I need to add that, as of yesterday, our two navies are in a stand-off in the South China Sea. It appears we've entered into an undeclared conflict, ma'am, and we're moving rapidly toward full engagement."

"Agreed. Time isn't on our side." Margaret nods. "China has the advantage, but our strength is that they don't know that we're aware. We must beat them at their own game, and to do this, it's vital that this operation remain covert. Move quickly and report regularly. I shall contact President Smirnov. The Russians may have field agents who might have information on *The Emperor*."

# Chapter 51

*I*nstructed to gather intelligence on China's new cruise ship, Russian Special Operations Forces, Spetsnaz, huddle to go over their approach to *The Emperor* one last time. The five highly-trained soldiers synchronize their watches at 01:00 hrs. Other than armed watchmen aboard the cruise ship, they've seen no movement, except for the heaving of the dock by which they hide. Shanghai's bright lights force the team to stay in the water, where the sea's darkness offers protection.

The team leader signals for his men to follow. They inch forward, keeping their eyes and silenced AK12 rifles focused on potential threats that might arise from the cruise liner. They need to inspect the vessel for evidence of missiles. As they near, they study the large glassed-in lounge on the deck. It appears that passengers occupy the area as images float across its windows. However, the ship isn't scheduled to depart for several days and should have no passengers as yet.

The team moves closer. The leader signals to two of the Spetsnaz soldiers and motions for them to climb the pulls on the ship's side. He steers the other two to spread out and wait. Once they near the deck, the leader motions when they can advance safely.

The two soldiers rely on stealth as they edge forward and approach the lounge. They notice moving forms and determine that they're electronic, not human. When the leader signals for them to enter, they go inside and find advanced ballistic missiles. They hear a noise. A guard approaches. The men crouch and point their rifles at the door.

The guard stops near the entrance and lights a cigarette. After inhaling, he walks away, humming to himself. Once his steps grow faint, the soldiers ease open the door, glance at their leader, and follow his direction as to when to climb down the pulls on the vessel's side.

*     *     *

In the late afternoon, while Margaret meets with her assistant, a text message from President Smirnov arrives: *The Emperor is loaded and ready to attack. Ballistic missiles. Note attached photographs and footage.*

Margaret's assistant goes over the schedule for the week, but Margaret only notices that the woman's lips move and doesn't take in the words. Her heart beats louder and louder. War is imminent. Perplexed, Margaret texts Ivan: *Thank you. We don't have much time.*

He replies: *Correct. The Emperor must be destroyed before it can launch. Call in your team. We must strategize to protect Operation Amira.*

"Madam President, are you okay? You seem distracted."

"My apologies. Something has come up, and I need to meet with the Chairman of the Joint Chiefs."

"I'll call him now, ma'am."

*     *     *

Within fifteen minutes, the Chairman joins Margaret. She shows him the photos and Smirnov's message, and then asks, "What are your thoughts?"

The Chairman remains silent, and his eyes drop to the floor, where he stares wide-eyed without blinking. Eventually, he looks up. "We need to sabotage the integrity of the ship."

"Can we do that?"

"We have no choice. O'Neil's people can initiate a cyber attack, which is our best option."

"Shall we call in the forces and meet?"

"Yes. I'll call the Chiefs. Sit Room?"

"Yes, in twenty minutes. I have a question before you make the calls—do you trust the Director?"

"O'Neil? Yes, I do. His predecessor was a traitor, but he and his fellow conspirators are gone. O'Neil's a patriot and is trying to rebuild the entire Intelligence operation."

"That's my take as well. Once we take this step, there's no turning back."

"Copy that."

Margaret cancels the rest of her appointments and gathers the folders from her safe. She heads to the Situation Room with a pace that leaves her Secret Service team scrambling. At the door, the new President takes a deep breath and pauses. She fears what lies ahead. Determined, she tells herself, *We're prepared. We won't get caught off-guard like with the USS Arizona.* Margaret takes another breath, straightens, and walks into the room. She's the first to arrive.

With a single-minded focus, she places the folders on the conference table and then walks into the adjoining fusion center, where thousands of bits of information get assimilated into daily reports.

"Gentlemen, please load these images and footage onto the Sit Room screens and include a visual of the port of Shanghai." She hands them a thumb drive.

"Consider it done, Madam President."

When Margaret re-enters the meeting room, the images from the Russian Special Forces show on the monitors: Two photos of the exterior of *The Emperor*, several pictures of the ballistic missiles hidden within the large enclosed deck lounge, footage of the moving "bodies," and a close-up of the port. She studies the dockyard. *The Emperor* lays anchored away from other ships.

The Chiefs arrive five minutes early. They greet Margaret with a salute and study the displays. The Chairman unrolls a large map of the East and South China Seas and says, "I told the Chiefs of a threat but didn't offer details. By the look of their expressions, they know what lies ahead of us."

O'Neil enters the room and finds everyone deliberating a battle he has yet to envision. Then he sees the screens and turns to look at Margaret. She acknowledges with a slight bend of her head. After studying the displays, he shakes his head and takes a seat along with the Chiefs.

Margaret stands and explains the developments. She underscores that *The Emperor* will depart imminently for its maiden voyage to Seattle. An urgent text gives her pause. Her face pales. After a deep breath, she says, "Gentlemen, I've just received a message from the Secretary of Homeland Security. They've begun retracing the steps of the Chinese visitors. So far, we have three terrorist cells identified, and …" Margaret stops reading and grimaces. "At two sites, they've uncovered capsules of an unknown virus. These soft-shelled containers were located on the underside of railings that visitors hold as they climb the stairs to the attractions. One grab and the virus would release. We're dealing with biological warfare."

She sits down and stares at her team. "This is a declaration of war." She puts the conference phone on speaker and calls the Secretary.

"You're on speaker," she alerts him. "The Joint Chiefs and Director O'Neil are present. We need regular updates. Separately, we need a list of all who would, potentially, benefit from a pandemic. Once you have that information, determine who's traveled to Beijing over the last three months. Bring me your findings ASAP. Lastly, get the virus capsules to Fort Detrick. We need a complete analysis."

Margaret takes a breath and turns to her team, "Do any of you have questions for the Secretary?"

O'Neil says, "The sites are specific. There's a reason for that. Check on security measures at each location, get employment records of guards, and have your teams review every inch of footage. Someone's looked the other way when this operation got set up. We need those traitors apprehended immediately."

"Other questions?" No one stirs. Margaret reminds the Secretary to call with any information and then says goodbye.

After she hangs up, O'Neil ventures a question, "Madam President, what prompted you to think treason is involved?"

"The attack is two-pronged. It involves aerial and biological warfare. My suspicion is that the biological prompted the aerial. Someone wants to so sicken the American people that we will do whatever it takes to survive. Who profits from such a catastrophe? Who wants control, and why? In this scenario, I believe China is an accomplice to something much more nefarious. Obviously, there's no better time to launch an attack than when we're in a weakened state, but to what end?"

O'Neil says, "Once you started down this path with Homeland Security, it clicked. I saw it myself. We have Americans involved in this insidious assault."

Pointedly, Margaret stares at O'Neil. "Do you think the cabal, associated with the assassination attempts at Begert Air Force Base, is relevant to this discussion?"

All eyes focus on O'Neil. He gasps and says, "Madam, Chiefs, we've identified our enemy. I'll contact the team investigating this traitorous group ASAP and provide a full report by the end of the day."

Margaret turns her attention to the group. "Gentlemen, as a first step, I suggest that we proceed stealthily to destroy *The Emperor*. Ten years ago, Israel and the United States created the Stuxnet worm, which successfully infested and destroyed a fifth of Iran's nuclear centrifuges as well as its computers. It brought a turning point in global military strategy. Since that time, I'm confident our capabilities have grown even more refined.

"My thoughts are that we can go to war and set the world aflame, or we can play China—and this cabal—at its own game. We identify the best techs for cyber warfare, and through the skill of these individuals, we dismantle *The Emperor's* missile control system through malware. Further, we handicap the ship's main control system so that it becomes dysfunctional once at sea. Following this, we move forward with Operation Amira."

"I've got the techs," O'Neil says. "One is in Hong Kong, the other is within Langley."

"Now we're talking!" Margaret smiles. Then she asks the Chiefs, "Do you concur?"

The Chairman responds for the Chiefs, "We're on board. Let's get this done."

"Thank you."

# Chapter 52

---

*A*cross the Pacific, in a small office overlooking a busy shopping area, a computer analyst from the Hong Kong University of Science and Technology gets interrupted by a phone call. He waits before answering. One—two—three rings.

"Yes? . . . What time? . . . Usual place? . . . Okay." He checks his watch, wipes the perspiration from his forehead, and closes his laptop. He needs to meet the courier in ten minutes.

An expert at cyber warfare, Chiang Wei studied the development and launch of the Stuxnet worm, and since then, has focused on delivery approaches that don't require direct contact. He climbs onto his bicycle and heads to the designated coffee shop near the university. After ordering a cup of tea, he joins a student at an outside table.

"Your instructions are inside the envelope," she states matter-of-factly. "There is to be no contact except through our usual means. I will need an update tomorrow."

He notices the curve of her neck and the way her dark black hair hangs freely over her shoulders.

"Chiang, did you hear me?"

"Yes, the usual means. An update tomorrow."

"Okay, then." She pushes back her chair and stands to leave.

"What's your name?"

"It doesn't exist to you." The young woman walks away and disappears among the street stalls.

Chiang opens the envelope. He scans the message, folds the paper, and sticks it deep within his tattered blue jeans. Nervous now, he checks to see if anyone watches, and then he gets up and walks away. Back at his apartment, Chiang unfolds the paper and reads it carefully. Afterward, he calls the listed number, enters his numerical ID, and waits for the response.

"The Chinese cruise ship, *The Emperor*, departs on its maiden voyage in two days. It carries ballistic missiles hidden beneath an outdoor glass lounge. The missiles must be deactivated, and once this is achieved, cripple the ship's main control system." He reads the coordinates and studies the attached photos.

The analyst is familiar with this cruise liner because the local news stations showcase *The Emperor* regularly, offering interior photos of the suites and dining halls. Chiang turns on the television and switches between stations. There it is—the luxury cruise liner. A drone flies overhead and shows viewers an aerial glimpse. Chiang studies the exterior glass lounge. *Easy to dismantle.* He watches as the images float by the glass windows and identifies that they're electronic devices to mimic human activity.

Chiang goes to his computer, stretches, and begins working. After several hours, he pauses and sends a text to his contact: *Having trouble. Need Jay's help.* A response directs him to text an encrypted number. He does so and receives contact information. *Can't override the control system.*

An immediate response says, *Back out. Introduce the Zenith crawler.*

Chiang tries the crawler, and it works. He sends a reply, *I'm in.*

At daybreak, Chiang makes a cup of tea. The crawler has infected the missile control system and progressively destroys its ability to activate. In another few minutes, it will become useless. Now, he must focus on *The Emperor's* main controls. If he builds in a timer, the ship will fail at sea.

As Chiang works, he covers his trail with a rootkit component that hides the damaging files from detection and only manifests as typical operation values to the users. The Captain won't suspect anything is wrong until his commands fail. When that occurs, it will be too late. He will have lost control of the ship and find himself in the middle of the Pacific Ocean.

Chiang smiles and looks off into the distance. Proud of his work, he knows his actions will stop the death and suffering of innocent people. He thinks back to the Tiananmen Square massacre and his classmates who lost their lives and shakes his head. There's no love lost between him and the Chinese Communist Party.

# Chapter 53

*A* FaceTime call from Ivan awakens Margaret at 05:00. Her morning is Ivan's afternoon—the result of a seven-hour time-zone difference. She stirs and then sits on the edge of her bed, stretches, and takes a deep breath.

"Good morning, my love. I had to call you early because I'm leaving for an official function in a few minutes. By the time I get home, you'll be at work."

"You can call me anytime, dearest." Her negligee only loosely covers her breasts.

Ivan moans when he sees her and whispers, "I can't stop thinking of you. Last night, the 5,000 miles between us disappeared, and there was only the two of us, suspended in time. I've memorized every curve of your body ..."

Margaret hears the interruption of distant conversation and assumes Ivan must leave for the formal affair. Before he can speak again, she says, "Darling, I know you must go. I love you dearly. We'll talk this evening."

She takes a deep breath and wonders when they'll see each other next. Margaret longs for his strong arms around her. She wants to forget about the Chinese incursion, the threats in the Middle East, and the looming financial crisis. She sighs, lost in her thoughts, and jumps slightly when a text arrives on her office cellphone. It's from Director O'Neil. *Hong Kong mission successful. Report forthcoming.* She smiles and stands. Now she can drink her coffee in peace.

Margaret leaves for her office earlier than she usually does and, on the way, decides to step outside. Her Secret Service team acts quickly and reminds her that she isn't to do such things.

"Gentlemen, it's only 06:30. I suspect the terrorists are sleeping, and I need fresh air." After a few side glances, the agents move out of her way and take their positions. They watch as she removes her shoes and walks barefoot on the grass. Beneath a large oak tree, Margaret closes her eyes and listens to the chorus of bluebirds and finches, of robins and wrens. Early morning has always been her favorite time of the day. She takes several deep breaths and returns to the agents. "My faithful friends, sometimes, we need reminding of the wonders of life."

Back in her office, an assistant brings the President a fresh cup of Kona coffee. Margaret takes a sip, and then glances at the framed quote on her desk, a gift from her father.

The soldier, above all other people, prays for peace,
*for he must suffer and bear the deepest wounds and scars of war.*
General Douglas MacArthur

She bows her head and prays quietly before she focuses on the report from the Fort Detrick Level 4 lab. A shiver runs down her back as she turns the pages and reads its conclusion: *The virus is a coronavirus infected with DNA from Ebola, Lyme, and HIV. It is unlike any natural virus that we have ever seen. This is a created virus, intended for bioterrorism. Consider it deadly.*

Margaret rubs at a nagging ache behind her forehead. *Did the teams retrieve all the capsules? Did they take precautions?* She re-reads O'Neil's text and responds, *Please check in as soon as you get to your office.*

O'Neil stops by her office before going to his own. "Good morning, Madam President. Something serious, I assume."

"Thank you for coming here directly. Before I explain, I want you to know that I'm deeply relieved your tech could dismantle the missile control system on *The Emperor*. That gives us breathing room, and we need it. There's more to this mess than we knew initially."

She hands the Fort Detrick report to O'Neil. "Look at the last page of this analysis."

The Director's face tightens while he reads. "You want to know whether or not we have all the capsules?"

"That and more. Might the Chinese have used other means to spread the virus? This has happened under our noses, George. How? The traitors involved must've hidden in plain sight, which tells me we're dealing with enormously powerful people. How did they elude us? They must be citizens we trust or at least listen to. Don't you agree?"

"Unfortunately, I do. You're thinking elected officials or appointees or pharma or ... ?"

Margaret nods. "Exactly, any or all of those. I also wonder if these attacks are related to the elusive cabal. Could you check with your team working on that investigation? While you do so, I'll call the Secretary of Homeland Security and ask him to come to the Oval Office as soon as possible."

✻    ✻    ✻

O'Neil paces as he speaks with the CIA team leader. He learns that seven people, three of them Americans, are under surveillance. The FBI and European counterparts assist. The leader warns O'Neil of mounting chatter focused on *Operation One World*. "Much of the chatter is encoded and not easily deciphered, but we anticipate more attacks on the United States, within and outside the territorial boundaries."

O'Neil frowns. "What's their goal?"

"That's just it, there isn't one. From all that we've seen thus far, members within the cabal have competing interests—dangerous competing interests. They use each other. The CCP appears docile, for instance, but our read is that it plans to take over the world. As for pharma, well, it wants control of the world's population. So, while the CCP plans to destroy, pharma offers a means to do so. It works for both, but the objectives aren't the same. That's just one example."

"Prepare a report ASAP. I need to have it on my desk by the end of the day."

O'Neil's face contorts when the gravity of the situation hits him. He glances over at Margaret. She nods and says, "It's worse than what we thought, right?"

"Correct."

Margaret's voice lowers, "Well, it's better we know now than when we launch Operation Amira. Tell me what you found out."

O'Neil repeats what the team leader told him and as he concludes, Margaret reminds him of one indisputable fact: the cabal is unaware that others know of their plans. Then Margaret says, "There's power in force, but also victory in surprise. We will prevail, George. Step-by-step, we will defeat their depraved scheme."

O'Neil nods. "As one of those steps, do you want me to oversee the ambush of the terrorist cells?"

"Absolutely. Do you have men you can depend upon? Most likely, the terrorists will be heavily armed, and because of that, SWAT teams need to conduct the synchronized raids. All electronics must get confiscated, and everyone present—arrested. I'd like your men to conduct the questioning. We need names."

"Today?"

Margaret nods. "We have little time and must act quickly."

"And ... covertly."

"You read my mind."

"In this case, it's easy to do. I've made inroads within the FBI, but I'm not satisfied with where we are just yet. I'll take the lead on this and will work with five agents only; all are former SEALs. I'd trust any of them with my life."

Margaret turns at the sound of a knock on her door. She looks back at George, "You're part of my team." As she hands him a business card, she adds, "Call me after the sweep. Use the number on the back."

The Secretary enters the office with a pile of papers. "I came as quickly as I could. We have all five cells identified—locations and names of owners or renters."

"Excellent. I've asked Director O'Neil to take the lead on this, but before he leaves, do you have a copy of the cell information for him?"

"Yes, I have one for each of you."

"Perfect. Director O'Neil, we'll talk later. Let me know if I can help in any way."

Once O'Neil has left, Margaret focuses on the Secretary. She thanks him for his diligence and goes over the reports. "Your list of potential profiteers from a pandemic is insightful. I see you've also tracked travelers to Beijing. Excellent. We need to continue down that path."

# Chapter 54

*A*t 15:00 in a neighborhood in each of five designated cities (New York, Atlanta, Chicago, Dallas, and Denver), SWAT teams led by a former Navy SEAL surround and break through exterior doors. The surprise raids result in a roundup of eleven women and seventeen men. Three subversives suffered gunshot wounds, four sustained broken limbs, and others received minor injuries.

O'Neil calls Margaret, "Madam President, the sweeps were successful. In addition to twenty-eight arrests, most non-U.S.-citizens, we now have damning evidence against China. Given the number of toxins we retrieved, their intention was to destroy the United States."

"Great job, O'Neil. Let's meet in the morning after you've had a chance to process the information. Thank you for everything."

"My pleasure, ma'am."

"One last thing—how are the SEALs?"

"Home again."

"I thought as much. Hooyah!"

Margaret no sooner disconnects than a commotion develops outside the Oval Office, and a handgun discharges. Margaret reaches into her desk drawer for her revolver just as the Secret Service rushes in.

"Ma'am, we just apprehended a Chinese national, who got past the inspection station. He claims diplomatic immunity and demands to speak with you. One of our own got shot in the arm."

"Book him. I have no time for terrorists. Director George O'Neil can handle the case. Just a minute, I'll call him now." Margaret punches in the number. "O'Neil, a few minutes ago, a terrorist made an attempt on my life. Yes … that is the case. I need you to handle it … Sounds good … They're transporting the culprit now."

Margaret turns back to the Secret Service agents, "Cuff the guy, silence him, and get him over to Langley. Exit through the rear. Make sure you have a full detail accompanying you."

After they leave, Margaret looks at her secretary. "Are you okay?"

"I've been better."

"Just so you know, I keep a gun in my drawer, and it's loaded. I wouldn't hesitate to use it if needed. I will do all that I can to keep you safe, no matter what."

Margaret walks to the exit door and realizes that people have congregated in the hallway and stand comforting one another. They all straighten when they see her.

"My friends, I don't know how this assailant got past our security, but I promise you, I will find out. Already, I've ordered footage from all cameras in the immediate and surrounding area. One of our brave Secret Service members took a bullet in the arm. Thankfully, his wounds aren't serious, but this never should have occurred. We rely on a highly-reliable x-ray screening process, but somehow, it failed to flag this man's weapon. The Intelligence department will interview each of you, and if you saw or heard anything, please share it with the agents. We must get to the bottom of this. Does anyone have any questions?"

"Do you know why the man wanted to shoot you?"

"I have no idea. I know only that the prisoner is a Chinese national. Other questions?"

"Will you speak with the Chinese President?"

"I have no immediate intentions to do so. I shall wait for the Intelligence team to get back to me. Other questions?"

"Do you think this has anything to do with the military buildup in the South China Sea?"

"All things are possible, but as I've expressed, I don't know. I wish I could offer insight, but like you, I'm baffled as to why and how this occurred and feel shocked that our area was violated. I've asked the National Guard to show a presence everywhere until this matter gets resolved. Thank you, all."

Margaret strides back into her office, settles at her desk, and rests her head in her hands. O'Neil texts her: *Assassin had inside help. Stay alert. I'm on my way.*

Margaret retrieves her handgun and puts it into her jacket pocket. She calls to her secretary, "Please, go home now. It's after five, and you deserve a glass of wine."

Her secretary stands in the doorway. "I have a lot of work to do, but tonight, I *do* need that drink."

Margaret stands and gives the woman a hug. They walk into the hallway together. "See you tomorrow."

When her secretary leaves for the evening, Margaret returns to the Oval Office and locks the door. She turns around slowly, takes note of the location of chairs, bookcases, and tables, and takes inventory of decorative items both high and low. Mentally, the President practices defensive moves and fingers the gun in her pocket. She has no fear. She's ready.

A knock sounds at the door. Margaret refrains from responding. Instead, she mutes the volume on her phone and texts O'Neil: *Are you at my door?*

*I'll be there in 5. I'm outside.*

*Someone's knocking, wanting in.*

*Don't open the door. Don't respond in any way.*

Margaret sits in a chair and turns it toward the door. Laser-focused, she takes her gun and points it toward the office exit. No further knocks sound, but a voice calls, "Madam President, I need to talk with you. It's an emergency. Please … wait, stop … I can explain …"

Sounds of yelling and struggle ensue.

Then O'Neil shouts through the door, "Madam President, I'm here. I've taken your visitor into custody."

Margaret opens the door. "What's going on?"

"My guess is, and it's only a guess right now, word has spread about the raids, and the Chinese network has decided you're to blame."

"Modesty aside, they're right about that. How did this guy get in here?"

"He and his buddy were part of the last public tour. They picked up guns in the East Wing restroom, where they stayed until directed to make their move."

"Who's behind this? Who hid the weapons?"

"We'll find out as soon as we can. Whoever it is, I don't believe that he'll live for much longer. These guys will want to clean up."

"Keep me updated, day or night."

Margaret goes back into her office, replaces her gun in the drawer, and falls into her chair. A text arrives from O'Neil. "That was fast," she mutters.

*Ezekiel Straits. Minor player in the National Economic Council. Loner, researcher, assignment—China. Found dead in his car. Parking structure just off 17th street. Bullet to the head.*

# Chapter 55

*T*he following morning, the Secretary of Homeland Security rushes to meet with Margaret about an urgent matter. Seeing him at her door, she motions for him to enter.

"We have a problem, Madam President." Out of breath, he pants. "St. Louis reports an outbreak of an unknown virus. Eight people are hospitalized and are in critical condition."

"But … as far as we know, the Chinese didn't visit St. Louis. Right?"

"Yes and no. We tracked each patient, and all of them attended the St. Louis Cardinals game yesterday at Busch stadium. They sat in section 451 but not in proximity to one another. However, each person would have used the same side rails to traverse the stairs. We've now secured footage of two cleaning staff affixing something under the stair railings three hours before the game commenced. Local police have identified these individuals and know where they reside. They plan to storm the apartment within the hour."

"Make sure the Chief of Police understands that we're dealing with bioterrorism. His team needs to wear hazmat suits. I'll text O'Neil. Go."

The Secretary darts out, and Margaret texts O'Neil: *URGENT!*

He calls straight away, "Madam President?"

Margaret explains the situation. "We have no time. Local law enforcement is going in. Get your men in the air. We need eyes and feet on the ground."

"Copy that. I'll report back as soon as I have an update."

\*     \*     \*

A SWAT team storms a St. Louis apartment located near the University of Missouri. One assailant tries to escape and is fatally shot. Three others are detained. The lead detective calls O'Neil.

"We've found boxes and boxes of unidentified medication in capsules, which fit the description you gave. From the looks of things, this was their headquarters. They've affixed a large map to the wall with big cities circled: NYC, Atlanta, Denver, Chicago, Dallas, and St. Louis. Also, several west-coast cities have arrows directed to them."

"Which ones?"

"Seattle, Portland, San Francisco, Los Angeles, and San Diego."

"The arrows originate from where?"

"Well, that's odd. It appears to be a location midway between the Hawaiian and Alaskan islands. Nothing's there."

O'Neil grimaces. "What about technology?"

"We've confiscated computers and cell phones. I'll send intelligence as it emerges. A hazmat team is going through the dwelling now. The terrorists aren't talking, but they will. I can promise you that."

"Best news I've had all week. My men are in flight, military chopper. Keep the prisoners separate. Guards at their cells always. No contact with anyone except men you trust, and make sure your guys wear body cameras. Mark my words, there will be attempts on the prisoners' lives, and we must stay prepared. The United States is under siege. The country as we know it is at stake."

\*     \*     \*

Two hours later, O'Neil meets privately with the President and offers a preliminary report.

"Police found four terrorists at the residence. From what neighbors have told us, two more remain at large. Local detectives are pursuing leads and have the apartment under surveillance. During the raid, one individual succumbed to a fatal gunshot wound. We have the other three in custody in individual holding cells, guards at each one. Computers, cell phones, drones, and documents have been secured.

"Separately, we've airlifted the boxes of virus capsules to the Homeland Security Level 4 Lab in Manhattan, Kansas. Its scientists will work in concert with Fort Detrick, and they've issued recommendations of treatment protocols for the virus victims now admitted to Barnes-Jewish Hospital in St. Louis.

"Ma'am, this was a coordinated attack on the United States. My team has begun processing the information both on-site and within Langley. They now have intel that China deliberately intended to destroy our nation's infrastructure. Further, from the map we discovered, *The Emperor* was en route to take out major cities on the west coast. You'll be pleased to know that it now sits dead in the ocean. Our operative dismantled the missiles with a malicious worm and obliterated the supervisory control mechanisms."

"All right! Now we have something to celebrate."

"There's more, ma'am. The Chinese strike group in the South China Sea has backed off and appears to be headed for *The Emperor.*"

"Even better news. When we meet with the Chiefs, could you summarize these new developments?"

"Consider it done."

"There's something more I'd like you to consider, George. You don't need to respond immediately. Take the week and think it through."

"You have my interest, ma'am. What troubles you?"

Margaret shifts in her chair and looks straight at him. "I need to appoint a Vice President and thought you might help."

"I'll do what I can."

"The thing is, I'd like *you* to become my VP. I respect you and enjoy working with you. More importantly, I trust you, impeccably. You're an invaluable member of my team. I know you don't like politics, but neither do I. It's one of those evils that snap at our heels, and either we walk faster or give it a strong kick. It is what it is. So, would you mull over the possibility?"

"I could, but I don't need to, Madam President. There's no one I'd rather work with more than you."

Margaret's eyes soften. "You have a family and a life separate from the public eye. Take a few days to think about the offer. I'll need to address the House and Senate, and if you're not hiding any nasty secrets, I'm fairly sure you'll get confirmed."

George chuckles. "Ma'am, in contrast to the work I do, my home life is simple. Kids are normal, wife is beautiful. What more could they be interested in?"

"You never know. Most of the elected officials are decent people. Unfortunately, the minority runs the show. If you're like me, you'll find that your military training helps when confronted with irrationality. I remind myself daily to stay the course, no matter what." Margaret checks her watch. "We'd better leave. It's time to meet with the Chiefs."

# Chapter 56

When she enters the Sit Room, Margaret does a double-take. The Chiefs have pulled up interactive maps on the monitors and posted strategic military positions for both land and sea. When they see her, they stand at attention.

"Gentlemen, at ease." She looks around the room, breaks a smile, and nods to each of the Chiefs. "I'm impressed. It appears we're ready to begin. Before doing so, I'd like to offer a few thoughts and then have O'Neil explain what occurred at the close of day yesterday and what happened today.

"My thoughts are just a reminder. We intend to free the Syrian people from a tyrant who has tortured and killed thousands. We join with Russia, Turkey, and our other allies to end this atrocity and establish stability. Our mission is a humanitarian one. We will deliver Hassan and his associates to Germany for prosecution. Our goal is to accomplish this with minimal human toll. With these comments as a backdrop, Director O'Neil, please cover recent events."

The Director recounts the attempts on the President's life, then proceeds to explain how the electronics on *The Emperor* have been destroyed, resulting in China's strike group moving to its rescue. Finally, he tells the Chiefs about the virus outbreak in St. Louis and the discovery of the headquarters for China's biological warfare in the United States.

The Chairman's eyes narrow. Like a hawk considering its prey, he says, "This is a declaration of war."

"Yes, you've called it correctly," the President says. "We can begin World War III legitimately—we have all the justification we need. Alternatively, we can outsmart them at their own game, and perhaps save humanity from unimaginable horror.

"You're expert strategists. I ask you to focus on the latter option. We can do this. We know China wants to destroy us. We know China effectively owns Iran, Pakistan, Afghanistan, and other countries through debt that cannot be repaid. We know they now occupy the Gulf of Oman and have armies on the ground approaching the Strait of Hormuz. What they don't know is that we're aware of their game.

"Today, we gather to review and solidify a plan to stop China's assaults on the world permanently. Time is of the essence. We're four days from launch on Operation Amira. I need your support." Margaret looks squarely at the Chairman and the Chiefs. Slowly, they indicate approval.

"General?"

"We're on board, but we're in this to win." The corners of his lips turn up, just short of a real smile.

"Agreed. Now, let's discuss strategy."

The Chairman asks each Chief to report in. The Naval Operations Chief of Staff speaks first.

"Madam President, the U.S. Navy has a strong presence in the Persian Gulf, particularly with the USS Gerald R. Ford and the USS Bataan. Since Admiral Parker informed us of the carrier's software vulnerability, our team has worked 24-7 to rebuild the entire control system. We've now protected the ordnance and nuclear weaponry. Further, the USS Dwight D. Eisenhower arrived in the Mediterranean Sea yesterday. These strike groups are prepared to respond mercilessly to any attack. Additionally, because of recent occurrences, our Sailors and Marines have all been briefed about the potential for biological and chemical warfare. They stand prepared.

"Thank you, Chief. Are your officers aware of the operation?"

"No. I've informed them that we're concerned about the military buildup in Iran. They're set to act at a moment's notice, and all units are at FPCON Delta."

"Excellent. Thank you."

The Army Chief of Staff straightens in his seat. "Madam President, the Army stands ready. We have close to 70,000 troops surrounding Iran. Afghanistan holds our largest contingent because we're presently engaged there. We also have numerous divisions in Qatar and Kuwait. Of notable importance to our success is our base in Bahrain. In addition to troops, this base is also a Special Forces Operations Center.

"Moreover, it houses our warplanes and spy aircraft. We and our allies launch from the Bahrain base. The Army bases and installations are all at FPCON Delta.

"On another point, Iran's missile arsenal is substantial. As we've discussed, it claims to have missiles aimed at thirty-five of our bases in the region. With Turkey and Russia's assistance via their S-400 anti-aircraft missile systems, we can turn this around and eliminate Iran's dominance in the region. Turkey's and Russia's hypersonic missiles can breach all known defense systems."

"You can depend upon our allies, Chief. Tell me, please, are your officers aware of Operation Amira?"

"No, ma'am. They only have an awareness of the buildup and threat."

"Excellent."

The Air Force Chief of Staff and the Commandant of the Marine Corps each take their turn to explain preparations. When they complete their update, Margaret asks again whether any officers are aware of Operation Amira. Both Chiefs answer in the negative.

Margaret says, "Gentlemen, this offensive will, ultimately, save lives and create the possibility of peace in the Middle East. We walk a path that few have thought attainable. We will make believers of doubters. The element of surprise is critical to this operation. From all that's been said, we've maintained silence. The combatants know our locations, but they don't know about our alignment with Turkey and Russia. Nor are they aware of our intentions. This gives us a powerful advantage.

"Tomorrow, we'll have a satellite meeting with the Presidents of Turkey and Russia. We'll explain our approach and hear theirs. Separately, I've promised to meet with the Israeli Prime Minister. He wants to partner with us. I've not responded to him, or mentioned his offer to anyone, because I'd like to hear your thoughts."

The Chiefs stay silent as they exchange glances then give the nod to the Chairman, who speaks for the group. Margaret is attentive to their unspoken exchange.

"Ma'am, Israeli involvement could only strengthen our operation. Their military is well trained, their commandos much respected, and they have air power we may need. Besides, they know the adversaries and are always ready to engage. If they say they'll partner, they will."

"Just so I'm clear, you advise an alliance with Russia, Turkey, *and* Israel."

"Yes. There's still too much up in the air, and with it, a risk we cannot anticipate. With Israel's backing, some of that unknown eases."

"What troubles you, General?"

He looks at Margaret squarely and says, "We're just days from launch and don't know who will replace Hassan, how to restrain the Syrian Army, or what will occur at the Presidential Palace in Damascus. This, while we face an approaching Chinese offensive, an Iranian missile attack, and battles in the Persian Gulf."

"All right. Thank you." She looks around the room and notes the heaviness. "Before we begin, are there any other comments?"

O'Neil clears his throat. "Yes. We've had initial contact with General Abadi, the Syrian General I mentioned to you earlier. We now know he's interested and willing to assist. Nothing has been promised or arranged. The General and his men are in the Aleppo area, where he oversees several thousand men. He guarantees their support. I await your guidance, Madam President."

Margaret turns to the Chiefs, "Gentlemen, what are your thoughts?"

They signal their support, and the Chairman says, "Let's make it happen."

Margaret nods. "Director, at the close of our meeting, contact your operative. Tell him that the coup will occur in four days. Outline the plans within Operation Amira. Explain that his new superior will contact him once Hassan is in custody. One of his first tasks will be to release all prisoners at the military penitentiary. I'm sure he knows that slaughterhouse well. Tell him that any soldier who resists the General's leadership should be confined in one of the emptied cells. We'll deal with any dissenters later.

"Tomorrow, we shall ask Smirnov how and when he will tell his military leaders about the operation and what he intends to do to bring his Army on board."

Margaret takes a breath and realizes that the room remains silent, and all eyes focus on her.

She turns to Director O'Neil. "The specter in the room is China. Can you give us an update on your intel?"

"Of course. We're tracking Sino movements both on the ground and in the Persian Gulf. They appear to be headed for the Strait of Hormuz. We're checking for chatter involving biological weapons, but thus far, we've heard none."

"Good to know. Thank you. Chiefs, given our recent experiences, we must prepare for a biological attack. Secure as many tactical gas masks as you can, rehearse protocols with the troops, and take all precautions. Any further thoughts?"

The Army Chief of Staff says, "Our embassies are vulnerable, ma'am. Particularly Baghdad. We need to get our people out."

Margaret nods in agreement. "What are your thoughts?"

"We send in Special Forces under cover of night and move the officials into Turkey immediately."

"Agreed. Please, proceed." She turns to the group. "Let's get to work, gentlemen. I'd like to see our positions on land and sea, your assessment of strengths and weaknesses, and how you will coordinate the siege."

# Chapter 57

——————

*M*argaret can't sleep and spends the night pacing and going over and over each detail of the plan and then creating a list of questions and concerns. When Ivan FaceTime calls, just hearing his voice calms her.

"Margaret, darling, what's wrong?"

"I'm worried. Maybe I've forgotten something. Maybe I've miscalculated."

"Oh, now I understand. Listen to me carefully. Do you think the Joint Chiefs are foolish men?"

"Of course not."

"Do you imagine your Chiefs would send thousands upon thousands of their men and women down a rabbit trap of your making?"

"Ah, no."

"But you imagine that, somehow, you've set things in motion that will result in catastrophe. You, personally, against their better judgments, have forced them to act."

"When you put it that way, it sounds ridiculous. I'm not forcing them to do anything. In fact, they created the plan."

"Exactly. I guarantee that if your Chiefs thought you illogical or off-base, they would say so. You work with some of the best military strategists on the planet. If they tell you it's a go, trust them. They don't pull punches and mean what they say."

Margaret takes a deep breath. "You're right, of course."

"How can anyone think about war and not know fear? So much is unknown." Ivan pauses and looks at her tenderly. "Maybe after our satellite meeting, you and I could take some quiet time. What do you think?"

"That would make me incredibly happy. I'll arrange for it."

"All right, my love, I'll see you shortly."

＊　　＊　　＊

The satellite conference-call with Turkey, Russia, and Israel is scheduled for 08:00. At 07:30, Margaret meets with the Joint Chiefs of Staff and the Director of National Intelligence to go over the most recent intelligence.

"I've loaded the aerial footage of China's advancing caravan," O'Neil says. "See screen three."

They watch intently for a few minutes, and then the Chairman shouts, "Stop it there!" The Chiefs rise and move to the display. "This is the evidence we needed. The Chinese are transporting ballistic and cruise missiles. Their goal can only be to destroy our strike group and, most likely, our bases in Bahrain and Qatar. China wants to cripple our defenses. This means Iran plans a full attack. Madam, we've just moved from coup to World War III."

Margaret's eyes widen, and her face pales. "What do you suggest?"

"We need to stop China."

"I ... ah ... I didn't expect this."

"Let me explain something, Madam President. Had you not fallen in love with an orphan and become alert to Hassan's reign of terror, and then decided to join with other nations to remove the Hassan regime, China and Iran would probably have caught us off-guard. We wouldn't have been prepared, as we are now, for the onslaught of their fury. Because of the steps we've taken, our task is a strategic one, not a hopeless defensive one. And, our greatest advantage is that it is WE who will surprise the enemy."

Margaret's jaw tightens. "Thank you, Chairman. Strategic we must be."

"I'm not one to spout things like this—" the Chairman says. "—but if anything counts as a miracle, this is one for the books. A mere child led us here, and because of her, we will be victorious."

The tri-country conference-call activates and interrupts the conversation. Margaret waits until all three leaders appear on the screen.

"Welcome, President Smirnov, President Ozdemir, and Prime Minister Fisher. Before we deliberate on Operation Amira, my team and I would like to offer an important update.

"Over these last few days, Chinese nationals have made two assassination attempts on my life. Six attacks involving biological weapons have struck at America's citizens—again perpetrated by Chinese nationals. Further, China launched its new cruise ship, *The Emperor*, bound for Seattle. Because of intel from Russia's Special Forces, we've learned it carries ballistic missiles. Our Intelligence division had an operative introduce an electronic worm and disable the ship and its weapons. It now sits somewhere in the Pacific.

"Most relevant for today's discussion is the information we have about the Chinese Army crossing the Pakistani and Iranian southern border, possibly headed for the Strait of Hormuz. We'd like to share that with you now." Margaret plays the video and watches the leaders' faces change from simple interest to pointed determination.

"From your expressions, you've drawn the same conclusions. We assume that China's goal is to eliminate the American carrier group and our bases in Bahrain and Qatar. Their overall objective? We suspect their actions are meant to cripple our defenses. If so, China and Iran plan a full attack.

"Gentlemen, it is the opinion of our military Chiefs that we no longer deal only with Operation Amira but face another World War. We have one invaluable weapon—the aggressors remain unaware of our partnership."

Prime Minister Fisher says, "First of all, thank you for your confidence in Israel. I'm honored to align with you for this operation. I agree with you, Madam President, on all points, but I'd like to add that since Iran is massively in debt to China, it is the latter who is the primary aggressor. This is a battle of biblical proportions, and Israel is obligated to do its part.

"As agreed, we've prepared to test a new intermediate-range ballistic missile over the Mediterranean the day before the operation. But, given this new information, I question the wisdom of such an act. It will elicit a response, that's true, but we may not have time for exercises. When we last talked, I also mentioned strikes against Hezbollah. I now believe we shouldn't do that because it could precipitate an early offensive from Iran and compromise the operation. I would like your guidance. We will ready our fighter jets and stand prepared to strike as needed. Our Special Forces are stationed across the region already and on permanent alert."

President Smirnov clears his throat. "Madam President and gentlemen, I hadn't expected this turn of events. Were it not for our collective decision to remove Hassan, we would remain wholly unprepared. Horrifying thought! Think of what that would mean for our people, our countries.

"Russia has thousands of troops in Syria. The day before launch, our officers will be alerted to the plan and will act quickly against the Syrian Army and any of its invading allies. I shall direct our Special Forces to infiltrate and provide intel that might guide our actions. Our aircraft, ships, and submarines stand ready. We'll deploy our S-400 in concert with Turkey's to eliminate Iran's missile silos. Finally, if China escalates, Russia commits to use the Avangard hypersonic glide vehicle. It's invulnerable, undetectable, and deadly."

President Ozdemir says, "Like my colleagues, I find myself utterly surprised at developments. Given how the situation has unfolded, I believe the United States *isn't* the only target. Smirnov, did you know anything of this before today?"

"No, nothing at all."

"And yet Russia has been a close ally of Syria. In fact, you even train its military. Correct?"

"Yes."

"You don't find it odd that you've heard nothing?"

Smirnov sits in silence. His face contorts while he considers the implications of Ozdemir's question. Finally, he says, "China wants control of the Middle East. It wants the oil."

Ozdemir nods. "And you, my friend, are in the way. It's not just oil they want, but also the bases and ports. Those 99 years they promised you for the use of Tartus, forget it.

"Iran makes a convenient bully for China to hide behind. We all know of Iran's deadly force, but I ask you, who provides Iran with its military prowess? So, China advances without attention, but it leaves a trail of death and destruction. It wants the oil, all of it. Russia is in the way, which tells me they've planned meticulously. But what about Saudi Arabia? Why take your missiles, troops, and airpower through Pakistan and ignore the Saudis? Does China have a strike group in the Arabian Sea? Has anyone seen any activity in Yemen? Kuwait? Iraq?"

Margaret motions to the National Intelligence Director and the Joint Chiefs of Staff to check.

Ozdemir shifts in his seat and looks at each of the leaders. "None of us expected this turn of events. Yet, here we are, and civilization needs us. Turkey will deliver Hassan and his associates to German authorities. We feel proud to do so. We'll also position our S-400s for firing at either Iranian missile sites or Chinese caravans. Smirnov and I will coordinate. Additionally, Turkey has thousands of troops at Syria's border and within Syria itself. We're ready to attack the Syrian Army and any intruding force aligned with that nation."

The sudden silence seems deafening, and then the Director of National Intelligence speaks, "My agents just texted. Our drones have filmed two Chinese Y-20s landing in Pasni, Pakistan. One delivered tanks and artillery, the other troops. We've also tracked a Chinese carrier group as it moved from the South China Sea to the Indian Ocean. I'm sure your intelligence has reported the same. For our part, we assumed this movement was related to the current tensions between India and China. I think we got that wrong. The strike group has now arrived in the Arabian Sea and approaches Oman. Just as alarming, two Chinese nuclear ballistic missile subs have entered the Gulf of Aden near Yemen. Per your request, I will have a report on Iraq and Kuwait imminently."

"Thank you, Director. The U.S. will prepare its F-22 Raptor fighters in Dubai and Qatar for attack. Our strike groups wait in position, both in the Mediterranean and the Persian Gulf. Our cruise missile-armed submarines also wait in place. The U.S. has about 1500 Marine and Special Operations Forces in both Iraq and Syria. And should we decide it necessary, we're ready to deploy B-2 Stealth bombers from the mainland."

"Madam President," the Director says. "I have another text from our agent working with General Abadi, the Syrian officer we discussed. Abadi told him of a stockpile of chemical and biological weapons stored beneath the St. Francis Church in Aleppo—enough to wipe out an entire country. He also claims that a tunnel runs from the church to a location near the Turkish border."

In clear view on the screen, Smirnov smacks his fist onto his desk. "Our Army is headquartered in Aleppo. Hassan plans to take them out. I'll have our Special Forces check on this immediately."

"I want my Commandos to accompany," Ozdemir says. "Let's talk after this and coordinate. I want to see what this bastard's got planned."

Margaret says, "Gentlemen, it seems we're all prepared. However, we plan to launch the day after Ramadan and, from all appearances, China and Iran will attack at the same time. Hassan, it seems, will come at us from within. Given all that we now know, should we commence Operation Amira a day earlier, on the final day of Ramadan?"

Smirnov says, "Our destroyer has cleared the Suez Canal and will dock at Tartus tomorrow morning. I agree to an earlier start. As for Hassan being an active player, I admit to having had my reservations. This past week, Hassan indulged my requests and even suggested a celebration at our base in Aleppo after the destroyer's launch. That struck me as out of character for him. Now, I'm sure he's planning something, and I suspect it involves chemical and or biological weapons. At least now, I can prepare."

The leaders deliberate for three hours, and together with the Chiefs, they craft a detailed strategic plan and establish Turkey's Incirlik Air Base as the Command Center. They partition the Middle East into sections and assign primary responsibility for each of those areas between Turkey, Israel, Russia, and the United States. The team maps out backup schemes for each component of the operation, and by the time the meeting concludes, each leader takes a list of tasks they must complete. Each of the four leaders is a military veteran. Each knows the reality of war. And each knows the uncertainty, fear, and devastation. But this is the first time they lead their military into a battle of this enormity.

A hush settles upon the team like a thick fog over a graveyard. Each person appreciates what they must accomplish. Every step must be chosen carefully, lest the ghosts of old awaken.

# Chapter 58

The Joint Chiefs of Staff and the Director of National Intelligence linger after the meeting. Margaret needs to call the Crown Prince of Saudi Arabia, and the leaders will assist with any questions that might arise.

"Madam President, I hadn't expected a call so soon after our last meeting."

"Nor had I, your Royal Highness. But a matter of extreme urgency has arisen."

"Please explain."

Margaret brings the Prince up to date and then focuses on her immediate concern. "The United States is collaborating with Turkey, Israel, and Russia to remove Hassan and deliver him to German authorities. We four leaders concluded a lengthy meeting a few minutes ago. We now realize that the situation has grown much more serious.

"We have surveillance of a heavily-armed Chinese force approaching the Strait of Hormuz. Two Chinese Y-20s have landed in Pasni, Pakistan, with payloads of artillery and soldiers. This discovery led us to—"

The Crown Prince grimaces and says, "To realize that China wants our oil."

"Yes. My military team then checked the area for further Sino incursions. We identified a Chinese carrier strike group in the Arabian Sea near Oman and two Chinese nuclear ballistic missile subs near Yemen."

"Do you have the coordinates?"

"Yes. I'll send them now." She nods to the National Intelligence Director, and he gets busy at his computer terminal.

After a few moments, the Prince says, "Received. Thank you. Please, continue."

"We also have evidence that Syria has joined with Iran and China. We assume its allies have done likewise. In which case, we stand at the brink of World War III.

"Had it not been for our intended operation, all of us would have been caught off-guard. Because of what we now know, we must launch an attack preemptively one full day earlier than intended so that it hits on the last day of holy Ramadan."

"Allah does not forbid a just war during the holy days. This is a war we must lodge. You mentioned your plan. May I have a copy? Saudi Arabia will get ready."

"Your Royal Highness, I'll transmit the information now. It is, of course, highly classified."

The Prince responds within seconds, "The packet has arrived. You can trust us impeccably. We will be prepared."

Margaret continues, "After our meeting, I'll alert our military leadership at the Prince Sultan Air Base. We'll ready our Patriot missiles for deployment, and also our troops and aircraft. I shall ensure they work in concert with you. Should we bring in the Stealth bombers?"

"Yes. We cannot over-prepare for a battle such as this."

"Two will arrive tomorrow."

After the call ends, Margaret takes a deep breath and turns to her team. "Gentlemen, there are a couple of important matters for us to settle. First, who will assume command at Incirlik?"

"Madam President," the Chairman says. "Because of the operation's complexity, we suggest multiple Commanders: The Chief of Staffs of the Army, Naval Operations, and Air Force."

"Excellent. After our meeting, prepare to leave immediately. Now to my second concern. To date, I haven't involved the Secretary of Defense or Congress. I need to do so now. Do you have any reservations about sharing the plan with them?"

The silence and side-glances alert Margaret to a problem.

O'Neil speaks for the group, "The Secretary of Defense is a political appointment. While he does have limited military training, he's never served in combat and wouldn't understand the critical nature of classified information. My recommendation is to delay talking with him until the actual launch. As for Congress, you might express concern over the military buildup we've detected and offer assurances that we won't attack unprovoked."

Margaret studies each of the Chiefs and realizes that they share O'Neil's perspective.

"Thank you. I will inform the Secretary just before we commence." She notices relief cross their features and decides to investigate why this is the case after the operation has concluded.

"Gentlemen, we are adjourned. Chairman and Director, I'd like to meet with you tomorrow morning. Same time, same place."

As Margaret gathers her files, she notices a text from Ivan. *My love, could we talk?*

She responds, *Yes, please call in 30 minutes.* Then Margaret notifies her assistant that she is taking time for lunch at her quarters.

# Chapter 59

The Russian and Turkish Special Forces teams meet at the St. Francis Church in Aleppo. They tell the parish priest that they need to examine the basement. The priest leads the way, and the officers discover a locked door. The priest explains that President Hassan keeps his most prized possessions there. He doesn't have a key and has never seen inside. A couple of soldiers break down the door and uncover an underground tunnel that leads to a cavern split into six rooms filled with vast stockpiles of chemical and biological weapons.

A track runs down the center of the underground cavern. Piles of rock at the sides of the rails indicate the cave was originally used for mining phosphate. Each team leader contacts their Commander and explains the discovery. Turkey's Commander tells his team to follow the tunnel to its terminus. The Russian Commander orders his men to stand guard within the church's confines and allow no one to approach.

The priest stands to the side, white-faced. Chemical weapons killed many of his parishioners. He now realizes that the church they trusted to save them also housed the deadly toxins.

"You cannot speak about this to anyone," the Special Forces leader tells the priest.

The priest looks at him with shock. "I will tell no one. How could I? But I plead that these vile weapons be removed from the church grounds."

"In time, Father, in time. We'll begin the extraction soon. Until then, talk to no one about what you've seen. In the wrong hands, this stockpile could destroy all of Syria."

*   *   *

Ivan receives the information minutes after the discovery by Spetsnaz, his Special Forces team. He shakes his head in disgust. *Hassan planned to kill me and all my men. He has just made my task an easier one.*

He calls Margaret. "Hello, my love. I've just received confirmation of the chemical and biological weapons housed under the St. Francis Church. It's worse than I'd imagined."

"Will you say anything to Hassan?"

"No. I've ordered Special Forces to stand guard within the structure and to hold firm. Unless Hassan's people go into the building, they should see no evidence of our intrusion. If the Syrian military notices anything, I'll tell Hassan that we've received threats and that I've taken extra precautions. I don't want anything to disrupt the destroyer's launch ceremony."

Margaret offers Ivan a tired smile. "Very believable."

Ivan's tone changes, "The reason I wanted to talk with you privately has nothing to do with Hassan or the operation per se. I just needed to tell you that I love you. I leave in the early morning for Tartus, where Operation Amira will commence officially. I know you believe in prayer. Please, keep my men and me in your supplications. This first step is critical. If Hassan backs out of joining us on the destroyer, the whole operation will fail."

"Even if Hassan doesn't cooperate, your sharpshooters atop the conning tower are at the ship's highest point. Probably, you have snipers on other vessels as well. From those heights, and with their skill, how can the operation fail? Dead or alive, Hassan will be gone."

Ivan shakes his head and smiles. "You amaze me. So it shall be, dead or alive. My precious spouse, I will call you before I leave for the airport, and before you fall asleep tonight in your bewitching sheer nightgown."

Margaret laughs and says her goodbyes. She picks up her papers, kisses Amira's photo, and heads back to the Oval Office.

# Chapter 60

The blare of pulsing sirens alerts everyone in the West Wing of a potential attack. Margaret, the Chairman, and Director O'Neil are meeting in the Situation Room when the alarms sound. Secret Service agents rush into the room.

"Per protocol, we're on lockdown, ma'am. There have been two incidents on the west coast. You need to look at the monitor."

Margaret's phone alerts her to a text from the base Commander at Vandenberg AFB. *Madam President, there's an incoming missile. Appears to be Chinese. We're launching an anti-ballistic rocket now.*

All heads turn toward the live feed. The anti-ballistic missile system at Vandenberg Air Force Base in California successfully shoots down an incoming intercontinental ballistic missile. A reporter shares cellphone coverage of the blast that lit up the early morning sky and broke windows in the area, and then states, "We have no reports of injuries."

Margaret gets a second alert on her phone and shares it with the Chairman and O'Neil. It comes from General Taylor, the Commander at Begert Air Force Base. *Madam President, a Chinese ballistic missile penetrated our air space. We neutralized it with the PATRIOT missile defense system. China has threatened our base multiple times. It instigated Admiral Parker's near assassination. I await your direction.*

"Gentlemen, China's recklessness leaves me speechless. They know we'll respond, and with force. Oddly, I believe they want us to do so. It doesn't make sense unless they wish to distract us from their invasion in the Middle East. Your thoughts?"

The Chairman says, "It's a tactical move. China has positioned itself for the real battle. However, we can't ignore this. We must respond."

"Agreed," O'Neil says. "Can we delay by demonstrating outrage and calling for an immediate investigation? Perhaps, we can send another carrier strike group into the Pacific?"

Margaret receives yet another text and says, "I have a lineup waiting to meet with me—the Secretary of Defense, the Speaker of the House, and the Senate Majority Leader. As soon as this lockdown lifts, I need to go." She texts her secretary and advises that she will arrive as soon as the Secret Service permits her to do so.

When the alarm signals that the lockdown is over, Margaret stands to leave. "Gentlemen, it is still your position that it's best not to discuss Operation Amira?" She notes their nods. "Okay, then."

She heads for her office.

"Good morning, Mr. Secretary, Madam Speaker, Majority Leader. I believe my first appointment is with the Secretary of Defense." With a nod to the Secretary, Margaret invites him into her office.

"I've just received word of the two airspace penetrations. Do you have more details for me?"

Margaret listens to the Secretary and realizes why her Chiefs advised her to remain silent about Operation Amira. The Secretary, a young man with high ambitions, wants a show of strength, along with press conferences and TV interviews. The missile attacks offer a platform for him.

Margaret keeps her features carefully neutral. "Could you represent me? I believe an in-person visit to Vandenberg and Begert is vital. I just met with the Chairman of the Joint Chiefs and the Director of National Intelligence. They report a Chinese build-up in the Middle East. I'm not sure what's going on, but a full investigation is required. We need to get to the bottom of this. Until we know, definitively, who orchestrated the assaults, and why, it's vital to refrain from divulging details. Just tell the Commanders 'the investigation is ongoing.' Also, please consult with the Navy about the possibility and wisdom of deploying an additional carrier strike group into the South China Sea. We can't be too careful."

"I totally agree, ma'am. You can trust me. I'm thorough and will keep you informed of my every step."

Margaret stands and extends her hand. "It was good speaking with you, Mr. Secretary. I'll await your call."

After the Secretary leaves, Margaret sends a quick text to the Chairman and O'Neil. *I now understand your reservations about the Secretary of Defense. I'm sending him to California to visit the two bases.*

O'Neil responds: *Well done, Madam President. I have good news: our Ambassador in Iraq, and his support team, have crossed into Turkey safely. They travel via military transport to Incirlik.*

Margaret texts: *What a relief. Thank you for letting me know.*

Margaret checks her watch. Ivan should have landed in Tartus. She sends a formal text. *Mr. President, could we meet via satellite?*

Ivan replies within seconds: *I'm on a diplomatic visit to Syria. Once I return to Moscow, my staff will contact you for a video link-up.*

Margaret smiles and then invites the leaders of the House and Senate to join her in the Oval Office.

They both express their concerns about the Chinese offensives and want to know what action the President plans to take. Margaret explains that the Secretary of Defense is headed to California to meet with the base Commanders and investigate each incident. "Additionally, I've authorized the launch of another carrier to the South China Sea. Once we obtain clarity about the enemy, we'll have the opportunity to respond directly."

She sits forward in her chair. "There is something more I wish to discuss. This morning, I met with the Chairman of the Joint Chiefs of Staff and the Director of National Intelligence. Both provided evidence of a military build-up in the Middle East that alarms us. Our allies have expressed concern too. Though I don't know the reasons for the increased activity, I suspect the intentions are sinister. As a precaution, our ambassador in Baghdad has relocated to Turkey. Our bases operate on high alert."

The Senate Majority Leader says, "Do you expect an attack?"

Margaret nods. "I do, especially given this morning's scare. However, I don't yet know when, where, or how. I can't even say whether or not America is the specific target. That said, we can't be too careful. I want to assure you that we'll respond defensively to any attack. At the same time, we will not act unprovoked. From all that I've been told, we're well-positioned."

The Speaker of the House says, "You have my support. You're not asking to declare war but attempting to avoid it. Our soldiers must respond if threatened."

"I agree wholeheartedly," the Senate Majority Leader says. "It heartens me to know we've moved our ambassador out of harm's way. We can only hope the action proves unnecessary."

The President stands and walks with the leaders to the door. "It's a privilege working with you both. Together, we'll emerge victorious." They shake hands and as they leave, the President turns to her assistant and says, "Please get Admiral Joseph Parker on the phone."

Margaret sits at her desk when the call arrives.

"Admiral, it's good to hear your voice."

"And yours as well. How can I help you, Madam President?"

"You've helped more than you imagine. When you alerted the Chief of Naval Operations to the software vulnerability in the USS Gerald R. Ford, he promptly ordered the reengineering of the entire system within the ship. Because of your actions, we can now respond to any threat that might arise in the Persian Gulf."

"And you anticipate threats, don't you?"

"Given the tensions that exist, anything is possible."

"Madam President, were I younger, I'd consider it an honor to serve under your command—particularly in that theater."

"Why there, Admiral?"

"The Middle East is critical to the world's energy needs. Everyone wants their oil, and as the demand rises, so will the conflict. What better place to serve than in an area torn apart by greed and ideology? Who knows, maybe we can make a difference."

Margaret smiles and nods. "Admiral, I work with an impressive team, and I consider you an integral member of that team. We're both being careful about what we do and don't say. I'd like to remedy that. Later this summer, I'd feel honored if you and Julie joined me for dinner at the White House."

Parker chuckles, "Yes, I suspect we do tiptoe around some topics. A conversation over dinner sounds like a great solution. Julie and I look forward to any opportunity to meet with you, Madam President."

"All right then, dinner it is. We can discuss the Middle East in depth at that time, as well as that mysterious meeting in Lofoten. My assistant will work with you in terms of a date. Until then, stay well, my friend. Ciao!"

# Chapter 61

*I*van arrives at the Tartus naval base in the early afternoon. Formations of sailors line the road leading to the harbor and stand at attention. The Commander of the fleet greets him with a salute and then leads him to the new destroyer. The two walk through the ship and talk about the next day's ceremony. After the briefing, Ivan asks if they could go to a quiet place to speak freely. The Commander takes him to the deck off the control center.

As he looks out over the Mediterranean Sea and breathes deeply of the warm ocean breeze, Ivan talks about Operation Amira. The Commander listens intently, asks only a few questions, and then responds.

"Mr. President, I've long hoped for a resolution to the Syrian crisis. The people are the victims, and they deserve better. You've given me hope in mankind, and I feel proud to serve under your leadership. I'll have everything prepared for the mission, including locked rooms and guards for the prisoners. We'll position sharpshooters in the destroyer's conning towers and that of its sister ship in the yard. The snipers won't miss their mark, should their skill become necessary."

"I trusted you'd have everything in place," Ivan says. A call from Hassan interrupts their conversation. "Excuse me just a minute, Commander, I need to take this."

Ivan grimaces and then offers greetings to his adversary. Hassan tells him of the buffet reception he's planned. Dutifully, Ivan expresses his gratitude and arranges to meet at 08:00 tomorrow. Then the Russian President turns to the Commander. "I'll need a handgun. Can you secure one for me?"

"Certainly, sir. I'll have a weapon to you within the hour." The Commander stands deep in thought as he stares out at the sea. With a slight turn of the head and a twinkle in his eyes, he says, "I'll enjoy tomorrow's journey more than others. There's nothing more satisfying than justice."

Ivan spends the night in the officer's quarters of the new destroyer. He thinks of his father, of his last courageous act, and decides that whatever lies ahead, he'll face it with the same fearlessness. Ivan sends Ozdemir a formal text before retiring, saying he looks forward to meeting him soon. After that, he messages Margaret and tells her that he will get in touch about her request for a meeting.

A knock rattles his door. Ivan peers through the peephole. When he greets the officer, the Commander hands him a semi-automatic pistol. With a salute, the man says, "Your Grach and ammunition, sir."

Ivan fingers the gun and returns the salute. "Commander, stay the course, no matter what Hassan's reaction might be tomorrow."

"Absolutely."

Before retiring, Ivan loads the weapon. It's been a while since he handled a Grach, but his instincts take over, and he feels at ease. Ivan lays on top of his bed and runs through each step of the mission.

At daybreak, Ivan rises and dons his dress uniform. He carries the side-arm in his pocket, under his jacket. In front of the mirror, he adjusts his cap and decides he's ready. He walks out onto the deck, where the Commander greets him.

"Mr. President, everything is in place. I've arranged for a show of strength with a line of armed sailors, three persons deep, on either side of the street leading to the port. Once Hassan and his entourage come into sight, our Navy band will play the National Anthem. I'll introduce the festivities and then ask Hassan to speak. When he finishes, I'll introduce you. Upon your final words, I shall step forward and explain that we're headed out to sea for our test voyage. We'll pull away from the dock immediately."

The band begins playing, and all on board the destroyer stand at attention. "It must be time, Mr. President."

Ivan acknowledges the Commander and walks over to welcome Hassan as he approaches in his limousine. The Syrian President climbs aboard the ship and exchanges pleasantries with Ivan. Everyone grows quiet when the Commander goes to the microphone.

"This is a time of celebration for the Russian Navy. We've looked forward to this day for quite some time. Our new destroyer strengthens the protection we can bring to the Syrian people. We feel deeply grateful to President Smirnov for his leadership and generosity, and we remain indebted to President Hassan for the use of this port and our continued friendship. President Hassan, could you, please, offer a few words?"

Hassan thanks the Russian military for their assistance in quelling the uprising, and then he thanks President Smirnov for his friendship over the last few years. He concludes by congratulating the Commander for his new destroyer and states that he hopes it never needs using in combat.

The Commander asks President Smirnov to come forward. Ivan adjusts the mic to his height and explains the pride he feels for his Navy. He mentions his gratitude to Syria and his fervent hopes that the discord between nations has resolved at last. Loud applause ensues.

The Commander shakes Smirnov's hand and steps in front of the microphone one more time. He explains that they will now take a brief cruise up the coast and then return for a buffet reception provided by President Hassan. He directs the band to play and motions for all those listening to join in singing Kalinka. Shouts of joy rise as the band plays the well-known tune. Some grab a partner and dance to the music. Others clap and kick up their feet rhythmically. All appear joyous except Hassan, who seems agitated.

"I need to get off the ship," Hassan says to Smirnov. But Ivan shakes his head and raises his shoulders as if to imply that he can't hear. Hassan yells, "I want off this vessel, now."

Smirnov signals again that he can't hear over the noise.

Hassan gesticulates wildly and fumbles for his phone when the ship clears the port.

Smirnov looks at the Commander. They both realize that foul play is afoot, and with Smirnov's nod, the Commander disappears to check for sabotage.

While dancing sailors crowd the deck, and the band plays the familiar tune, the Commander and his officers inspect the destroyer for explosives. The day before, one of Hassan's men installed a direct line to their President. Because of this, the Commander orders that the communication center gets checked first.

Hidden behind the console, under a maze of wires and transmitters, a single timer counts down to a hellish end. Hurriedly, the officers dismantle the trigger and track its death-dealing charge. Once removed, the Commander looks at his men. "Stay the course. We will play this cat-and-mouse game until we receive orders to do otherwise. Stay alert. Be brave. We will prove victorious."

When the Commander returns to the festivities, he signals Smirnov. With a slight nod, Smirnov has Hassan and his two statesmen handcuffed. The three fight the guards but unsuccessfully. The sailors take the prisoners below deck and put them into separate locked rooms.

Hassan demands his release. "You will pay for this," he shouts while he pounds on the door. "The fires of hell will rain down on you."

Smirnov texts Ozdemir. *We're ready. Three passengers.*

When the vessel nears Cape Apostolos Andreas, the northern-most tip of Cypress, two Turkish military helicopters approach, accompanied by fighter jets. One lands, and the other hovers in place. The Russian guards gag each prisoner, put cloth bags over their heads, and take them to the chopper. Ivan watches as they clear the horizon and then gazes at the Commander. "Well done. Now it begins. Stay focused and alert."

The second helicopter lands to collect Ivan and his Secret Service team.

Ivan's helicopter reaches altitude, but a crackling voice from the destroyer's communications system comes over the radio. The Commander shouts, "Incoming! Incoming!"

A loud explosion follows his warning. Sonic waves rock the chopper violently and send it into a spin. The pilots regain control but with zero visibility. Thick, dark red smoke blinds them. Another radio transmission reaches them. Though static breaks it up, they hear, "… missile … neutralized. Thank you, Israel."

As soon as the chopper lands at Incirlik Air Base, Ivan rushes to the Command Center. The American Chiefs of Staff and Turkey's military leadership focus on a large screen that shows a collage of camera feeds. Ozdemir stands to the side, talking on the phone with the Israeli Prime Minister. Ozdemir thanks the Israeli PM for his help.

Ivan signals he'd like to take the phone. Ozdemir gives him the handset. "You saved my destroyer, Prime Minister. Thank you. I'm ready to return the gesture."

After the call, the two Presidents stand shoulder-to-shoulder and study the screen.

"It's good we're friends, Smirnov."

Ivan offers a side-glance and a nod. "Da."

"When this is over, let's talk about the cabal."

Ivan turns and faces Ozdemir. "You're aware of them?"

"Of course," Ozdemir snaps. "Their tentacles stretch far into the Middle East. And now is the perfect time to dismantle them."

"Let's include Adler. Her CIA and other teams have information that could help us. Between our three countries, we'll get the job done."

An urgent phone call interrupts their conversation. The American Commander at the Prince Sultan Air Base tells the Chiefs of Staff that China's subs in the Red Sea have crossed into the Saudi territorial waters.

"The Saudis ask that we deploy the Patriot missiles. They believe—and I believe—a Chinese strike is imminent."

After a brief consult between the Chiefs, the order is given. "Deploy the Patriots."

When the rockets strike the subs, an immense fireball lights the expanse of desert and sea. An iconic mushroom cloud rises into the blue heavens far above. The Commander takes a step back with a horrified expression contorting his features. He realizes what this means. The Chinese had planned a nuclear attack—so much worse than a third World War.

The Commander sends an urgent message to the Joint Chiefs. *China intended a nuclear attack on the Saudis. Expect the same in the Persian Gulf.*

✳    ✳    ✳

The Joint Chiefs confer and deploy the B-2 Stealth bomber. They notify the military leadership at Qatar and tell them to take all precautions. Then they order the strike on China's carrier group, which has moved dangerously close to that area.

The monitors show live operations. Over sand dunes and oil refineries, the B-2 bomber carries its deadly cargo. The two pilots activate the satellite-guided missiles and begin the countdown to when they must detonate. With the target visible and the payload ready, they discharge.

The first missile hits the carrier, next the cruiser, and then the two destroyers. Shockwaves travel across the horizon, breaking windows and sending people running. Huge mushroom clouds rise, announcing the defeat of the aggressor's dreams. Higher and higher the clouds travel and take center stage. The Middle East has awakened. Life can no longer be as it was.

At the Command Center, trepidation silences all who watch the drama unfold on the screen. None of them have ever seen such a sight, and they shudder at the ramifications. Turkey acts first and directs the S-400 precision-guided munitions at Iran's two largest missile silo complexes. Russia follows its lead and aims its S-400 missiles into two more silos and strikes Iran's uranium stockpile. Like dominoes lined up in a sequence, a chain reaction ignites.

Under General Abadi, the Russian and Syrian troops storm the military penitentiary and release political prisoners tortured for their beliefs, while incarcerating the guards who administered the pain. They then rush into the Presidential Palace, fend off heavily-armed guards, and arrest all those working for Hassan. F-22 Raptors fly overhead and provide reconnaissance while they attack enemy tanks and artillery deployments.

Separately, Israelis bombard the Iran-backed Hezbollah strongholds in Lebanon, while Saudis hit the Houthi rebels in Yemen. Meanwhile, the now-vacant American embassy in Baghdad burns to the ground to the shouts of glee from the Quds Force, part of the Iranian Islamic Revolutionary Guard Corps. As the crowd's fury intensifies, the sky darkens with swarms of American and Israeli fighter planes. With deadly force, the jets deliver one hit after another to the Iranian embassy, also in Baghdad, until only rubble remains.

In the Persian Gulf, the USS Bataan takes fire from an Iranian destroyer and responds aggressively. Bataan's attack jets scramble and lift-off the ship to dump GPS-guided bombs on the destroyer, but not before a missile hits a conning tower on the Bataan. Along with attack helicopters, the bombers move to Iran's tank brigade, which approaches the shoreline rapidly. They deploy a battery of missiles and terminate the Iranian military advancement. Amphibious vehicles from the Bataan head to shore with 2,000 Marines. Israeli fighter jets join the American planes and, together, they clear a path for the Marines.

The USS Gerald R. Ford strike group enters the Strait of Hormuz. Its airborne jets expect to engage. Two ballistic missiles penetrate the airspace. The Patriot anti-ballistic missile system in Dubai intercepts the rockets. F-22 Raptor bombers storm the sky. They head for coordinates south of Jiroft and assail the target with successive strikes. Like an eruption of Mount Vesuvius, flames and debris shoot high and scorch the once-blue sky.

While the battle in the Persian Gulf escalates, a Chinese nuclear-armed strike group approaches the USS Theodore Roosevelt carrier group in the Pacific Ocean. Command Center personnel spot the two carrier groups, and then watch as jets and helicopters take off from each U.S. ship and Sailors disappear below deck. Moments later, the dark shadow of the B-2 Stealth bomber spreads across the carrier. In rapid succession, the bomber discharges and hits each Chinese vessel. The explosions send tsunami-sized waves north and south. Fireballs shoot into the stratosphere, and then consuming mushroom clouds choke the fires of hell.

Ivan's eyes narrow and grow dark as he watches. He side-glances Ozdemir, who gives him the nod. They agree. Unspoken but understood, they know what must be done to end China's invasion.

Smirnov picks up his phone. "Deploy the Avangard. ... Yes, as we discussed. The CCP's compound and the nuclear base on the outskirts of Harbin."

Ozdemir says, "You've saved mankind."

On another screen, they watch as the Russian hypersonic Avangard breaks through the atmosphere atop an intercontinental ballistic missile and hits the CCP's compound. The building erupts in flames, and then— as if in slow motion—the structure crumbles. Dust and debris cloud the screen and block the image.

On the next monitor, one more Avangard rides an ICBM and strikes China's nuclear base on the outskirts of Harbin. The earth erupts as explosion after explosion rips it open until only immense craters remain. Multiple fireballs shoot into the atmosphere, and monster clouds of radioactive debris engulf the billowing swells. The ground shakes with a magnitude 9.6 earthquake that races through the province and topples buildings and destroys bridges. The devastation creates a wasteland. As far away as Sapporo in Japan, windows shatter, and people run from their homes and into the streets. The missile hit China's nuclear storage center.

The Command Center falls silent. Faces freeze blank. All present gape at the screens in disbelief.

Smirnov finds himself trembling. He turns to Ozdemir. "I didn't know."

"How could you know? All we can do now is wait."

"For what?"

"To see if the world has awakened. To see if it now remembers."

"What are you talking about?"

"There ... see!" Ozdemir points to one of the screens. "Do you see? The Iranians are retreating. They've dropped their weapons and are going home."

On the middle monitor, Chinese troops retrace their steps and head back to the Pakistani border.

Ozdemir says, "That's what I waited for. All those souls who vanished in an instant are helping us remember. China thought it could control the world. It tried to destroy the United States and thought it could take over the Middle East. Now, China may have lost even its own country.

"None of us want war, Ivan, not really. We think we want power, but once tasted, we need more. There is no quelling the hunger it brings. But, perhaps now, its shackles have broken, and its darkness lit for all to see."

Ivan drops his head and then turns to look at Ozdemir. "Do you know about my father's dying word?"

Ozdemir shakes his head.

"He tried hard to speak, but the only word he could utter was *family*." Ivan struggles with his emotions.

"Your father was a great man. You see that now. He often spoke of the human family, how we needed to learn to live in harmony. It was his hope, and it became mine as well. If enough of us remember our dreams, we have a chance. Do you need me to show you what I mean?"

Ivan wipes away a stray tear and nods. "That would help."

"Okay, let me make a call." Ozdemir punches in a number and says, "Bring the gift to the Command Center."

A couple of minutes later, a door opens, and Ivan hears a familiar voice.

"Papa, Papa," a child cries and runs into Ivan's embrace.

The Russian fails to control the tears that pour down his cheeks. He holds little Amira.

The girl whispers, "I've waited for you, Papa. I knew you would come for me."

Ivan holds her even tighter as he weeps.

The wolf will live with the lamb,
the leopard will lie down with the goat,
the calf and the lion and the yearling together,
and a little child will lead them.

**Isaiah 11:6**

# Postscript

he Syrian War began as a peasant protest. It became a conflict between radical and moderate forces (ISIS and the Free Syrian Army), and Sunnis and Shiites (Iran and Hezbollah against Saudi Arabia and Turkey), and has led to tensions between the East and West (Russia and the United States). And then China got involved.

From a humanitarian perspective, half a million Syrians have perished. Ten million more have become displaced. Most reside in Turkey, homeless, hopeless, and in poor health. High Commissioner Filippo Grandi, of the UN Refugee Agency, calls Syria "The biggest humanitarian and refugee crisis of our time, [ and ] a continuing cause for suffering."

The Syrian people need their country returned to them. They need, as King Abdullah has proposed, an intra-Syrian conciliation committee representative of the people to forge a future for Syria. Reforms must be activated so that the people can live in "dignity, glory and pride." His proposal is rational, and it is achievable with our participation.

All sides must lower the bar of hatred. Initiatives that foster goodwill must replace old ideologies of terrorism and war. We need to change the story—our story—to one in which we are family.

# Glossary

**Avangard**: Russian-made hypersonic boost-glide missile system. It travels in speeds up to Mach 27, making it apparently invulnerable to existing systems. It is nuclear-capable.

**B-2 Stealth Bomber**: American-made strategic bomber with stealth technology. It can fly from U.S. bases to anywhere in the world within hours. It can carry 40,000 lbs of conventional and nuclear weapons.

**Ballistic missile**: A missile initially powered by rockets that then follows an unpowered trajectory arching upward before descending to its target. These missiles carry nuclear or conventional warheads.

**Carrier strike group**: A Navy operational formation that includes an aircraft carrier of approximately 70 fighter jets, a guided-missile cruiser, two warships, and a flotilla of six to ten destroyers and/or frigates. The CSG holds upward of 7,500 sailors.

**F-22 Raptor**: American-made stealth tactical fighter aircraft. Primarily used for air battles, it also has other capabilities, such as ground and electronic warfare.

**FPCON**: Within the U.S. military, force protection condition (FPCON) is a counter-terrorist threat level. There are five FPCON levels. *Delta* is declared for high states of alert and when maximum security measures are needed.

**S-400**: Russian-made anti-aircraft weapon system. It is, arguably, one of the most advanced systems available. It can also be used for ground targets.

**SEAL**: U.S. Navy *Sea, Air and Land* Special Forces. Highly specialized and trained.

**Spetsnaz**: Russian Special Forces. Highly specialized and trained.

# About Gwen M. Plano

*G*rowing up in Southern California, Gwen M. Plano loved learning, and she loved imagining stories, some grandly epic, all personal and heartfelt. She taught and served in universities across the United States and in Japan, then retired and focused again on her stories. Her first book, *Letting Go Into Perfect Love*, is an award-winning memoir recounting some of her struggles in life while providing insight into the healing process. Gwen shifted to fiction after this first book and joined forces with acclaimed author John W. Howell in writing a thriller, *The Contract: between heaven and earth*. Its sequel, *The Choice: the unexpected heroes*, soon followed, this time a solo effort. *The Culmination, a new beginning*, is the third book of the series. Gwen lives in the Midwest with her husband, traveling and writing, sharing those stories only she can imagine. Learn more at https://www.gwenplano.com.

# Fresh Ink Group
### Independent Multi-media Publisher

Fresh Ink Group / Push Pull Press

Hardcovers
Softcovers
All Ebook Platforms
Audiobooks
Worldwide Distribution

Indie Author Services
Book Development, Editing, Proofing
Graphic/Cover Design
Video/Trailer Production
Website Creation
Social Media Management
Writing Contests
Writers' Blogs
Podcasts

Authors
Editors
Artists
Experts
Professionals

**FreshInkGroup.com**
**info@FreshInkGroup.com**
**Twitter: @FreshInkGroup**
**Facebook.com/FreshInkGroup**
**LinkedIn: Fresh Ink Group**

# Read Book #1, Prequel to *The Choice*

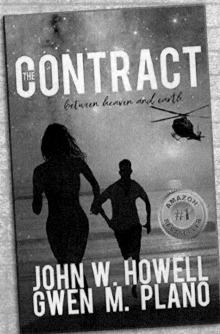

The earth is under the threat of international warfare. In heaven, a divine council contracts with two souls to avert the disaster. Navy SEAL Brad Channing and teacher Sarah O'Brien become heaven's reps to avert the disaster. On a strategic Air Force base in California they discover a conspiracy to assassinate the U.S. president and achieve global dominance. Even as the military appears to be protecting the president, it is not clear who can be trusted. Only Brad and Sarah have any chance of preventing worldwide conflagration. *The Contract* thrills with twists and surprises even as Brad and Sarah explore their earthly and heavenly romantic desires.

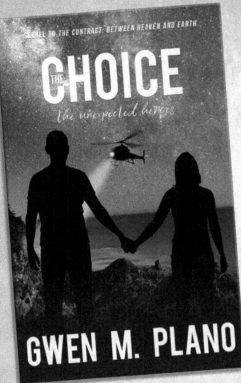

**The Choice: unexpected heroes** is the sequel to *The Contract: between heaven and earth*. In the first book, a catastrophic political event threatens Earth. The heavenly leadership decides to execute extraordinary measures to ensure the survival and long-term viability of the planet. Two volunteer souls return to Earth and take human form as Brad Channing and Sarah O'Brien. They are ultimately successful in preventing the catastrophe, but lose their lives in the process.

The Choice picks up where the first book ends, at an Air Force Base in northern California. The base commander invites Brad's former Navy SEAL instructor to help him determine who is behind the murder of Brad and Sarah. It is evident that their deaths are part of a bigger plan, and the commander has an urgent need to thwart that plan.

A mystery unfolds which implicates key Washington D.C. officials. A confidential team studies the evidence and pursues leads. Eventually, they uncover a traitorous conspiracy that has as its goal: world domination. The pressing question is who can be trusted and who cannot.

**Read it now!**